What readers are saying

FOREIGN RELATIONS

and

The Val & Kit Mystery Series

FIVE STARS! "Blimey! What fun! . . . . These girls bring a sense of humor and a lot of fun to their search for who dunnit. I so enjoyed traveling with them across the pond for their latest adventure. They always keep me guessing until the end—not only about the who but the why. I especially liked the thoughtful way this book navigates the delicate challenges experienced by older children and their parents after divorce. Well done."

FIVE STARS! "Loved this fun book and a chance to catch up with my two favorite girl authors (and detectives). I particularly enjoyed that it was set in England as I am an Anglophile and some of the observations were so 'spot on' . . . a really great story that captured my attention from beginning to end. Just waiting to see what comes next and if Val will ever find a 'friend' and settle down? . . . Please keep the books coming, Val and Kit!"

FIVE STARS! "This is my favorite series. I know I could be BFFs with Val and Kit. Characters are real. Writing is smart and funny . . . who could ask for more?? Well, I could . . . more books, please!!!"

FIVE STARS! "Better than bangers and mash! These two ladies in England . . . what can possibly go wrong? A marvelous adventure punctuated with enough wit, humor and suspense to keep me a fan of Val & Kit for a long time."

FIVE STARS! "When meeting an old friend for coffee and a chat, do you think to yourself 'Wow, I really miss them. Why do we wait so long to catch up?' That is exactly how I feel every time I read a Val & Kit Mystery. Like I just sat down for a hilarious chat over coffee and cake followed by wine and chocolate. These girls are a hilarious mix of Laurel and Hardy with a dash of Evanovich sprinkled with Cagney & Lacey. Comedy, love and mystery: a brilliant combination."

FIVE STARS! "Easy reads, page-turners and full of fun can describe this series. Though these books aren't deep and overwrought, the characters are wonderfully developed. I can see each of them so clearly in my mind's eye. For me that's the mark of a good read. Delightful and entertaining. I can't wait for the next installment. Thanks, Roz and Patty!"

FIVE STARS! "This series is a fun read. There's friendship, suspense, mystery, humor and a bit of romance for good measure."

FIVE STARS! "Fun series. . . . just finished reading all . . . and am already missing the stories. The characters were fun to follow as they solved the murders."

FIVE STARS! "I love these stories . . . I was reading in the car and laughing out loud. My husband looked over and just shook his head. Thanks again for another good one."

FIVE STARS! " . . . Val and Kit . . . the combo is dynamic. What one doesn't research, the other imagines. . . . They could have been the love children of Erin Brockovich and Columbo! . . . They mix their fun-loving, diverse personalities with a by-the-seat-of-your-pants investigation. . . . Val and Kit are a couple of sometimes-serious, wise-cracking hometown gals."

Foreign Relations
A Val & Kit Mystery

Rosalind Burgess
and
Patricia Obermeier Neuman

Cover by

Laura Eshelman Neuman

Copyright © 2017
Rosalind Burgess
and
Patricia Obermeier Neuman
All rights reserved.
ISBN-13: 978-0-692-91250-8
ISBN-10: 0-692-91250-9
www.roz-patty.com

Blake Oliver Publishing
BlakeOliverPublishing@gmail.com
This is a work of fiction.

Also by
Rosalind Burgess
and
Patricia Obermeier Neuman

The Disappearance of Mavis Woodstock
A Val & Kit Mystery

The Murder of Susan Reed
A Val & Kit Mystery

Death in Door County
A Val & Kit Mystery

Lethal Property
A Val & Kit Mystery

Palm Desert Killing
A Val & Kit Mystery

Dressing Myself

Acknowledgments

As always, we are indebted to our copy editor, Sarah Paschall, and our beta readers. Without them, our book might look like one of those *can you read this* tests, with missing letters and even words. And special thanks to Anna Belle Hunt and the Tracy women (Melissa, Emma, and Anna Lydia) for their help with the cover photo shoot and to Laura Eshelman Neuman for creating our cover and our bookmarks. We're also sending ENORMOUS thanks to our fact checkers across the pond, Jill Reeves and Jennie Farrell! Last, but certainly not least, thanks to one of our favorite dogs, Brew, whose name we borrowed for our book's English coffee shop, Brew Ha Ha.

We dedicate this book to our readers.
We love you every one.

Foreign Relations
A Val & Kit Mystery

The Val & Kit Mystery Series

CHAPTER ONE

When a man is tired of London, he is tired of life. Samuel Johnson, a British essayist and poet, wrote this in 1777. Imagine how he might have upped his opinion if he'd been able to walk across the River Thames on the Millennium Bridge; take a ride on the London Eye, with its spectacular view of the capital; or visit the dazzling Tate Modern art museum.

Kit James and I were in London, and I was giddy with excitement. In my nontransatlantic life, I am a Realtor working for a small outfit in Downers Grove, Illinois. My boss, Tom Haskins, owner of the company that boasts four full-time employees, including himself and me, claims to have been to the city several times. He assured me we could see the whole place in about forty minutes.

"In 1777, maybe," I'd countered.

"Nah, it would have taken even less time back then, Kiddo."

"How could it, seriously?" I had laughed. "Tom, are you sure you've actually been to London, because—oh, forget it."

"I've been, and just remember, Val, they're not big on ice over there, so don't go nuts. And they drive on the wrong side of the road, so make sure you look both ways when you cross the street."

"Hmm, wouldn't that apply to any city?"

"Just do it."

Forty minutes, indeed! We spent twice that amount of time in the Tower of London gawking in awe at the Crown Jewels.

***

I had booked us a room at Queen Anne's Chambers, a hotel located within walking distance of a lot of famous stuff, not the least of which was Buckingham Palace.

"So, which is it?" Kit asked when I first told her about our travel plans. "Are they chambers or a hotel? And what do they mean by chambers, anyway? Why don't we just stay at a Hilton?"

"No. We can do that anywhere. Queen Anne's place sounds so . . . English."

"Okay, but your Queen better have decent Wi-Fi, that's all I'm saying."

On our first day in London, ignoring any jet lag, we took a boat ride on the River Thames. Together with a million or so other tourists, we embarked at the majestic Tower Bridge and set sail down the river toward Greenwich, where, if nothing else, we could set our watches to mean time, whatever that actually means.

As our vessel glided lazily on the water, our tour guide explained points of interest on either side of the river. To our right was the site of the original Globe Theatre, where Shakespeare himself had ruled the roost, and the pub next door, where his actors ran to change costumes, among other things. To our left were shimmering towers of glass where Cher and Robert De Niro supposedly owned apartments. During our brief sojourn in London I'd already become accustomed to the amazing architecture that spanned hundreds of years in the blink of an eye, from the timber used in Tudor England in the 1500s to the innovative glass and steel of the twenty-first century.

Our jam-packed four-day extravaganza included afternoon cucumber sandwiches and tea at The Savoy Hotel, champagne cocktails at The Ritz, and a couple of shows in the famed theaters of the West End.

"Do you think King James ever thought about refurbishing?" Kit asked, as we settled into our snug seats in the Dress Circle of the theater named for him.

"Funny you should ask that." I consulted the playbill I had purchased with a ten-pound note. "They did refurbish several times after the original structure was built in 1688. Last update was . . . let's see . . . oh, 1790."

"I thought I recognized this green velvet."

On our last evening in London, we joined the throng of people strolling along the Thames embankment, heading toward Westminster Bridge. Across the river we took in the splendor of the Houses of Parliament, bathed in gold as the sun began its descent. We stopped to take phone pictures, wedging between two Canadian twentysomethings with Maple Leaf appliqués on their backpacks and an Asian couple who had some serious cameras dangling from straps around their necks.

"It's really a beautiful city," Kit said, surprising me a little. She is not a big fan of old-timey stuff.

"Yes," I agreed. "It's bloody magnificent."

***

For the remainder of our time in England, our plan was to rent a car and drive a couple of hours out of London to enjoy a stay in the County of Sussex. There my daughter,

Emily, had found a cottage for us to lease. Her husband, Luke, had been transferred for a year to Chichester, a nearby city where he did, well, whatever it is he does . . . something in computers (I'm never exactly clear what).

"Are you sure we're on the right road to the village?" Kit asked. "I think we've passed those sheep at least three times."

The sky was clear and very blue, the weather was warm, and we appeared to be the only car on the two-lane road. Even with the wind blowing through the rolled-down windows, Kit's chin-length auburn hair cascaded perfectly, outlining her face and making her appear like a model doing a shoot for fabulous fiftysomethings.

Mine, not so much. Wind tunnel came to mind when I pulled down the visor to grab a look at my blond bob in the mirror. I snapped it back quickly and turned to watch as we sped past the seemingly endless green pastures. The dozen or so sheep, all staring at us transfixed, did indeed look familiar. "The guy in the pub told us this was the way to go," I said.

"The one with the lazy eye?"

"No. Not him. The one in the other pub. He was sitting on his own in the corner and looked a bit like Charles Manson."

"Oh great. You took directions from a death row inmate? Where was I?"

"Well, he's no longer—oh, never mind. You were in the restroom. He told me he had great respect for Americans, in particular our marching bands, and he admired our ability to throw a parade."

Seeming not to care about the Charles Manson look-alike or his opinion of Americans, she asked, "Don't you mean I was in the *loo*?"

She took her eyes off the road for a few seconds, turned toward me, and we both burst into a peal of laughter. I was consumed with joy to be with my best friend of more than forty years and driving on the wrong, or at least the

4

other, side of the road in a car that was not much bigger than my microwave oven.

And it was true that we'd taken ourselves on a little pub crawl on the way to our destination. The King's Head, The Queen's Arms, The Prince's Big Toe (okay, I made that last one up). After another five miles or so, a sign appeared in the hedgerow along the road.

Village Centre Ahead.

"That's it!" I yelled. "We just passed the sign. Look! There's another one."

LITTLE DIPPING. Population 576.

Kit slowed the car down as we entered a street lined with shops and small restaurants on one side and a church behind a large expanse of green on the other.

"Look for Magpie Lane," I said, as she slowed the car even more and the street became transformed by houses on either side, some with thatched roofs. "Oh, here it is. Turn here. Number 6. Oh my, it's adorable."

We had arrived.

***

"I'm Brown Owl," the woman announced, as soon as I opened the front door of our cottage. She said it with such authority, she might have been informing me she was the prime minister.

"Okaaaay." I extended my hand to shake hers. "It's very nice to meet you, Miss . . . Ms. . . . Mrs. Owl? Did you say Owl?" She was tall and thin, with overly permed short gray hair. She wore an expensive-looking tailored suit and sensible lace-up shoes. I noted her pallor and thought she could have benefited from a little makeup. "Kit," I yelled over my shoulder, my voice easily reaching down the short hallway to the small kitchen.

"What the hell kind of oven is this?" she yelled back. "Am I supposed to cook in this thing—"

"Kit, dear, we have a visitor, Ms. Brown Owl—"

"Brown *what?*" Kit appeared behind me, a kitchen towel draped over the shoulder of her cashmere sweater. She looked surprised to find a woman rather than an actual owl. "Kit James," she softened her tone and extended her hand in greeting.

"Brown *Owl.*" The woman laughed a little. "Sorry; that might sound strange to you, but it's how we sometimes address the leader of the Brownies. Some packs don't stick to the tradition, of course, although here in Little Dipping we do. But please call me Vera. Vera Wingate. I run the pack over at St. Matilda's. I thought I'd just stop by and welcome you to our village . . ."

She hesitated so long I decided she would probably rather be doing more important Brown Owl stuff. I noticed beads of perspiration on her top lip, which was surprising, given the mild day. Finally, with a shake of her head, as if to clear it, she spoke again. "The oven, by the way, is an AGA. And yes, you'll probably be using it—if you plan on cooking, that is."

Just then a little girl stepped from behind her. She was wearing a blue-and-white-checked dress, belted at the waist, that appeared several sizes too big for her tiny frame. On her head was a navy beret from which several unruly red curls had escaped. "Are you from America?" she asked in a voice too loud for her slender body.

"Yes," I said. "We are. Please, come in, ladies." I leaned back, giving them space to pass through. Charming as our cottage was, and although larger in square feet than my own tiny apartment back home, the walls separating the individual rooms made it appear much smaller.

Vera Wingate put her hands on the little girl's thin shoulders and steered her past me and into the living room. "This is Ivy," she announced. "She insisted on coming with me."

"Well, hello, Ivy," I said. "That's a very pretty name."

"No, it's not. It's poison. And I didn't insist on anything, Brown Owl; I just happened to be going in the

6

same direction." Freeing herself from her elder's grip, her eyes darted around the small room before she plunked down on the end of the old brown chesterfield (which we Americans call a couch). "So, are you two from Florida or what?"

"No." Kit sat down next to her. "Not Florida. You're thinking of Disney World, I bet."

"No, I'm not," Ivy said. She had picked up a small silver bell from the end table beside her. "Are you from California, then?" She studied the bell.

"No, sorry; nowhere that exciting."

"Texas?" She shook the tiny bell and then returned it to the table.

"Wrong again."

"New York?"

"We're from Illinois," I cut in, saving Ivy the arduous chore of naming all fifty states.

"Never heard of it." She sniffed, her ginger eyebrows raised in disbelief that there was such a place. "What's there?"

"Chicago, for one thing," Kit said. "You seem to know so much about America, Ivy, I'm sure you have heard of that."

"No, but my dad probably has. He's been all over the world."

"Good for him," Kit said, trying to sound impressed. "So . . . Brown Owl . . ." She turned her attention away from the child and toward the older woman.

"Vera, please."

"Vera. Can we offer you coffee or something? Tea, perhaps?"

"Got any cake?" Ivy asked. She had crossed her thin legs in a mature fashion that looked all wrong on someone so young. I noticed one of her white knee-length socks was twisted around her ankle.

"Ivy, that's very rude," Vera/Brown Owl admonished. "And pull your sock up."

"I like your dress," I said to Ivy, although it reminded me more of a candy striper's uniform than something a little girl would wear. "It's very pretty."

"No, it isn't. My dad was in the navy once, and he had a very nice suit."

"Ivy, your sock," Vera repeated. "Fix it." And then, turning back to Kit, she said, "Thank you, but no, we won't stay for tea. Another time, perhaps. Just wanted to pop in and say hello."

Reluctantly, Ivy stood, muttering as she did so. "Yanks don't know how to make tea, anyway; my dad told me that." She began pulling up the errant sock, but it immediately fell back down around her ankle. "Have you ever met Taylor Swift?" She looked up at Kit.

"Yes. Many times," Kit lied. "Have you?"

"No, but I don't reckon she's all that."

"I'll be sure to tell her what you think of her—"

"Nooooo," Ivy began to wail, "don't you dare go and tell her—"

"For goodness' sake, Ivy," Vera said, "don't you know when someone's pulling your leg?"

"Oh." Ivy stopped wailing. "She shouldn't tease children. It's not very nice."

"How old are you, Ivy?" Kit asked sweetly.

"How old do I look?"

"Hmmm." Kit rested her chin in her hand, as if deep in thought. "Let's see . . . twenty-six?"

"Don't be daft. I'm nine."

"She's eight and very naughty." Vera looked annoyed.

"You're just confused again," Ivy said, but the look in her eyes convinced me she was taunting this Brown Owl. I had no doubt Ivy was eight.

"I can assure you the other Brownies are much better behaved," the Brownie leader said.

"Is Emily here?" Ivy changed the subject quickly, which seemed to come naturally to her.

"Emily? You know Emily? She's my daughter."

"Yes. I was here when she came to rent this place for you. She doesn't look like you; she's very beautiful, and she's an actress, you know. She lives in Los Angeles; that's in California. But her husband, Luke, is working in Chichester for a little while. He's the IT person; that means information and technology, and he specializes in programming nautical code. He likes the Chicago Bears. Emily does too, of course, but I think I can get her interested in Manchester United. They play football, but my dad told me you call it soccer in America, which is so dead wrong."

"Well, I expect you'll bring Emily around to your way of thinking, Ivy," I said.

She dug her hands into the pockets of her dress. "Yeah. Emily's really nice. I hope she gets that part in the play they're doing at The Beamlight Theatre. She's a brilliant actress."

"Really?" I hadn't spoken to my daughter since we'd arrived in Little Dipping, so I wasn't really up on the latest Emily news, but it seemed she had a fan already. And I was also grateful to learn what it is my son-in-law does for a living. "I thought Emily had already been cast in the play."

"Nah." Ivy took a seat again and leaned over to carefully roll both her socks around her ankles. "She's only the understudy. That means if Doreen gets herself killed, then Emily can go on—"

"Ivy!" Brown Owl said. "What nonsense you talk. No one is getting killed."

"Probably not. But Doreen—she's my sister—isn't half as good as Emily. Did you fly here on a plane? 'Cuz you know, you could have come by boat. My dad was on loads of boats. Of course you wouldn't want to be on the *Titanic*. That hit a big iceberg, and everyone died."

"Not everyone." Kit said it kindly, but I still couldn't believe she was actually correcting this little girl.

Ivy just shook her head and adjusted her navy beret, roughly shoving some ginger curls back in place. "Most of the Irish did, like Leonardo."

9

"He wasn't Irish, ya know." Now Kit's kind tone held an edge of smugness, and I *was* impressed with her sudden cinematic knowledge. Generally, she either talks or sleeps through a movie.

"Yes, he was," Ivy insisted.

"No, dear. Actually, he was from Wisconsin." Now Kit looked triumphant.

"Wiswhat?" Ivy scrunched up her little face. "Where's that, then? It must be somewhere in Ireland, right?"

"Wisconsin is the state that borders Illinois to the north, in America, where we come from, remember?"

"If he was American, why was he staying down in the bottom of the ship with the poor people?"

This would have been a great opportunity for Kit to teach Ivy that not all Americans are rich. But no. "Good question," she said instead. "He should have been in first class, and then he might have made it."

"Oh, for goodness' sake," Vera Wingate interrupted them, and I was grateful. "Enough with you, child. Let's leave these two ladies in peace." She yawned. "Forgive me. I didn't get a very good night's sleep." Then she reached for Ivy's thin arm with her own thin arm and gently pulled her off the couch. "I live three doors down, at Number 9, so if you need any help, please give me a knock. And welcome again. Hope you enjoy your stay in Little Dipping."

"Phew," I said, as I closed the door after our visitors left. "She's really a little pistol, isn't she?"

"Yeah, but I kinda liked her."

"Yeah, you would. And by the way, how did you think we were going to make them tea? Or coffee, for that matter. I hope we *can* get a decent cup of coffee in Little Dipping."

Later, when I was upstairs unpacking in one of the two bedrooms that were separated by a rather large and obviously remodeled bathroom, I heard Kit call me from the floor below.

"Hey, Valley Girl, did you move that silver bell thingy?"

"What?" I called back down, leaning over the banister.

10

"It's gone. Remember? It was on the table by the end of the couch."

"Why would I move it?" I went down the steep stairs. "Really? It's gone?"

"Yeah." Kit was sitting in the same spot the disgruntled Ivy had occupied an hour earlier. "I think the little stinker pocketed it."

And once again we both burst out laughing.

CHAPTER TWO

"Missing?" I heard Emily ask with alarm. "You mean missing like . . ."

Her voice trailed off, and I couldn't hear the response from whoever it was that had knocked on our door, so I rose from the table to join them.

It was our second evening in Little Dipping, and the four of us were enjoying the fruits (rather meat, bread, and cake) of Kit's labor at the AGA. I'd had no doubt she would soon be its master.

After dining out the night before at The Lady of Shalott, a local pub, she'd insisted she would make our Sunday dinner. Emily and Luke were thrilled at the thought of a home-cooked meal and lavished Kit with thanks, but I knew the truth was, she was itching to put her culinary skills to work after almost a week away from her own kitchen. Especially since she'd been so disappointed in the pub's fare.

"How can anyone ruin a shepherd's pie?" she'd demanded. I was thankful she was asking only Emily, Luke, and me, and had resisted her first inclination to complain to the cook. But she barely pecked at her food as she continued her critique, apparently deciding to fill up on wine instead, so I wasn't sure she was really giving it a fair chance.

I would have been happy eating dirt, so enthralled was I by the entire village even before we had explored it after church the next morning. I felt as if we'd been set down in the middle of a Jan Karon novel, and even Kit's grousing about her meal that evening couldn't shake my sense of peace.

She was tipsy by the time we walked the short distance back to our cottage, and I thought she spoke too loudly when we were in front of Vera Wingate's cottage. "So is Ivy Vera's daughter?" She waved her arm toward 9 Magpie Lane.

I shushed her.

"You met them?" Emily sounded surprised.

We'd been so excited to see her and Luke when they'd arrived, not long after Vera and Ivy's departure, that we hadn't even mentioned our visitors. Instead, we'd fixed the tea Luke had brought, and spent hours catching up and hearing stories of Chichester, Little Dipping, and The Beamlight Theatre before going to the pub.

Luke chuckled. "Ivy," he said. "If you think she's something, wait'll you meet her mom."

"So Vera is not her mother," Kit said, echoing my own thought. "Anyway, I liked Ivy," she added.

Ivy's mother, it turned out, was Claire Scoffing, a name that suited her well. We met her at church, and I instantly saw where Ivy got her . . . I could only say *attitude*, although it pained me to accuse an eight-year-old of having an attitude.

"Ivy told me about you Americans," Claire said, by way of introduction, when her young daughter dragged her by the hand to where we were standing outside St. Matilda's.

"Yes, this is my mother, Valerie Pankowski, and our dear friend Kit James," Emily said.

I saw Luke put his arm around his wife's shoulders, as if she might need protection from Claire Scoffing.

"So you're renting the Gaston cottage?" Claire pushed a silky lock of black hair behind one ear, revealing a diamond stud so large I decided it wasn't actually a diamond.

"I don't know. Emily made all the arrangements—"

"Yes," my daughter spoke up. "It's the Gaston cottage."

"Oh dear," said Claire, in an ominous tone. "I hope you'll like it."

"It's absolutely charming." Kit sounded defensive, as if she'd built or at least decorated it herself.

"Oh, it is that, all right," Claire said. She took Ivy's hand to lead her away. "Nice meeting you," she said in her offhand manner, even though she had never officially introduced herself.

We learned her name from Luke only after they departed. "She's a piece of work," he added. "Hardly the welcoming sort the rest of the villagers are."

And the next few hours bore that out, as we walked along the cobblestone sidewalks, peering into shop windows and stopping for a cup of tea at The Crawley House café. I was tickled to see how many people my daughter knew, and it was obvious they all thought as highly of her as Ivy did.

Emily gave us a tour of The Beamlight Theatre, and it turned out to be Luke's first close-up of the ornate venue as well. It was an impressive structure for a small village. "So, Ivy tells us you're an understudy for her sister," I said as we followed along behind her. "How old is her sister?"

"She's eighteen." Emily motioned for us to take seats in the front row.

As we faced the heavy velvet curtains that hinted at the drama they would reveal when drawn open, I felt an excitement begin to form in the pit of my stomach. I could only imagine how they must make an actress like Emily feel. Still, an *understudy*? And for a young girl? Of course Emily, though in her twenties, could pass for a teenager herself.

14

"She's a major talent, believe me," my daughter responded to my unspoken thoughts. "I'm honored to be her understudy. And it's a proverbial foot in the door." She smiled.

That's my Em. An attitude that gives the word a *good* name. I had no doubt the other participants in the play already realized what a gem they had in her, with her good nature and work ethic. *She's her mother's daughter,* I immodestly thought. And I added—since they were *my* thoughts and could offend no one—*certainly not her father's.*

The mere thought of my ex, though, took me away from the conversation I so wanted to be involved in— hearing about our daughter's part in the current production. Instead, I wasted precious moments feeling irritated at David's presence on the isle. I knew he was here somewhere, coincidentally spending several months in England on business. I wondered if Emily had heard from him yet.

" . . . Mom?" her voice caught my attention.

"Hmm?" I had no idea what she'd just said.

"Val, are you okay?" Kit grinned. She loves to tease me about my daydreaming, but I just hoped she wouldn't press for what I was thinking. I avoided talk of my ex-husband with our daughter as much as possible. She was grown and gone by the time we divorced, although she must have seen it coming her whole life. Still, he was her father. "What were you thinking about?" my friend pushed.

"This beautiful theater and all the history it holds. Wouldn't these walls have stories to tell—"

"Um, yes. That's what I just said." Emily looked at me, puzzled.

"Yes, I'm agreeing. Now tell me more about this Doreen." I remained unconvinced that she was worthy of a better position than my Emily.

"Well, as I said, she's fresh out of school and pursuing an acting career. I don't think she'll be in this village theater long—she's really good."

"Then maybe in the next play, *you'll* get the lead. And *you'll* have an understudy." I couldn't believe it, but I sounded exactly like my own mother.

"Yeah, maybe," Emily said.

"I'm just glad our girl is so happy here." Luke put his arm around Emily and gave her a squeeze. For the millionth time I felt so grateful he was her husband. Oh, I knew that Emily being content in England made his job easier, but I also knew he genuinely wanted my daughter to enjoy her time here and be successful. I was only slightly worried that her year in England would slow down her budding acting career in America.

"Oh, me too," I said. "I think it's fabulous that you found a place to keep up with your acting, Em. I'm sure they're thrilled to have you." I reached across Kit's lap and squeezed Emily's hand.

Kit stood up before I'd even removed my arm. "Shall we move on?" she said. "We'll be back for Saturday night's performance, right?"

"Right," Emily said. "But you can sneak into rehearsals before that."

"I can't wait," my pal said, "except that I don't want our vacation to go by so fast."

"Me either," I said, emphatically enough that I saw all three of them study my face. "It's just so peaceful here. Heaven on earth."

If I'd known what was ahead, I might have said *hell* on earth.

***

After our Sunday stroll, we returned to our own cottages—Emily and Luke lived a five-minute walk away—for naps. Well, Kit didn't nap; she planned and prepared our dinner. And in typical Kit fashion, it was a traditional English-countryside dinner that included Irish soda bread, whole trout, and stout cake. The Lady of Shalott would have done well to hire her.

"So tell us more about this Claire Scoffing," I said, after Kit had filled all our wineglasses.

"You pretty much saw for yourselves," Luke answered. "That's just how she is. Curt. Self-absorbed. Superior."

I nodded. "I could see Ivy growing up to be just that."

"I like Ivy," Kit reminded me. "She's refreshing, ya know. Not your typical eight-year-old."

The rest of us nodded in agreement, but it was clear we weren't sure that was a *good* thing. Kit just shook her head, as if we were missing the point.

"What about Doreen, her older sister?" I asked. "Is she like their mother?"

"Not at all," Emily said. "And she and Ivy have different fathers. Maybe that explains why *they* are so different."

"Ivy sure thinks the sun rises and sets on her father," I said, hoping our use of the word *father* wouldn't make Emily think of her own.

"His ex-wife sure doesn't." Luke gave a mirthless chuckle.

"So they're divorced," Kit said.

"Yes. Are you surprised?" He chuckled again.

"Does he live around here?" I asked.

"Oh, who cares about him. About them," Emily said in uncharacteristic abruptness. "Tell me what's going on back home. How's Tom? And Billie and Perry? And how are Grandma and William?" She held her fish-laden fork midair, waiting for me to begin my answer.

I swallowed my last bite of soda bread and then took a sip of wine, feeling like I was taking Communion. Then I filled her in on my boss and officemates. Easy fodder for evoking a few laughs.

"And Grandma and William?" she asked about my mother and her husband, after I'd finished my last Perry story, the one about his botched Botox.

17

"They're good," I said, after a brief pause.

"Mom, is there something you're not telling me?"

Damn. I couldn't fool my daughter. I'm a terrible liar, but had thought maybe I could pull one off by omission. "Well, William's undergoing some tests. I'm sure it's nothing, or I wouldn't be here." That was only partially true. I'd felt torn between ditching my mom and ditching Kit. But both my mom and William assured me that *his* kids were coming up from Illinois to be with him and I'd only be in the way. I wasn't sure how to take that, but finally decided to take it to my advantage. It wasn't without more than a pang of guilt, however. "He's had some health issues they haven't figured out yet," I said. "They're doing some tests."

"Oh." That seemed to satisfy her. I supposed she assumed I wouldn't be in England if it were *really* serious. My guilt intensified.

"Could you please pass the bread?" Luke asked, as he reached for the butter.

I picked up the basket and held it out toward him. That's when we'd heard the knock at the door and Emily ran to answer it.

I soon joined her, and by that time the man was talking loudly enough for Kit and Luke to hear from the table, where they remained eating their fish and soda bread.

"She's missing," the man said. "She left for church at nine o'clock, and no one has seen her since."

CHAPTER THREE

The man was tall, over six feet, with black hair cut short, showing off his handsome face.

"Come in." Emily opened the door wider to let him in and stepped aside so he could pass her in the small hallway. "This is my mother, Valerie Pankowski."

"Are you Ivy's father?" I asked as I led the way to the dining room, where Kit and Luke still sat at the table.

"No," he said, extending a hand in greeting to them. "I'm Alistair Carlisle, Doreen's father. Doreen is Ivy's half sister. I take it you know Ivy."

"Yes," Emily said. "Doreen and Ivy are both nice girls. We saw Ivy this morning at church with her mother. But we didn't see Doreen."

"Right." Alistair's face took on a perplexed look. "Apparently, she left the house before her mother and sister, but never showed up. I was supposed to take her to lunch, but no one has heard from her. I'm just scouting around."

"Come sit." Kit rose and indicated the living room.

"Thank you, but no. I should continue looking for Doreen. Claire—my former wife, her mother—thought she might be here with Emily. You are both in the play, I understand." Did his eyes linger on my daughter just a few seconds too long? Or was I just being a mom?

"Yes," Emily said. "But I'm so sorry; I haven't heard from her today."

"Right," Alistair said again. "Well, I won't keep you from your dinner." He glanced at the dining room table. "Looks delicious, by the way. I guess I'll go visit some of Doreen's other friends. Maybe they have seen her. This was my first stop. Ivy said you and she were great mates." He looked at my daughter.

"I like Doreen very much." Emily followed Alistair to the front door. "Is there anything we can do?"

"No, I don't think so. But of course if you do see or hear from her, please tell her to ring her dad." He turned at the front door and gave us a little salute. "Teenagers, huh?"

"He seemed nice," I said, as soon as Emily closed the front door and returned to the table. I was really just fishing for *her* impression of him.

"Yes, doesn't he? Doreen adores him. Although she says he's a terrible flirt." Her quick chuckle was replaced by a look of worry as she sat down next to her husband.

Luke immediately began rubbing her forearm. "I'm sure she'll be okay," he said, but Emily didn't look convinced.

An hour later, after they had both left, Kit and I cleared the table, taking the dishes into the small kitchen.

"No dishwasher," Kit remarked needlessly.

"Here's one." I raised my hand. At home, although my apartment came equipped with all the modern conveniences, I rarely use my dishwasher. Mainly because I so rarely cook anything.

"Okay, you can dry." Kit turned on the faucet and then squeezed some pink liquid into the sink. A torrent of bubbles rose into the air.

"I wonder if Alistair is a bit of a womanizer." I handed Kit a dirty plate. "Maybe that's why he and Claire divorced."

"Yeah. I could see that. But I think any man might want to divorce Claire Scoffing."

I pondered this while Kit pondered who knows what as she washed and I dried. Later, when the dishes were clean and stacked away, we retreated to the living room and turned on the Samsung Smart TV, landing on an old episode of *Law & Order: Special Victim's Unit*. "Perfect," we said in unison.

"Just like home," I added.

***

"Ah, my two favorite Americans!"

We had awakened early, eaten a sumptuous breakfast prepared by Kit (who was forming a relationship with the AGA), and made a few calls back home. Emily had told us she was going to sleep late and study her lines before going to rehearsal, and we'd assured her we could entertain ourselves.

So we walked to the high street to browse and buy gifts to take home. Before long we found ourselves outside the pub.

We glanced at our watches and decided it would be foolish not to go in.

"Good morning," Kit replied to the large florid-faced man behind the bar who was busy drying a beer glass with a dish towel. The pub was empty, so we took two stools at the bar.

"What can I get you ladies?"

"Hmm." Kit glanced at her watch again. "What do we want at eleven thirty in the morning?"

"The missus is cooking bangers and mash today, lunch special." He turned to a small blackboard behind him that did indeed list bangers and mash, along with various pies, some containing meats and other ingredients I would not necessarily have wrapped in pastry.

"Okay, I'll bite," I said. "What exactly are bangers? Sounds dangerous."

"Sausages. And some of the best on offer today, all the way from Cumberland. Comes with mashed potatoes and fried onions."

"Did your wife make the shepherd's pie we had Saturday night?" Kit asked.

The man threw back his head in a hearty laugh, his rosy cheeks jiggling. "Yeah," he said, when he was able to contain himself. "She's not the greatest cook in the world, but she tries her best, bless her."

Just then we heard a loud yell from someone out of sight. "Pinky!"

He put down the glass and draped the towel over his shoulder, like Kit always does. "Whoops. Better go see what The Duchess wants." He laughed some more, shaking his head this time. "Have a think on what you want, and I'll be right back."

He returned a few minutes later, wiping from his moist eyes the kind of tears that come with great joy, not sadness.

"I'm Kit James, and this is Val Pankowski." Kit stuck out her hand.

"Pinky," he said. "Good to know ya. So, are you ladies brave enough to try the bangers?"

"I think I'll have the ploughman's lunch," Kit said, to my surprise. "French bread, assorted cheeses, and pâté," she explained to me.

I was no foodie, but I guess I shouldn't have skipped the cuisine section of the guidebook.

"Me too," I said.

"Right you are. And to drink? Fancy a shandy to wash it down?"

"What's that?" I asked.

"Beer and lemonade, fizzy lemonade to you. Think of Sprite."

"Sounds good," I said, although I thought the combination might suck.

Pinky caught the look on my face and threw out a big laugh. Then he turned to grab two glasses from the shelf behind him. And soon our ploughman's was served with half a pint of shandy. Both were delicious.

"So, Pinky." Kit dabbed at her lips with a red paper napkin. "We hear Doreen Carlisle went missing last night. Any news?"

"Not that I've heard," he replied from farther down the bar where he was dipping several glasses into a small sink full of soapy water. "Duchess!" he yelled, twisting his head slightly. "Did Doreen show up?"

"Nah, not yet," she yelled back.

"There you have it." Pinky nodded. Apparently, The Duchess was the final authority.

"Well, that's worrisome," I said.

"Nah, not really." Pinky took a glass from the suds and passed it under the running tap water. "That girl has legged it before."

"Legged it?" I asked.

"Run away," Kit kindly translated for me. I wondered when *she* had become the expert on British vernacular. I watched as she picked up a slice of cheese and began nibbling on the end. "Wow, this is excellent cheddar," she said. "Where does it come from?"

Pinky leaned his beefy elbows on the bar, an earnest look on his face. "Costco," he whispered, and then roared his signature laugh.

As the pub began to fill up, we finished our meal without the benefit of Pinky's wit. When we were done, we paid our bill and waved good-bye.

"Have a nice day, ladies," he yelled while laughing. "See ya."

"I think a walk might be in order," I said.

"That sounds good," Kit agreed.

And so we left the dimly lit pub for the glorious sunshine outside and began ambling along the high street. The shops had already become familiar, and I loved how good the people watching was. A man in a three-piece suit trailing a dachshund on a leash hurried past us, a young woman with pink hair talked on her cell phone as she pushed an oversize stroller housing twin boys, and an elderly lady inched along with a walker.

"Ya know, we should do more of this," Kit said.

"Walking?"

"Yeah, when was the last time we—"

"Hello! Yoohoo!" a voice called out. We turned to see Brown Owl/Vera Wingate coming toward us, waving. "Out for a stroll, I see," she said, getting closer.

"Hello, Vera," I called, as Kit and I stopped and waited for her to catch up.

"We heard that Doreen didn't come home yesterday," Kit said when Vera reached us. "Do you know anything?"

"Phew." She waved her hand in front of her face as if swatting a fly. "That one's a runner. She'll be back."

"Well, that's good to know," I said.

"Yes," she went on. "Her father stopped by my cottage last night looking for her. As if I'd know where the girl is."

"Us too. He was worried."

"Hmm." Vera pursed her thin lips. I noted that she had put on a little makeup, but her choice of tangerine lipstick looked garish against her pale skin. "Bit late in the day for that, I'd say."

"What do you mean?" Kit asked, but Vera had already begun walking away.

"Can't stop; must dash," she said, although she was doing anything *but* dashing. Her steps were slow and deliberate. "Have a nice day, ladies."

We watched her back as she wearily moved forward. It made me feel tired just watching her. "How about a nap?" I asked.

"Good thinking."

We both quickened our pace toward Magpie Lane, and when we turned the corner, I saw a small girl leaning against the fence in front of our cottage.

"Ivy!" Kit called to her, as the child looked in our direction and waved. "What's up?"

"I got out of school early," she said.

"Wanna come in and have a soda?" Kit opened her purse to extract her door key.

"Soda?" Ivy scrunched up her nose as if at a bad smell. "Why would I want soda? Are we going to bake something?"

"Oh, I mean pop. A drink, ya know." Kit looked flustered, a rarity. "I think you call it a Coke, but we have a lot of different flavors."

Emily had stocked us up with a wide variety of canned drinks, so I figured Ivy would delight in making a choice.

But no. "Got any cake?" she asked. Clearly, we were going to have to stock up on cake as well if we expected visits from this little person.

"I made a stout cake yesterday," Kit said. "Will that do?"

"Does it have chocolate icing?"

"Ya know, you are rather picky for a—"

"What about chocolate biscuits? Got any of those?"

"Come in, and we'll have a look."

***

Ivy was wearing the same dress we'd first seen her in, and I assumed it was a school uniform. She sat on the end of the couch, as she had on her last visit, and I caught her glancing at the end table where the missing silver bell had stood. She held a glass of orange soda and chomped down on a Snickers bar Kit had produced from her purse.

"So, has Doreen returned?" Kit took her own seat at the other end of the couch.

"Maybe. I haven't been home yet."

"Goodness, does your mother know where you are right now?"

"Of course she does."

"Are you sure?"

Ivy carefully put her glass on the table and produced a cell phone from her pocket. "I sent her a text. See?" She waved the phone at Kit as proof of her action. "She's not home from work yet, anyway. She works at The Cut Above; that's a hairdresser on the high street. But not on Fridays, 'cuz that's when she cleans the vicarage, and sometimes I go meet her there if she's running late; but she doesn't make me work. I usually just play a game on my phone—"

"So your mother is very busy," Kit said.

"Like all mothers." Ivy sounded wise beyond her years.

"And she must be so worried about Doreen."

"Yeah, probably, but Doreen runs away a lot. I think she'll be back soon this time, because of the play and stuff. She really likes that bloody play."

"Ivy," I said, "should you be saying *bloody*?"

"My dad says it sometimes."

"Really?" I said, not going any further. I certainly didn't want to discipline someone else's child. "Well, I hope Doreen comes back soon; her father was worried about her."

Ivy didn't respond, but instead took the final bite of her Snickers. Then her eyes darted between Kit and me, her head moving as if she were a spectator at a tennis match. "He's not taller than my dad, you know."

"I'm sure he isn't," Kit said kindly. "Ivy, what does your dad do?"

Ivy took a long drink of soda, holding the glass with both hands. Her arms looked so thin, it seemed the weight of the drink might be too much for her. Before answering, she returned it to the end table. "Dunno. I haven't seen him for a while."

"Oh, I'm sorry," I said.

"Yeah." Ivy suddenly looked sad. She leaned forward to pull up her sock. "But I expect he'll come back soon."

***

Ivy eventually received a text from her mother telling her she was home from work. As we said good-bye at the door, the *Law & Order* theme song filled the cottage, signaling an incoming call for me. Ivy spotted Emily's face on my iPhone.

"Tell Emily I said hello; tell her to text me," she called, as she skipped down the path from our cottage to the street.

"Hello," I said into the phone to my daughter. "Your admirer was just here. She wants you to text her."

"Mom," I heard Emily's hushed tone. "I'm at The Beamlight. We haven't even started rehearsal yet because . . . the police are here. They found something."

CHAPTER FOUR

I don't understand why the police haven't contacted *me*," Doreen's father said.

"Well, Mr. Carlisle—"

"Please. Call me Alistair."

"Alistair," I said. That was the easy part. I thought of David and wondered for the first time if we'd caused others to feel this awkward. Probably the least of what a divorce does is to make others uncomfortable.

"You were saying?" he nudged me.

"You have to forgive my friend." Kit grinned her *gotcha* grin. "She gets lost in her own thoughts."

And you love catching me, I thought, but didn't say. I'd kept poor Alistair Carlisle waiting long enough. *Or was he poor Alistair Carlisle?* I remembered Vera's implication that his worry over his daughter was a bit late. "Your wife, er, your ex-wife told the police *she* would let you know," I said at last. "But I'm sure they'll be around to see you soon." *Sooner than you'd like?* I wondered.

He shook his head in disgust, but I wasn't sure if it was at his ex-wife or the police. Probably both.

Kit and I had hightailed it to The Beamlight with Luke after Emily hung up on me without giving further explanation. There we met up with not only her but the police, Claire Scoffing, and the rest of the cast and crew— except for Doreen, of course.

The police, it seemed, had found something suspicious in the nearby woods. More accurately, a young man jogging there had come across something he thought he should report to the police.

I explained to Alistair Carlisle now, as we sat in the small living room of our cottage drinking the tea Kit had brewed, that the jogger had stumbled over a woman's shoe that lay under a thick patch of ground cover. As he bent to pick it up, he noticed off to the side some papers that turned out to be a script. A script for the play *The Taming of the Shrew* with Doreen Carlisle's name written in the top right-hand corner of the cover.

"This Darren McCoy took the script over to The Beamlight, since he saw lights on," I continued. "And of course someone there called the police because Doreen hadn't shown up for rehearsal."

"My wife—my ex-wife—why was she there?"

"She said she'd gone to The Beamlight hoping Doreen *would* show up for rehearsal," Kit said.

"Of course. I should have thought of that." Alistair shook his head in apparent regret.

"Well, no one's thinking clearly, I'm sure, in these, um, scary circumstances," I said. I felt guilty myself for not having contacted him after we left The Beamlight. We had agreed only to have Doreen call him if we saw her, but still, any father deserved to know the latest about his missing daughter. And something about Claire should have told me she wouldn't really see that he did.

When we'd arrived at The Beamlight, we'd seen a portly policeman standing in front of the stage talking to the others, who sat in the first few rows of the theater. It looked like he was performing a one-man show. And not a comedy, judging from his serious countenance.

We took seats behind the others. I was still trying to catch my breath after following Kit and Luke as they'd trotted halfway through the village to Pembroke Lane and then headed up the small hill toward the theater and the woods behind it. I hadn't realized Kit was in such good shape.

" . . . speak to each of you individually," the officer was saying. "We no longer think Doreen has just, er, taken off for a bit."

"Oh, Luke," I heard Emily say with a groan, as Detective Portly paused and looked into the faces of all of us seated there, one at a time. She and Luke were holding hands.

"I'm not so sure about that, Officer Downey," a tall slender man said with the volume of a great stage actor, as he stood up from his seat in the front row. "This is the very reason I had grave concerns about casting her in such an important part. She's done this before, you see, disappearing at an inopportune time." He shook his head.

"Sit down, Jeffrey," the officer said. "We have reason to believe it's different this time."

"Why—"

"That's all I can say right now. You'll have to trust us." It was an order, not a request, and the inspector sounded as if he didn't give a damn whether Jeffrey chose to trust him or not. "As I said, we'll be speaking to you each individually. And we need to do it at the station, so if you'll all get yourselves there now, we'll dispatch with the whole thing in the most expedient manner. But first, sit just a minute." He then held up one hand, thrust his index finger out, and proceeded to take a head count.

"He obviously doesn't want anyone here to escape interrogation," Kit whispered to me. A little too loudly, I thought.

"Write your name, address, and phone number on here, please, and then head over to the station." He handed a clipboard to the end person in the first row, and then he folded his arms across his chest and watched us sign our names before heading out.

Luke and Emily returned to their cottage after grabbing some leftovers from our fridge, and Kit and I had just decided we'd get in our jammies and watch TV, when Alistair Carlisle knocked on our door. "I thought I'd stop by to make sure you still haven't heard from Doreen," he said.

"Come in," Kit had urged. And over tea, we did what his ex-wife had neglected to do. We brought him up to date.

"I'll let you lovely ladies get on with your night," he said when we'd finished. "Sorry your stay here is turning out to be less than peaceful." He set his teacup down on the end table.

That's when I noticed the missing bell was back.

***

"How did you even get this number?" I asked my ex-husband. "And why—"

"Emily gave it to me," he said, his tone adding an unspoken *of course*.

"I don't see why—"

"She wanted me to find out a good time for you. And Kit, of course."

Well, I had to give Emily props for extricating herself from any communication between her divorced parents. That hadn't always been the case, and I'd been painfully aware of how difficult it had been for her to participate in the volleys between David and me. *Dad says he's fine with Christmas Eve instead of Christmas Day. Mom says New Year's works better for her. Dad says he'll be out of town then. Mom says forget it.* Well, usually it was David who said that last one, but it's the sort of discomfort we'd caused Emily. And now it seemed she wasn't going to let herself be a part of it. No

31

doubt Luke had coached her, and I gave silent thanks once again that she'd married him.

I climbed out of bed and headed toward the kitchen, where I was glad to see Kit already had the coffee going. *No time is good for me,* I wanted to tell David, but I thought of Emily again and how much she wanted us all to get together, so I decided to be the reasonable one. David, not so much. He insisted he had to have dinner with Emily and Luke *this* week. Something about an unbelievably busy—and important—schedule he had that would preclude his seeing Emily and Luke if he didn't do it now. But he was in London for three months, for Pete's sake. I found it hard to believe—or at the very least irritating—that this was his only free time to see them. Apparently, he wasn't even able to come to her play on opening night—or any night.

"How about tomorrow evening?" I asked, because I just wanted to get it over with. I saw Kit look up from the *Hello!* magazine she was reading.

"I already have a dinner scheduled for then, so—"

"Then don't ask me what's good for *me*. Tell me what works for you," I said through clenched teeth, but he didn't seem to notice. Big surprise. I saw Kit roll her eyes and return to her magazine, as if to say *oh, it's only David.*

"How about lunch tomorrow?" he asked. Of course. He no doubt had something much better planned for the nighttime.

"Sure."

"Can you come to London? We could—"

"I am not coming back to London until we head home," I said. I wasn't going to let him or anything else rob me of a whole day in this bucolic setting. And then I remembered Doreen and thought *too late.* But all the more reason not to waste time on *David.*

"Fine," he said. "I'll come there. I'll be there at noon. Tell me where."

"Ask Emily," I said, and then hung up, feeling like a bad mother for throwing him back her way.

"What was that about?" Kit closed her magazine and set it aside. Then she placed both hands on her coffee cup and raised it to her mouth. But instead of taking a sip, she merely looked over the edge, her brown eyes expressing the curiosity that got her in trouble as often as not.

"We're meeting him for lunch tomorrow."

"You, not we. Not me, anyway. Did you notice this thing?" She indicated a large glass container with a metal plunger. It was half-full of coffee.

I ignored it. "C'mon, Kit, you know I need you."

"You do not need me. You'll have Emily, surely. And probably Luke. This, my dear, is a cafetière. I found it in one of the cupboards," she said.

"Don't change the subject. And don't make me beg, Kit. I *always* go along with you, and on far more nerve-racking things than lunch with David." I didn't add that I needed her along *especially* since Emily and Luke would be there. They were half *his* people. I needed a peep that was all my own, and I had clearly won Kit in the divorce.

"Fine. But don't blame me if there's a scene. Ya know, I can't stomach him."

"*Really*? Why'd you wait this long to tell me?"

"I thought wearing black to your wedding was a clue."

"You were a vision in fuchsia, and you know it."

"Yeah, I was pretty hot back then. But next time you get married, let *me* pick the bridesmaid dresses."

"As if." I gave her a hug on my way to sit down across from her. I could always count on my Kitty Kat.

***

After we'd had a buttered crumpet and a banana, along with a second cup of coffee, Kit and I got dressed for the day. And since I still hadn't heard from Emily, we decided to walk over and see if it looked like anyone was up. I knew Luke should be at work in Chichester by now, but it had no doubt been a late night, or at least a restless one, even after

33

they'd returned from the police station. I knew they might both be sleeping in.

There was a light on in their breakfast nook, however, so I tapped on their front door. Softly, in case the light had just been left on overnight.

Emily soon appeared at the door, eyes puffy from sleep and her long blond hair tousled but gorgeous. "Good morning, Mom." She didn't sound happy.

And I should have known why.

She opened the door wider, and we followed her to the kitchen and helped ourselves to fresh coffee. "Dad called," she said.

I figured from her tone of voice that he'd made some disparaging remark about me or had somehow shared with her the tension of our phone call. I regretted telling him to ask Emily.

"Yeah," I said, trying to sound natural, if not chipper. "Did you guys decide where we should meet?"

I thought Emily looked surprised, as if she expected me to berate her dad, or perhaps to give her *my* side of the story. But I resisted the urge and renewed my vow to hide from her my undying disdain for her father. "Yeah. We're going to eat at The Crawley House at noon, and then I'm going to give him a tour of the village and The Beamlight. *If* we're allowed in there, that is."

"What do you mean? Isn't Jeffrey the director? Surely he would let—"

"It's not Jeffrey. It's the police. Tim—he's one of the townspeople in the play—just called to say rehearsal has been cancelled for tonight. The police have the place sealed off or whatever they call it. Like it's a crime scene." She arched her eyebrows in disbelief, and I found myself wistfully admiring my own blue eyes—the younger version, of course. "I think it's Doreen's shoe they found in the woods. Only one shoe. It smacks of foul play to me, for sure. And I'm guessing the police have reason to believe . . . well, I'm not sure what. But Doreen was involved in the

34

theater, and the shoe was found near there, as was her script, so I guess it makes sense . . ."

"Well, honey, no worries. If your dad can't see The Beamlight tomorrow . . ." I bit my tongue so I wouldn't add *too damn bad he can't come for your actual play*. And then I wondered if the theater would even be *open* for the play.

Man, I thought, *this week isn't turning out as we'd planned.*

***

"Did you tell Em about Ivy and the bell?" Kit asked. We were having lunch at Garibaldi's Famous Pizza, a cute little restaurant located on the high street. I wasn't sure where, or why, the pizza was considered famous, or even who the namesake Garibaldi was. As far as I could tell, the establishment was owned and operated by an Indian family with the last name Singh who had hailed from New Delhi a few generations earlier. Regardless of its dubious fame, the pizza was delicious. As we'd weaved our way through the crowd to an empty table, I'd overheard more than one group talking about Doreen Carlisle or the theater or both. I also heard the word *shoe* more than once.

It was creepy.

"What bell?" Emily asked.

"It's not a big deal," I dismissed the topic. And then I decided I'd rather talk about the mischievous Ivy than think about what might have happened to her older sister. "There was a little bell on the end table that went missing during her first visit and reappeared during her last one."

"Oh," Emily said, as if she didn't want to be bothered with such a triviality when she had a friend and fellow cast member who might be in jeopardy. She nibbled at her kale salad.

"Ivy reminds me of me when I was little," Kit persevered, trying to lighten Emily's mood, I felt sure.

Emily scooted her chair back and stood. "Excuse me. I have to use the ladies' room."

"Who'da thunk it?" Kit said, when Emily was out of earshot.

"Who'da thunk what?" I took a bite of my pizza, still wondering why in the world Emily would order a kale salad when there were so many more delectable items on the menu.

"That we'd find ourselves smack-dab in the middle of a murder mystery in this quaint little village."

"Kit! No one has said anything about murder. And consensus seems to have it that Doreen most likely has snuck off for a bit, surely to return."

"Hah. It seems to me police consensus has it that Doreen's shoe was found in the woods, along with her script, and it's likely that nothing good can be deduced from that."

I hate when Kit uses words like *deduced*. Nothing good ever comes of *that*.

We ate in silence until Emily returned, and she had nothing to add to the conversation—or lack thereof.

***

On our way out of the pizza place we met Claire Scoffing. She had her long black hair pulled into a ponytail, this time showing both earlobes and her too-large, too-fake diamond studs.

"Any word?" Kit put a hand on her arm. It didn't seem Claire was going to slow down for even a *hello* otherwise.

"About Doreen?" she asked, and I half expected Kit to say *duh*.

"Uh, yes," she said instead, removing her hand, but maybe only because Claire pulled her arm away.

"Yes and no. No word from Doreen, but we do know the shoe they found is not Doreen's."

Like a wicked stepsister insisting the shoe should fit her, Kit said, "How can that be? I mean, Doreen's script was right there. How can the shoe not be hers too?"

"Because it's a six and a half, and Doreen wears a size five."

CHAPTER FIVE

How tall *is* this Doreen?" Kit asked, as soon as we were clear of Garibaldi's, and Claire Scoffing. "What adult has feet that small?"

"It's English; their shoe sizes are smaller than ours," Emily said, as the phone in her jeans pocket began to chirp. "Excuse me. I have to take this." She stepped to the edge of the sidewalk, the phone now to her ear.

Kit and I moved on, stopping to gaze in the window of a shop that seemed to sell only hand-knitted items. Through the glass we saw a magnificent display of sweaters, hats, and scarves. But I kept one eye on my daughter, watching her facial expression go from shock to delight.

"Right, okay, no problem. I'll be there," I heard her say before she tapped her screen to end the call. Then she ran to catch up with us, linking her arms between Kit's and mine.

"That was Jeffrey." She sounded a bit breathless. "The director. Rehearsal is back on, and he wants me to come in early."

"Is there news?" I asked. "Did the disappearing Doreen show—"

"No. Doreen still hasn't been heard from. But since the police have confirmed the shoe is not hers, they've released the theater, and it's all systems go."

I wasn't sure if I was happy or not to see the bright light radiating from Emily's eyes.

"So, you know what this means?" she continued.

"The understudy goes on?" Kit kissed Emily on the cheek.

"Yep. Me. Meet Katherine Minola. The shrew that needs taming."

"Honey, that's . . . that's . . ."

"Exciting," Kit finished the sentence for me.

"Of course. It's just that—"

"Oh, Mom, it's the lead in *The Taming of the Shrew*—"

"Yes." I felt—and probably sounded—a little annoyed. As if I didn't know the name of the damn play she'd been talking about for days.

"Shakespeare, Mom."

"Yes, I get it. I wasn't thinking Woody Allen wrote it."

"And in England, of all places to get the lead. Wow!"

"You'd be fantastic in England or Timbuktu," Kit said.

We walked a few more steps, and then Emily stopped. "I really should head home and study my lines. Jeffrey wants me at The Beamlight in an hour. Do you mind if I—"

"No, honey, you go do what you need to do," I said. "We'll talk later."

"Hey, I'll ask Jeffrey if you can sneak in and watch the rehearsal. I'm sure he won't mind."

She gave us both a kiss on the cheek and ran ahead, her phone once again stuck to her ear.

"So," Kit said, as she linked her arm through mine, replacing Emily's, "what are you thinking?"

"Just that . . . well, of course it's great that she gets the lead. But I wish she wasn't quite so . . ."

"Happy?"

"Well, yeah; I mean, it's just that under the circumstances—"

"Looky here, it's not Emily's fault that Doreen took off. Don't ruin it for our girl."

I patted Kit's arm, which was still looped around my own. I love how much she cares for Emily. "You're right," I said.

"Of course I am. And remember, *the play's the thing.*"

"What does *that* mean?"

"It's from *Hamlet.* Everyone knows that."

"Not everyone knows that, and what does it—oh, good grief, please don't tell me you're suddenly an expert on Shakespeare."

"Let's go back and look at that knitting shop. I thought I saw something in there your mother might like."

***

"Hiya." Ivy was waiting for us at our front door, sitting on the steps and raising her arms as if she were part of a spectator wave at a baseball game.

After the knitting store, we had stopped at Marbles Grocery at the far end of the high street, within walking distance of our cottage. It was a six-aisle shop stocked with all the basics for survival plus many exotic items that thrilled a foodie like Kit. I watched her pick up a jar of ginger and then stare into space for a few seconds, like a child who's just spotted Santa and his sleigh through her bedroom window.

"We need hand soap," I reminded her, taking the jar and returning it to the shelf. A quick calculation told me that the regular Marbles customer would have had to lose her real marbles in order to shop there; the prices seemed ridiculously inflated.

"Yeah, hand soap." Kit sighed. But I could see she was mentally floating through her recipe files for something that called for ginger.

"Hi, Ivy," Kit and I called back in unison now.

The little girl stood and ran toward us, taking one of the heavy plastic shopping bags from Kit. "Got any cake in here?" She slipped her arms into the straps of the grocery bag and wore it like a backpack.

"As a matter of fact, we do." Kit smiled.

"You shouldn't shop at Marbles; it really is better to go to Tesco—much cheaper."

"Yeah, well, we didn't feel like driving today," I said. "And by the way, does your mother—"

"Yes." Ivy trudged ahead of us. "I texted her. She knows where I am."

"Ivy," I said, reaching the front door and digging in my purse for the key, "who normally looks after you when you get out of school?"

"Depends." She walked ahead of us into the cottage. "So, you heard about the shoe, right? Not Doreen's. Of course I coulda told them that. Dopey Downey should have asked me. He's really up himself—"

"Well, whatever that means, he is a policeman, right?" I said.

"Yeah. But he's heavy-handed. I mean he's dramatic. No, wait, I mean he—ooooh, chocolate and coconut!" She set the shopping bag on the kitchen counter and removed a cake Kit had paid a small fortune for.

"To your liking, missy?" Kit laughed.

"Oh yeah. To my liking, all right."

***

"So, Ivy, when you said you knew the shoe wasn't Doreen's, *how* did you know that?" I asked.

We were at the kitchen table, where Ivy was consuming a huge slice of the cake accompanied by an equally large glass of milk.

"Because she wears those French high heels with red soles."

41

"Ah no, honey. Those are Christian Louboutin's," Kit said, making it clear that a Louboutin was more likely to be found on the moon than in Little Dipping. "They cost a fortune."

"Yeah, that's them. She got them at the charity resale shop on the high street. You should go there; they have good stuff."

"But even so," Kit pressed on with her case against Doreen owning such shoes, "they are very, very expensive."

"Her dad, Alistair, paid for them. He's got lots of money. He gets her whatever she wants. And believe me, she'd never lose one of those shoes."

"Ivy," I said, watching her take a gulp of milk, "do you like Doreen?"

Ivy waited to answer, seeming to give the question much thought. "Yeah, of course. She's my sister. Sometimes she straightens my hair for me. And she does take me to the pictures, but only if it's something *she* wants to see."

"But you don't seem very concerned that she's missing. I would be so worried if it were *my* big sister."

Ivy gulped some more milk. "The good news is that now Emily gets to play Kate, and she'll be soooooo good."

"But Ivy—"

"Seriously. She's a much better actress than Doreen. Jeffrey should have given Emily the role in the first place. I don't know what he sees in Doreen. You know—" She stopped midsentence, concentrating hard on her chewing.

"What?" I asked.

"I really do like this cake. But I also like strawberry stuff."

***

"I'm really cross with your daughter," Jeffrey said, coming toward us from the center aisle of the theater. "She lost her bloody script, of all things, and we retrieved only half of the one found in the woods. It's really not on. I'm

42

Jeffrey Hastings, by the way." He stopped talking long enough to offer a limp hand. The way he extended it, I wasn't sure if we were supposed to shake it or kiss it.

He was handsome, I couldn't help but notice, with chiseled features and bright blue eyes that matched the blue in his plaid shirt. But his blond hair was a little too long for my liking. "I don't think we were officially introduced last night," he continued. "Emily said you were coming to watch the rehearsal, which is okay, but make sure you sit in the back and of course—" He put an index finger to his lips. "Absolute silence."

"Nice to meet you," I said, in what could only be described as a stage whisper—appropriate, at least.

But he had already turned and was hurrying back toward the stage, where I could see Emily and several other actors waiting for him.

"Huh," Kit responded in a normal whisper—nothing staged about it. "Who the hell does he think he is?"

"He's the director, remember—"

"Yeah, and I'd like to tell him where he can direct—"

"Kit. *Shush.*"

We took two seats at the end of the last row, after I gave Kit the same look I used on the ten-year-old Emily whenever I took her to the theater and she began talking loudly. As instructed by Jeffrey Hastings, we sat in silence and watched the rehearsal.

I was overcome with pride as Emily, in her skinny jeans and Vineyard Vines T-shirt, somehow transported herself back to Padua, Italy, in the late 1500s (these two facts about the play I learned from Google). Her English accent was perfect, as I knew it would be. Emily's ability to imitate any accent had kept her father and me enchanted from the time she was a little girl in her first starring role. She was six, and the school production was called *Fun Day at the Zoo.* Back then she was somehow French. Her father and I were amazed at her linguistic skills, even though we didn't know any actual French people to compare her to.

Now, after twenty minutes of the five actors onstage running through a scene, Jeffrey began waving his arms in the air. "People, people! Stop." I wasn't sure if Emily could see us, but she stared out to the back of the theater and then stamped her foot heavily on the stage.

"Was that acting, or was that real?" Kit asked.

"Don't know; I think acting. Emily's not a foot stamper."

"It was good, either way." Kit nodded.

"Okay, people," Jeffrey's voice boomed. "Take fifteen minutes and then let's try to remember we are having dinner in Renaissance Italy, not Little Dipping's Burger King." He actually bowed with an enormous flourish after he finished speaking. Then he flapped his hands in dismissal, and the actors dispersed.

Emily came running down the aisle and took a seat in the row right in front of us. She turned around and said, "Hey, you guys, thanks for coming."

"Are you okay?" I asked. She looked flushed as she took a clip from her pocket and somehow raised her long blond hair into a fashionable twist.

"I'm good, Mom. But poor Jeffrey is not cool."

"Is this his full-time job?" I asked. He certainly had the air of someone whose livelihood depended on the play's success.

"Oh no. He's a pharmaceutical salesman. But he takes this seriously. And there are too many things going wrong for—"

"Not the least of which is that one of his cast members is missing."

"Yeah," Emily said. "Still no word, but everyone around here seems to think that's kinda how Doreen rolls. More than a few people are amazed that Jeffrey ever cast her in the lead in the first place. I don't know what's up with that."

"They're not upset that you got to take over, are they?" I asked. A sudden tiny fear ran through me. I had been on the sidelines of so many of Emily's productions, I knew how jealousy could grow rampant among cast members. Not to mention their mothers.

"Oh no, everyone is so nice." She smiled her glorious smile, and my fear vanished. How could you not love her?

"So, Jeffrey said you lost your script. What was that about? I thought you had it glued to your body."

"Hmm." She sprang the clip from the back of her head and shook her hair loose. "I don't know what happened. I had it last night. Luke went through the lines with me. But after lunch today I ran back to get it and couldn't find it. Maybe he picked it up by accident. He had a big stack of papers in his briefcase when he left this morning. But no big deal. I know the lines. What did you guys think?"

"I thought it was mahvelous, dahling. Simply deeeevine," Kit purred, patting Emily's hand. "Can't wait to see you in costume."

"Yeah. I have a fitting early tomorrow morning, then dress rehearsal will be Friday night." She rubbed her hands together with glee, and I thought once more how lucky she was to be able to work at her craft.

Soon Jeffrey appeared on the stage, clapping his hands and calling out, "People, people, let's do this!"

***

An hour later we were back at the Gaston cottage, in our jammies, in front of the enormous television watching *Blue Bloods*.

"Does it sometimes feel like we never left home?" I asked. We were curled up at either end of the couch, watching Tom Selleck address a contingent of his NYPD officers.

"Yeah. Maybe we should watch something British?"

"Er, I don't think it would be appropriate to switch Tom off in the middle of his address."

"Right. Hey, how about a glass of sherry?"

"What? Where'd you get that idea?"

"I saw an unopened bottle in the kitchen cabinet. I assume it was left by the previous renters, or maybe the owners. Wanna have a sip?"

"Sure. I don't think the NYPD can stop us."

Kit rose from the couch and disappeared into the kitchen. But she reappeared two seconds later holding up what looked like a silver teaspoon with an intricately carved handle.

"Looks like the Little Dipping kleptomaniac has struck again. There were six of these spoons in the kitchen drawer. When I was looking for an opener just now, I counted only five. One missing." She leaned against the door frame and crossed her arms. "Whaddya think?"

"Maybe we should talk to her, because she did at least return the silver bell."

"Someone did."

I smiled. "Maybe we should pat her down next time she's over."

Five minutes later we returned to New York, while sipping from two elegant, but rather small, sherry glasses.

CHAPTER SIX

If I had to hear the horrible news that a body had been found, it couldn't have come at a better time: during a most uncomfortable lunch with David.

For starters, he'd kept us waiting thirty minutes.

"I'm so sorry, Luke. I know you have to get back to work . . ." I had plucked my phone out of my purse that rested at my feet to check the time and also to see if maybe I'd missed a text from David.

But no. He wasn't that considerate.

Then again, I hadn't totally figured out just what my phone could and couldn't do on this side of the pond. Not to mention I didn't know what David's was capable of.

I decided to continue to bite my tongue, even though we were now fifteen minutes into our wait. What if he'd been killed, driving on the wrong side of the road, or what if—

" . . . you do realize, right?" Kit asked, and it was clear she was addressing me.

"What?" I leaned down and returned my phone to my purse.

"Val, for crying out loud. Wanna join us?"

"Sorry; I was just wondering where David could be—"

"It's not your worry," she said, "and certainly not for you to apologize for him." She looked at Luke as if to say *don't you dare blame Val for this.*

"No one needs to apologize," he said, and I thought *bless you.* I could see Emily's discomfort growing, and I vowed to chastise Kit as soon as we were alone.

But she beat me to it. "Oh, never mind me," she said. "I'm sorry to be so rude. I'm just irritated with Larry." She looked at me and said, "*Husbands. Men.* I'll explain later." Then she took a sip of her wine, followed by a big sigh. "Of course no one needs to apologize about David, not even David. If Luke doesn't have to worry about the time, the rest of us certainly don't. We're on vacation." She gave us a big smile, but I knew it wasn't easy. She really, really does not like my ex-husband.

"So Emily," I said, "you have rehearsal this afternoon? Still no word about Doreen?"

Kit rolled her eyes at me, as if to say *you don't think we would have heard?*

"Yes and no," Emily said, picking up her own wineglass and taking a sip. "I have rehearsal, and Doreen's whereabouts are still unknown. I feel so guilty."

I knew she felt guilty, but she *looked* happy. So I decided to follow Kit's lead and be happy *for* her. If Doreen was too irresponsible to take advantage of such an opportunity, there was no reason for that to spoil Emily's joy. Or mine. "Oh, honey, just enjoy your good fortune. I'm sure Doreen will show up, all full of apologies and—"

"Yeah, and reclaim her role." Now Emily didn't look so happy.

"You don't think Jeffrey would *give* it to her, do you?" Kit looked appalled at the idea. "Surely he wouldn't be that stupid *twice.*"

"Who knows? I'm an outsider, after all."

"Yes, but an über-talented one." I glanced down at my phone, which I had strategically placed in my purse so I could check the time without actually removing it. David was now twenty-eight minutes late.

"You can say that again." Luke patted his wife's arm.

But before any of us had a chance to, David swooped into the café.

Luke and Emily rose from their chairs before the door had even closed behind him. He gave Luke what appeared to be a bone-crushing hug and then held Emily at arm's length, the better to take in the sight of his little girl. But she wasn't little, and he'd spent a lifetime foregoing opportunities to lay eyes on her. "How are you, sweet pea?" he asked, and then he took her in his arms and held on as if for dear life. *What the heck?* This was a side of David I hadn't seen before. *Was he dying or something?*

At last he let go of Emily, and as she eased back down into her chair, he turned his attention to Kit and me. "Ladies." He nodded in our direction but made no move to bestow a kiss or even shake a hand. Whew.

Kit merely nodded back, but I can never allow any awkward silence, especially with Emily and Luke watching. "Hello, David. Please, sit." I motioned to the only empty chair, the one between Emily and Kit. My stomach roiled, as if in anticipation of a scene. I tried to make eye contact with Kit to give her a *please don't* look, but she avoided my gaze. "How is your time in England going?" I asked. Like I cared.

But I did care that he looked so much better than the last time I had seen him. He was thinner, and although he had lost a little hair on top (the good news), he had cropped what remained very short, giving him an almost-military appearance. It made him look younger (the bad news).

"Couldn't be better." He whipped his napkin onto his lap. I noticed that he was dressed very casually. Golf shirt and khaki pants, instead of the formal suit he used to favor, even for informal occasions.

"What are you doing in England, anyway?" Kit found her voice. It wasn't a question of interest, more a *what the hell right do* you *have to be here?*

"Um, have you ordered?" David looked around the table.

Kit spoke before anyone else had a chance. "We should have." She glanced at her watch, and I almost expected her to announce the time and mark David tardy. "You're—"

"No, we haven't," Emily said. She handed her father his menu and opened her own. "Hmm . . . everything here is delicious."

"Good," David said. "I'm famished."

"Aren't we all," Kit muttered.

***

After we'd dined on English fare (I'd chosen lamb with mint jelly and roasted potatoes) and small talk, having agreed to sip our coffee and wait a bit before ordering dessert, Kit addressed David again. More civilly this time. "So, David, what brings you to England?"

"My daughter being here isn't enough?" he asked, wasting his charming grin on my friend. "That's why you and Valerie are here, right?"

Valerie? I wasn't sure he'd *ever* called me that. Certainly not in any of our good times.

"It was my understanding you already had plans to be here." Kit stared at him as she lifted the coffee cup to her lips. She set it back down without sipping and spoke again before David had a chance to. "I think I'd like another glass of wine. Does anyone else want one?"

After we all had a glass in hand, Kit raised hers in a toast. "To England," she said. "Whatever the reason." She took a sip and turned her head to look at David again. "And *why* are you over here? I mean, besides Emily."

"Emily," David said, turning his head away from Kit, "did your grandmother get ahold of you?"

50

"No." My daughter looked alarmed. "Why would Grandma be trying to get ahold of me?"

"Why would my mother be trying to reach Emily?" I asked, thinking immediately of William and his tests. But why *Emily*? "And why would she call *you*?"

David gave a grim chuckle. "Yeah, I was never her favorite son-in-law."

"Yes, you were," I assured him. "You were her *only* son-in-law."

He ignored me. He's always been really good at that. "She didn't say, although she did ask me if I knew about . . . what's her husband's name?"

"William," I said. "What about William?"

"I don't know," David said. "She just asked if I knew he was undergoing tests. Which of course I did not."

"Of course not. Why should you?" I asked.

"Mom," Emily said, sounding like a mother addressing her child instead of vice versa. An *unruly* child. Then she looked at her father. "That's all? That's all Grandma said?"

"She also said there was nothing to worry about. That's what she wanted you to know. There's nothing to worry about. I promised her I would tell you in case she didn't reach you."

"Why didn't you just say so?" I asked him, although I wasn't sure I believed him—or my mother.

"So Jean knew you were in England?" Kit asked. "Does *she* know why you're here?"

"Actually," David said, his gaze remaining on Emily, "I was about to get to that." He drew in his breath. "I have some big news, and I guess this is as good a time as any . . ." He lowered his arm and brought it back up with Emily's hand in his. Looking at our daughter as if none of the rest of us existed, he spoke softly but with great glee. "Honey, I'm getting married again. To an English girl, er, woman."

I pretended not to see Emily look in my direction, and pulled my wineglass up to my face, wishing it were about a hundred times bigger. I felt Kit jab my thigh under the table, and I gave her ankle a little kick. Our version of body language that we've perfected over the decades. I knew she had just conveyed *what the hell*, and I was certain she'd understood my *no shit*.

"Dad, when . . . who . . ."

"Um, congratulations," Luke spoke up, but his voice lifted enough to turn it into a question, like he was asking Emily and me, if not Kit, if it was okay for him to offer good wishes.

"Yes, David," Kit said. "Congratulations. Who's the lucky girl, er, woman?" Her voice reeked with sarcasm, no permission asked and none needed.

"David," I said softly, trying to temper Kit's comment and improve the scene for my daughter, "that's wonderful news. I'm happy for you." *But sad for your intended*, I didn't add.

"Dad, who . . . how long . . ."

"I've been seeing her for over a year, Em. I hadn't planned to make a big deal of my announcement, but since I'm over here when you are . . ." He took a drink of wine. "I'm here to meet her family," he said.

"Didn't you want her to meet yours, I mean *me?*" Emily asked. "And Luke?"

"Of course. And she will. I just wanted to tell you first." He looked rattled and took another drink.

I watched my daughter and felt certain I could read her thoughts: *I assume she's been in the United States with you; why the delay?*

Apparently, David could read our daughter's thoughts too. "You were busy getting ready to move, and I was in Chicago and you in LA . . ."

Emily picked up the dessert menu, no doubt dismissing her dad's feeble excuses as meaningless. I wanted to tell her *fuhgeddaboudit—who knows why your dad does or doesn't do what he does (or doesn't)*. I didn't want her to feel hurt.

Luke obviously didn't, either. I saw him put his arm around his wife and draw her closer. "We look forward to meeting her, David." My son-in-law looked across the table at me as if checking to see if he should ask my forgiveness.

Well, I definitely did not care to meet her, so I was staying out of the conversation. I tried to give Luke an *it's okay* smile, however. I really did not give a crap.

Really.

"Who is she, Dad?"

"Heidi Kellogg."

"But who is she?" Emily sounded like a prosecutor pushing for the truth. The whole truth and nothing but.

My discomfort had grown downright painful. So maybe I did give a teensy crap. "I'm going to have this cherries jubilee." I tapped my menu. "I love cherries."

I saw David give Emily's hand a squeeze and heard him say, "We'll talk later. I'll introduce you."

Emily withdrew her hand. "I think that's a good choice, Mom. I'll have the same."

Luke looked relieved to have something else to do, as he called our waitress over.

But before she asked for our dessert order, the young redhead made it clear that she wanted to share something with us. She'd no doubt just heard the news herself and just *had* to tell someone. We happened to be the first "someone" she saw. Her green eyes were wide as she looked around the table at each of us in turn. But even though her pencil was poised over her order pad, she still didn't ask what we wanted for dessert. Instead, she said, "Did you hear they found a body?"

***

When we learned the waitress could not tell us *whose* body had been found, we hurried out of the café, our appetites for dessert obliterated by the news.

David followed the rest of us, clueless and only slightly curious. He seemed more eager to hit the road—and return to Heidikins?—than to learn what we so desperately wanted to learn.

"Dad, why don't you go back to Hei—to London? I'll call you later. We'll pick a better time for a visit."

He seemed thrilled to oblige as he peeled himself off our little group and made his way to where he'd parked his car.

"Thanks for lunch," Kit called after him, and I wondered if he could tell her tone actually said *good riddance*.

I wasn't sure where we were headed. Emily was in the lead, and I thought she was maybe going to the police station. But surely . . .

And then she stopped in her tracks as we learned whose the body *wasn't*.

A young woman was heading toward us on the pathway, her dark hair flowing behind her. She was tall and slim and wearing high heels that made her appear even taller. When we met up, she towered over Emily as my daughter threw her arms around her and shouted, "Doreen!"

"Oops," Kit mumbled for my ears only. "Looks like the lead is back. Damn."

"Kit, will you be still." I wanted to hear every word. I wanted to know what the heck was going on.

"Doreen. I was so scared," Emily said. "I was so sure . . . we just heard a *body* was found. And I was . . ."

Doreen started crying now, soft sobs. She dabbed her eyes, and when Emily didn't continue, she finished for her. "So sure it was me? I wish. No, it was that poor, sweet Brown Owl. Vera Wingate. She was stabbed to death."

CHAPTER SEVEN

Here, drink this." Kit handed me one of the little sherry glasses filled to the brim with the ruby-red liquid. "Are you upset? Because you—"

"Yes, I'm upset." I took the glass from her outstretched hand and set it down on the end table. I was sitting on the couch, my legs drawn up underneath me.

"Was it the lamb? Because it looked a little undercooked to me." She joined me on the couch.

"The lamb was fine—good, it was good." I was wearing a pair of hand-knitted slippers that I'd bought at Knit One, Purl Two, the yarn shop we'd discovered on the high street. I'd also bought my mother a tea cozy that was fashioned after a honeycomb. I thought it was sweet, but I was pretty sure she would find it objectionable and never use it. "How was your lunch? What did you have again?" I asked.

"Steak and ale pie. It was delicious. I'm going to try to make it when we get home. Are you upset with David—"

"Duh." I picked up the sherry glass and took a gulp. "Why are these glasses so small?"

"I think you're supposed to sip sherry, ya know, not gulp it down like a longshoreman."

"Longshoreman?"

"Okay, a stevedore . . . I don't know, just don't gulp."

"Why is my mother calling David?" I asked. "To my knowledge, she hasn't spoken to him since the damn divorce—"

"Ah." Kit leaned back and sipped her drink. "To *your* knowledge. She might FaceTime with him every day, for all you know."

"Hah. I doubt that very much. She's still working on how to send a text. The last one I received from her was confirming her dentist appointment."

"So she called David to find out what's going on."

"Why didn't she just call me?"

"Because you give her a filtered version—"

"I do not. And besides, how does David know what's going on?"

"With *him*, dummy. She probably turned on her supermother-Jean radar and learned he's getting married. You probably wouldn't tell her that until David and Heidi were celebrating a wedding anniversary."

"Ugh." I finished my sherry in one last gulp and handed her the empty glass. "Isn't it just so typical of him, making his big announcement to his daughter when she's at lunch with other people?"

"Who cares? So he's marrying Heidi and will live happily ever after in Switzerland."

"What?" I called to her. She was back in the kitchen, hopefully refilling my glass. "Switzerland?"

"Yeah, from the book, where Heidi ran around the Swiss Alps with her grandpa and was forever yodeling—"

"Very funny." I took a sip from the glass she handed me.

"*Are* you upset that David's getting married?"

"Of course not." I reverted to gulping this time. "I just hope Emily is okay with it. What do you think?"

"I think Luke went overboard sucking up to his father-in-law."

"Nooo. Luke was just being nice. He's always nice."

"Maybe too nice?"

"Kit, Luke is a great guy." I pulled one foot out from under me and began poking my finger through the stitches in the slipper around my toe. "So, what about poor Vera?"

"Yeah," Kit mused. "We'll go check out her cottage later." On our return home we had noticed a police car parked outside her place.

"Er, no," I said emphatically. "We will stay out of it."

"Just walking past it won't hurt. It's not like there's any crime-scene tape to stop us."

"Because it's not the scene of the crime. She was found in The Cut Above, remember?"

"Yeah, I think I remember what Pinky told us fifteen minutes ago."

We'd stopped into the pub to buy a bottle of sherry, at Kit's insistence, and he had given us some scanty details of Vera's death. All had been confirmed by his wife, The Duchess, via her megaphone yelling from the kitchen, or wherever it was she hid. She had advised us that Vera was found in the bathroom of The Cut Above by Claire Scoffing, and she appeared to have been stabbed at least twice.

"Sorry." I glanced at my watch with its rubber strap, the one I'd purchased from the sale bin at Target. "We could go to the theater and catch the rehearsal."

"Yes. The question is, will Emily still be playing the lead now that Miss Fancy-Pants has turned up? Did you get a load of those shoes?"

"I thought she was very lovely."

"But she was overly dramatic, don't you think?"

"Emily said she'd call me as soon as she had news," I said, ignoring Kit's remark. I wasn't willing to have an argument over Doreen's dramatics. Instead, I took my phone out of my pocket. No messages or missed calls. But before I could return it to my jeans, it rang. "Shoot. It's David." I looked at Kit.

"Answer it."

"I don't want to speak to that jackass—"

"Answer it," she repeated. "Maybe Heidi pushed him down the mountain and he can't get up." She was laughing at her own humor as I hit the answer button.

"David," I said, taking another sip of sherry.

"Val, I just wanted to check on you."

I should have laughed at the idea of him showing any concern for me. But instead, I said, "Check on *me*? Why?"

"Because I kind of sprang the news on you today. I just hope you're okay with it."

"What news are you talking about?"

"My ... er ... Heidi ... you know, about getting married. I wasn't sure if that was the best way to handle it."

"Oh, *that*." I winked at Kit. "I'm very happy for you, David."

"Whew. That's so good to know."

Again, I almost laughed. The line between us remained silent for a few seconds, and I enjoyed it. Normally, I'd be babbling to fill up the dead air, but this was rather nice, and I hoped he was squirming.

"So," he said at last, "I guess I'd better get going. Good news about Emily."

My ears pricked up like a retriever who'd just heard a car backfire half a mile away. "Emily? What do you mean, *Emily*?"

"Just that she gets to keep the lead role. It was bothering her, since this Doreen has turned up, and—"

"Wait. Since when do you know what's bothering her? And how do you know, anyway?" The thought of my mother calling my ex-husband was bad enough. But Emily calling him with news before she called me was too much.

"I just spoke to Luke. He phoned me," David said, sounding innocent, but he didn't fool me for a moment. His voice had taken on a have-I-said-the-wrong-thing tone.

"Right," I said, backpedaling as I watched Kit flip a finger, a middle one, in the general direction of my phone and David. "Yeah, it's great, isn't it?"

"Of course I had no doubt the director would keep her in the lead."

"Really?" I stopped for a few seconds, wondering where he got his fantastic insight. And then I couldn't resist. "Why exactly did you have no doubt? Where do you get your freaky perception?" I gulped the rest of my sherry, a good quarter of an inch at least. Why *did* these glasses have to be so small? I handed the empty glass to Kit and shut off my phone, not bothering to wait for David's response. "Get me another drink. Please."

"Wow." Kit took the glass but didn't move. "You gave it to him good. He's probably so scared right now."

"He said—"

"I heard what the moron said." She still wasn't moving. "Don't let him get to you, Valley Girl. And I told you your son-in-law was getting sucky."

"Please just get me another thimble of sherry."

"Why don't we go for a walk instead?"

"You're as bad as David. We are not going to visit Vera's house, so just forget it."

"Okay, okay, we'll walk in the other direction. Promise."

***

The other direction led us past the post office, a stationery shop, and Fine Wine Time (did the owner actually try saying that three times before naming the establishment?). Eventually, we arrived at The Lady of Shalott. Without hesitation, we went in and took two seats at the bar.

"Finished your sherry already, ladies?" Pinky headed in our direction.

"We didn't even open it yet." I watched him laugh. His merriment was infectious, and for no other reason, I found myself laughing along with him. "I'll have a shandy," I said, getting comfortable on the stool.

"I'll have a glass of pinot," Kit said. "You do have pinot, right?"

"What kind of a pub would it be if we didn't have pinot? Okay . . ." He turned to the shelves behind him to study the stack of bottles. "Remind me . . . which one is pinot?"

"It's the bottle right in front of you," Kit said, "the one that says *pinot* grigio on its label."

We watched Pinky grab the bottle and remove the cork. "Ha. Just kidding. Sorry, but this one isn't from California. It's . . ." He held the bottle closer to his face, putting on a pair of reading glasses that were hanging from a chain around his neck. "Let's see . . . oh, Italy. It's Italian."

"Good enough. Do you even sell wine from California?"

"Hell yes." Pinky removed his glasses. "But it's cheap plonk. I give it to the locals. Save the best and most expensive for my American visitors."

We all three laughed, not that it was particularly funny, and then I heard a ping from my phone. A text message from Emily. *J says I can keep the lead. Yippee! Drop by the theater tonight if u want. Love u guys.*

"Hmm." I showed the message to Kit. "Good of her to let me know."

"You're not upset with *her* now, are you?" Kit took a sip of her Italian pinot as Pinky left to serve another customer. "Because really, you—"

"Nooooo." I took a long sip of my shandy from its regular-size glass. "That would be petty."

"Exactly. If you're mad at anyone, be mad at Luke—"

"I'm not mad at anyone. Let's just enjoy our drinks."

She nodded. "Good idea. Say, Pinky," she called down the bar, and he slowly made his way back toward us. "What's the story on Vera Wingate? It's so sad about her."

Pinky leaned on the bar in a conspiratorial manner. "Yeah, I liked Vera. She could be a bit snobby and generally came in here only when she was collecting money for one of her charities. But she was a good person."

"Does she have family around here?"

"No, never married. No kids. Never heard of any brothers or sisters."

Before we could respond, he twisted his head slightly and yelled behind him, "Duchess, did Vera have any family?"

"Her dad died when she was young," came the reply, "and her mom passed away several years ago from some strange disease. She has a sister in Scotland, older than her. Hasn't seen her for a while, I heard."

"So." Pinky returned his full attention to us. "There you have it." He grinned, looking proud of his wife's knowledge.

"It must come in handy, being married to Wikipedia," Kit observed.

"Yeah, it does," he agreed, "only The Duchess is much faster."

"Do the police have any leads?" Kit looked over his shoulder and nodded, as if giving Pinky a message to pass on to the know-it-all Duchess.

"Nah," Pinky answered without getting verification from his other half. "But give 'em a chance. The police aren't too swift around here, so they'll probably bring someone in from Chichester. But it's not like *CSI* on the telly, where they only have to run the dead person's knickers under a microscope and five minutes later they've got the name of the killer's grandmother and what kind of car she drives."

***

"Can I buy you beautiful ladies another?" We both swiveled on our stools to see the tall man standing behind us.

"Alistair," I said. "How are you? How's Doreen? We're so glad—"

"Perhaps you would join me?" He turned and indicated one of several empty tables that lined the far wall of the pub.

"Sure." We got down off our stools, and Kit picked up her glass.

He put an arm around both of us, pulling us close to him as he escorted us to the corner table, where he seated us each in turn. "What are you drinking?" he asked.

"Pinot for me," Kit said.

"Nothing for me; I'm fine." My shandy was only half-gone, and as much as I liked it, I knew it was too sweet to be doing my figure any good.

We watched Alistair at the bar. He had to wait a few minutes to get Pinky's attention, even though the pub was nearly empty. I noted that when Pinky did eventually address him, there was no joking or laughter. Pinky handed him two glasses and took Alistair's money without comment.

"So, thank goodness Doreen is home and safe," I said, as soon as Alistair sat down between Kit and me.

He nodded while taking a gulp of his beer. He was even more good-looking than I remembered, from when he was at our cottage looking for Doreen. The lower part of his face was partially covered with one of those trendy half beards so many men sport, the kind where you never know if it's intentional or if they just forgot to shave. Either way, in his case, the errant whiskers seemed a perfect complement to his permanent swagger. He swallowed some beer and then put his glass on the table. "Yeah, she gave us all a big fright. But not for the first time."

"Where is she now?" Kit poured the contents of her almost-empty glass into the full one.

"She's with her mother."

"Right," I said. "I understand your ex-wife found Vera's body. That must have been awful."

"Yep, I suppose it was."

"But . . . what about Doreen? Where was she, and when did she surface?" Kit, who likes to get right to the point, was in good form today.

"Ah." Alistair took up his glass. We waited while he swigged his beer. "That's just the thing. Although Claire called the police to report the . . . er . . . to report finding Vera, it turns out that Doreen was there first. She'd made plans to meet Vera at The Cut Above before it opened. And . . . well, I guess you know what she found. Seems like Doreen called her mother, and then her mother called the police." I noted that Alistair seemed remarkably calm as he shared the horrible details.

"Hmm . . ." Kit sounded as blasé as Alistair. "Any idea why Doreen was meeting Vera at the salon?"

"Don't have a clue. I haven't really had a chance to talk to Doreen yet. I understand she and Claire have both been at the station giving statements, but the police let them go since they haven't finished at the crime scene." He paused for only a second before abruptly changing the subject. "So, is everyone here treating you ladies right? Are you having a good time?"

Good time? Was he kidding? It seemed ludicrous to ask such a thing. Who has a good time when there's a dead body on the doorstep? We both ignored his question.

"That doesn't seem right," Kit said. "Or maybe that's just the way things are done here."

I frowned in her direction. "How do you figure?" I asked her. "What doesn't seem right?"

She smiled her beaming smile. "Nothing. But let's just hope Doreen doesn't do another runner."

And then the smile was wiped from Kit's face.

CHAPTER EIGHT

A man I'd never seen before approached our table. And whereas Kit's face had lost only its smile, Alistair's lost its color as well.

"Don't get up." The lanky man with ginger freckles that matched his hair put a hand firmly on Alistair's shoulder to make sure his order was heeded. "I'll just be a minute here. Sorry to interrupt, ladies." He nodded at me and then at my pal.

I didn't need the help of Dennis Culotta, my detective friend (Kit would say boyfriend) back home, or anyone else, to know this was Ivy's father. The resemblance was startling.

"Devon." Alistair's brown eyes narrowed in fury—or was it fear? "What are you doing here? I thought you were in—"

"Yeah, I bet you did. But our ex-wife tells me there's a bit of a problem here in our little corner of the world. I thought I better come check it out."

"It's none of your business what goes on here."

I saw Kit arch her eyebrows in a look of confusion and great interest.

"I have a daughter here." Devon sat down next to Alistair and thrust his face just inches from the other man's, his hand still gripping Alistair's shoulder. "And I mean to see that *your* daughter—"

"That's quite enough." Alistair manned up and stood up, and Devon rose with him, as if they were duct-taped together. "You leave Doreen out of this."

"Here, here." Pinky had shuffled over to our table and was busy separating the two men, who continued nevertheless to look each other in the eye. They were the same height and of similar build. I wondered who would have won the brawl that Pinky might have interrupted. "You gents simmer down and sit down or take it outside. Or I'll sic The Duchess on ya." He looked at Devon Scoffing and gave a forced laugh. Then he glared at Alistair Carlisle.

I felt Kit's foot hit my shin under the table, and I half expected her to blurt out a *what the hell.* But I knew she was enjoying every second. I also knew she would make it her— *our*—business to find *out* what the hell.

I sighed. "Kit, I think we should get back to the cottage. Emily will be—"

Surprisingly, she removed her purse strap from her chair and stood. All the while, I continued to watch the three men move their eyes among each other as if waiting to see who was going to comply with Pinky's order first.

And then Kit and I made our way out of the pub, seemingly unnoticed by them.

Out on the sidewalk, I started in the direction of the cottage as Kit headed the other way.

"Where are you going?" she asked.

"What do you mean, where am I going? Where are *you* going?"

"To watch Emily rehearse. Why else do you think I'd leave that compelling drama in there?" She turned toward the pub and gave a nod.

65

"Oh yeah." I'd already forgotten about Emily's texted invite.

Kit resumed her walk toward The Beamlight, and I fell in step alongside her.

***

As we made our way down the aisle in the darkened theater, I didn't notice until it was too late that Doreen was seated in the front row. By the time I saw her, we couldn't avoid her.

Awkward.

I felt grateful for the required silence that allowed me to merely smile and nod at Doreen. But it wasn't too dark for me to notice that she did not acknowledge my muted greeting.

Not one to let a situation remain ambiguous, however, Kit whispered, "Hi, Doreen."

Bye-bye, ambiguity. Doreen looked directly at Kit and said nothing. Then she returned her glare to the stage in front of us.

Well, I knew she wouldn't be *happy* about Emily getting the lead, but I'd hoped she would understand.

So much for that hope.

I'd gotten stuck taking the seat next to Doreen, since Kit had passed it up. I felt and saw Doreen move her body as far away from me as she could, leaning against the armrest on that side. Then, as if that wasn't far enough away, she stood up and moved across the aisle to a seat in the second row. I watched in amazement—how could she be so blatant?—and then turned my attention to the stage.

Emily was speaking, and Doreen was immediately relegated to the recesses of my mind. My daughter really *is* an amazing actress.

***

66

Whenever Emily had retreated from center stage, my thoughts reverted to Doreen. I was dreading the end of the rehearsal, when we'd have to face her in the bright light. How would she treat us? And how would she treat *Emily*? Would there be a scene? They were both, after all, actresses, with scenes being their stock-in-trade.

But I needn't have worried. At least not about that.

When the lights went up, I snuck a glance across the aisle, moving only my eyes, to take in the second row. But Doreen was not there. I looked around the entire theater and still no Doreen.

Now I prayed that she *had* done another runner. Or whatever they called it. I breathed a big sigh of relief, however temporary.

"You okay, Val?" Kit seemed to have forgotten all about Doreen.

"Well, Doreen kind of freaked me out. But she's gone."

"Ah, forget about her. She got what she deserved. And I'm sure she'll get over it." Kit stopped talking, but I could see her mind working. "Ya know," she said at last, "it's a little odd that as soon as she returned, she found Vera's body. Makes you wonder where she *was*. And what she was doing."

I was glad to see Emily approach and hoped it would make *Kit* forget Doreen, as she'd advised me to do.

"Hey! Thanks for coming." Emily gave us each a quick hug. "I've gotta stay a while—"

"Sure. No problem. We can wait outside—"

"No, Mom. You never know how long Jeffrey might keep us. Especially since we open so soon." She gave a shudder of nervous excitement.

"You can't walk home by yourself—"

"Sure I can. This is Little . . . um, I won't. I'll text Luke to come for me."

"Promise?"

"Promise." Now she gave us each a peck on the cheek and hurried off to join the rest of the cast, who were already being lectured by Jeffrey and his waving arms and pointing fingers.

***

My first thought when I awoke the next morning was, *I hope Emily made it home safely.* But I shrugged off the worry. I would have heard from Luke if she hadn't. I resisted the urge to text her and *just make sure*, knowing I would risk awakening her.

I saw our visitor as soon as I entered the living room. She was sitting on the couch, arms folded, legs crossed, one foot wiggling up and down. "There you are," she said. "I thought you'd never wake up. Where's your friend?"

"Ivy! What are you doing here? How did you get in?" I was immediately nervous.

"I just turned the doorknob." She uncrossed her legs and picked up the bell from the end table. She gave it a little ring.

"Kit's still asleep," I said, shushing her. "You mean the door wasn't locked?" I couldn't believe we'd forgotten to do that. But maybe . . .

"Or else it's broke."

"Broken," I said, and then I wondered if British English had the same rules as American English. And who cared? "Ivy, come sit in the kitchen with me."

She followed, and we both sat down at the table.

"Have you seen your father?" I asked her.

"What do you mean? Of course I've seen him." Ivy avoided my eyes as she reached her hand to the side of her nose and scratched it.

"I mean recently. Like yesterday. Or this morning."

"No," she said. "He's been gone a long time."

"Where does your father live?" I asked.

"On his boat. I think." She stood up, obviously uncomfortable with my questioning, and I felt horrible. She was just a child.

"I'm sorry, Ivy. I didn't mean to be nosy. We Americans—"

"Yeah, my dad says—"

"I'll make coffee," Kit's voice caught us by surprise. We hadn't seen her enter the small kitchen. "Hi, Ivy. Why aren't you in school?"

"There's no school today."

We both turned our attention to Kit, who was already busy with the cafetière. Secretly, I preferred the Mr. Coffee sitting on my kitchen counter at home, but if Kit missed her fancy Krups coffee maker, she never said. After giving the cafetière several hefty plunges, Kit carried it over and placed it on the table.

"Ivy, when did you last see your dad?" she asked.

I tried to catch my pal's attention and somehow convey the message not to interrogate our little friend. I'd already done enough of that.

But Kit remained oblivious, and Ivy seemed to warm up to her in a way she hadn't to me. Humph. "He came last Boxing Day," she said. "It was my best Christmas *ever*. He had the biggest box of crackers you've ever seen."

"I bet they were delicious," Kit said.

"No, not the kind you eat. He got them at Harrods, so you know they cost him a packet."

"In America, ya know, crackers are people—"

"Kit, obviously she's talking about something else."

"Okay, so what are crackers?" Kit asked our young friend.

Ivy gave a little squeal and proceeded to describe trinkets and small treasures encased in a wrapping that popped when opened. "We each had one on our plates. Mine had a teensy game in it. I lost it," she added, sounding as sad as if it had been a chess set made of marble. And then just as quickly, she brightened. "And my dad brought me this locket." She looked as thrilled as if he'd presented her with the Crown Jewels, and she drew her hand to her neckline, pulling the necklace out in front of her chin to show us the heart shape. It had already taken on the tarnished look of cheap metal.

"That's lovely," Kit said.

"Yes," I murmured, and then remained quiet. I had a feeling Kit could get way more out of Ivy than I could. Or die trying.

"Where does your dad live?" my friend asked. Aargh. That's the question that had frozen Ivy from me just moments earlier. Kit waited patiently for her little pal to answer.

And she did, blithely elaborating for Kit. "He lives in Liverpool. In a harbor. On his boat. Liverpool is called the World in One City. That's how cool it is. And my dad lives there." She looked as proud as if he were its mayor.

Do they have *mayors in England?* I wondered. But I wasn't about to interrupt Kit's roll. *Ask away,* I mentally ordered her. We do read each other's thoughts, but I doubted that was necessary in this case. No one could have *stopped* her from asking away, I felt sure.

"Does your dad work in Liverpool?" Kit took the cup of coffee I handed her and carefully sipped at the hot brew.

"Of course," Ivy said, but I thought she looked . . . guilty? Embarrassed? "What are you two going to do today? Did you go to rehearsal last night? Was Doreen there? I bet Emily is waaaay better than her. Did you get to see?"

"Um, about Doreen." Kit set down her coffee cup. "She was there, yes. But she seemed very unhappy. She didn't seem to want to talk to us."

Or even sit by us, I wanted to add. But I really hoped Ivy would forget I was in the room. I stayed silent and continued to drink from my own cup of hot wake-up potion.

"Don't pay any attention to Doreen," her little half sister said. "Did you know she found Brown Owl . . . dead?" Tears popped into Ivy's eyes, tears that belied the seemingly contentious relationship she'd had with her Brownie leader.

She wiped them away almost as fast as they appeared. "Doreen doesn't care about anyone but Doreen. She's like her father."

"You mean her father cares only about Doreen? Or that he cares only about himself?" I asked.

Kit glared at me as if I'd been correcting grammar, but I wasn't. I wanted to know who it was that Alistair *did* care about.

As I'd feared, I seemed to have shut Ivy up. "I gotta go," she said. "My mum wants to take advantage of her shop being closed to spend the day with me."

"About the shop . . . ," Kit said.

But Ivy had scurried out of the room, and then we heard the front door open and close.

"Boy, do we have our work cut out for us." Kit finished her coffee in one last gulp and then poured more.

I put my crumpet in the toaster. "What in the world do you mean by that?" But I was afraid I knew exactly what she meant. Expecting Kit to ignore the murder mystery that had turned my Jan Karon setting into a Sue Grafton whodunit was like expecting my mother to ignore anyone's poor grammar.

Kit didn't answer me, so I dropped it. I'd just keep her busy, too busy to butt in where she wasn't wanted or needed.

"Want a crumpet?" I asked.

She nodded, and I added another to the toaster. We never have them back home, but when in Rome . . . or England . . .

When we'd finished our buttered crumpets and second cups of coffee, we walked into the living room on our way up to the bedrooms to dress for the day. I'd convinced Kit we still had more shopping to do before we got totally tied up in the play once it opened. We both saw it at the same time, just as we approached the table at the end of the couch.

Emily's lost script.

CHAPTER NINE

O h, what a tangled web we weave . . . ," Kit said dramatically, taking the heretofore missing script from my hands.

"Are we quoting Shakespeare again? Go on, enlighten me; tell me what everyone except *me* knows. Oh, wait—did one of the Kardashians get her hair caught in a—"

"Me first in the bathroom." She turned and ran up the stairs.

"And?" I yelled after her. "Who said it?" I waited at the bottom of the stairs long enough for her to dig out her phone and google it.

"If you really must know, it was Walter Scott," she finally called down to me. "It's from a poem . . ."

"And?"

"And . . . everyone knows *that*."

***

Fifteen minutes later I was sitting in the living room waiting for Kit to finish getting ready. As I flicked through the pages of the script, I marveled at the elegant words attributed to the characters by The Bard. Ten minutes after that I looked up when I heard Kit descending the stairs.

"Ya know," she said, "there was a good-looking sweater in the knitting shop—"

"Knit One, Purl Two?"

"Yeah. I might get it for Larry. What do you think?"

I smiled, thinking fondly of Kit's husband. "Yes, that would be a great idea for him. Perfect for golf. So you're not irritated with him anymore?"

"Humph. Say, maybe you and I should take knitting lessons."

"Er . . . have you forgotten that I actually have a job?"

"Exactly. Knitting would be perfect for you . . . ya know, when you're sitting around empty houses waiting for suckers—"

"Buyers."

"Okay, buyers to show up."

"Forget it. That's when I balance my checkbook and pay my bills."

She went to her purse and took out her lipstick before moving to the gilt-framed mirror by the front door. "Okay, just giving you options. So, about this script turning up. What do you think—"

She was interrupted by a light tapping on the door. We looked at each other in the mirror. "Open it," I said, from my seat on the couch.

A familiar face greeted us. Detective Constable Downey, still looking portly in his navy suit, his double chin straining against the collar of his shirt.

"Sergeant Major!" Kit said.

"Actually it's only Detective Constable, I'm afraid. May I trouble you for a word?" He raised his right hand to show what looked like a plastic identification card encased in a wallet.

"Of course." Kit opened the door wide to let him pass, and from her position behind him I saw her eyes widen as she indicated the script I was holding. "Come in. Let's go to the kitchen. I'll make us some coffee."

"That's very good of you, but I won't keep you too long."

Before joining them, I slid the script under one of the throw pillows on the couch.

***

Detective Constable Downey was seated on one side of the wooden kitchen table, Kit and I across from him. He undid the buttons on his too-tight jacket. But he didn't loosen his tie, and I wanted so much to reach across and do it for him.

"So, you two ladies are visiting us from . . . er . . ."

"America," Kit piped up.

"Excellent."

"I'm Katherine James, and this is Valerie Pankowski."

"If I'm not mistaken, I believe I saw you . . ." He squeezed his hand inside his jacket and removed a notepad. "Let's see . . . Monday evening, when we were investigating a report that young Doreen Carlisle was missing."

"Yep," Kit said. "We were there. Did you ever find out where Doreen was?"

"Who knows, with that one. Complete waste of resources, looking for her."

"Well, at least she came back safe and sound," I said.

"Hmm," Downey said.

"Let me get you some cake." Kit went to the waist-high refrigerator and bent down to open it. She returned a second later with the remains of the chocolate-and-coconut cake she had bought for Ivy. As she placed a small plate before our visitor, I plunged some ground coffee into the cafetière.

"That looks rather good," our policeman said as Kit cut a slice of the cake. "Mmm . . ." He took a bite and widened his eyes in appreciation. "This is lovely. So, let's see. Oh yes, about Vera Wingate. As you probably know, Miss Wingate lived three doors down from you—"

"She was single?" I asked.

"She was a widow."

"Right. Only you said *Miss*, and so I guess I just assumed—"

"Slip of the tongue. Pardon me." Popping another piece of cake into his mouth, he took a long gulp of coffee from the mug I slid his way. "So, as her neighbors, did you know her at all?"

"We just met her on Saturday, the day we moved in," I said. "She came by to introduce herself."

Kit added, "And then one more time, on the highway—"

"Highway?" DC Downey looked perplexed.

"She means the high *street*," I clarified.

"Yeah, what she said," Kit confirmed. "But we didn't really talk long."

"So you really didn't know her. Would you mind?" As he spoke, he cut a smaller slice of the remaining cake.

"No, we didn't really know Vera at all," Kit said. "But we heard she was found at the beauty shop, stabbed to death."

DC Downey lowered his head and shook it. "Bad business. Very bad business."

Kit leaned forward across the table. "Is it true that she was found by Doreen Carlisle?"

"Um . . . I'm not supposed to discuss the case . . . you understand."

"Of course; I guess that would be totally against police procedure." She leaned back and smiled. "And especially not with outsiders who have been here only two minutes. Can I pour you more coffee?"

"Yes, that would be lovely, and please . . . Ms. James, is it?"

"Kit; call me Kit."

"Kit." He smiled. "We here in Little Dipping don't like to consider anyone, no matter how short a time they've been here, an outsider. We are one big happy family."

"Oh, you—we—certainly are. We love it here, don't we, Val?"

"Yes, we've gotten to know several people in such a short time. Everyone seems so nice."

"Yes, yes." Kit nodded vigorously, then drew her perfectly threaded eyebrows together. "Hmm, except for that one guy in the pub yesterday. Val, what was that man's name?"

"Darwin? No, wait . . . Devon."

"Oh, him?" DC Downey shook his head in disgust. "Total waste of space."

"He's Ivy Scoffing's father, right?" Kit asked.

The constable raised his eyebrows; his look conveyed it was anyone's guess who Devon Scoffing might have fathered. "He was in the pub, you say. I hope he didn't bother you. Actually . . ." He leaned forward across the table to talk in a loud whisper, and Kit and I leaned forward, too, although we could hear him perfectly well. "Claire Scoffing has a restraining order out on him; he's not supposed to be anywhere near her—or Ivy."

"Really?" I still leaned forward. "What did he do?"

"What do any of them do?" was his highly unsatisfactory reply. I waited a second for him to continue. "He was released from prison a month ago. Served only eighteen months, mind you, of a two-year sentence. That's the way it is nowadays. We catch 'em, and the courts give 'em a little holiday, courtesy of the taxpayer."

With this little revelation, both Kit and I sat up, and I hastened to fill the DC's coffee cup while Kit put the last slice of cake on his plate. "So, he was definitely not around last Christmas?" I asked.

"Oooh no; he was banged up in Woodhill Prison, serving at Her Majesty's pleasure. A real mean bastard he is too. Oh, sorry, ladies. Forgive my language."

Kit and I made the same gesture, waving our hands in the air like there was no way to offend either of us.

"So." DC Downey carefully put his coffee mug on the table. "How many times did you see Scoffing?"

"Just once," Kit said. "We were in the pub with Alistair Carlisle, and he came over to our table."

"Yes," I took up the story. "He was a little aggressive toward Alistair, and so Kit and I decided to get out of there."

"Very wise."

"You could check with Pinky. He saw the whole thing."

"Will do." Downey took out a short pencil, licked the end, and wrote Pinky's name on a fresh page in his notebook.

"So who do you think stabbed Vera?" Kit had risen and was clearly looking for something in the cupboard to entice the DC to stay. She returned with a package of chocolate-covered cookies. Like a dealer at a high-stakes poker game tempting a gambler, she placed a few on Downey's now-empty plate.

"Oh, ta," he said, taking one. "These are my absolute favorite."

"Back to Vera." Kit had her elbows on the table now. "Any thoughts on who did it?"

"Or why." Downey flicked a stray crumb from the corner of his mouth with his tongue. "Motive, you see. That's what we need. Seals the case every time. Not that we've had many cases to seal around here."

"Of course." Kit sounded irritated at his lack of information, and I gave her foot a kick, afraid she'd lean across the table, grab Downey by his lapels, and shake what he knew out of him.

"Detective," I said, as a way to distract him from Kit's obvious annoyance, "Pinky thought you might be bringing some officers from the Chichester police station to help with the investigation." I might just as well have accused Downey of being an incompetent idiot.

"Hmm. Possibly. It's not confirmed yet. And not that we need 'em, although our force here in Little Dipping is small, and like I said, we're not used to murder."

"If anyone can solve it, you can." Now Kit sounded confident, and Downey took another cookie.

"Yep, probably. I suppose I should get on. We're just doing a door-to-door check to see if the neighbors saw anything strange or unusual on the day of the murder."

"Wish we could help you more," I said.

He got to his feet, brushed a few crumbs off his jacket, and returned the notebook to his inside pocket. "One final thing, ladies. You say you saw Devon Scoffing in the pub, but did you ever see him with Vera? Or maybe hanging around Magpie Lane, that sort of thing?"

We both shook our heads. "Did they know each other?" Kit asked, leading the policeman to the front door.

"Oh, we all know each other in a place this small. Most of us, anyway. But I'd be particularly interested if you saw Devon Scoffing close by."

I opened the door, and he stepped outside.

"Were they friends?" I asked.

"On the contrary, dear lady. She was the one who turned him in."

CHAPTER TEN

What did Devon do, that Vera had to turn him in?" Kit pushed past me and stepped outside, as if wanting to make sure she got an answer before DC Downey slipped out of our clutches.

"Receiving stolen goods."

"Oh dear; that certainly wouldn't have made her very popular with him—"

"Sorry," he said to Kit, "but I have to get on with *this* crime. Far more important, you see." And he continued his walk away from us. But before he got too far away, he turned and called back, "Thanks again."

Looking as dumbfounded as I felt, Kit stepped back inside, and I closed the door behind us. "Well, that was interesting."

"Ya think?"

Before I could expound on what I thought, my phone rang. I pulled it out of my purse and saw that it was Emily.

"Hi, Mom. I, um, wanted to ask you something."

Now what? I wondered. I could tell by her voice something was up. *Had another body been found? Had Luke been arrested for Vera Wingate's murder? Were David and Heidi going to have a baby?*

"What's up?" I asked, shutting my thoughts off and hoping to end my suspense.

"Well, I . . . now just think about this, Mom. Don't say no without considering it."

"Emily, what on earth are you talking about?" I was growing more concerned. How often did I say no to her, for Pete's sake? The number of times in her life that I'd turned her down for anything could probably be counted on one hand.

"Well, I had this idea, when I first heard you were coming. And then I didn't think it was going to work out. But now I think it could—"

"Emily, will you just tell me?" I sat down on the couch, thinking I might need the support. Kit joined me, her expression asking *what's going on?* I shrugged as I waited for Emily's answer.

"You see, Mom, Luke has this guy from work who's coming to the play Saturday night. And, um, we thought you might like to meet him."

"Well, of course I'll meet him, if he's coming to the play." Was *this* all she had to tell me?

"I mean, we think you might like each other. We kind of told him . . ."

"Told him what, Em?"

"Well, that maybe he . . . he and you—"

"Emily, you mean you're trying to fix me up with him?" I stood and looked down at Kit with my *what the hell* look, as if this were all *her* fault.

Now *she* shrugged.

"Mom. Don't be that way. It's just that Luke works with—well, kinda *for*—this really nice guy. He's British and really charming," she said, sounding like me trying to entice a buyer to check out one of my new listings.

Did he offer a game room and a three-car garage? But I wasn't in the market for a house. Or a man.

"Emily, I'm not looking for a man," I pushed all the authority I could through my phone's mouthpiece.

"But Mom, why should you be alone? Especially now that . . ."

"Now that what? Now that your father has Heidikins?"

"See? It does bother you. And of course it would. You're young and attractive and—"

"Emily, where is this coming from?" I began to pace around the small living room, aware that Kit's head turned whenever I did as she continued to follow the conversation.

"It's not coming from anywhere. Luke's boss is an eligible bachelor, you're an attractive single woman . . ."

I felt certain she was beginning to realize how ridiculous she sounded.

But no. She continued. "Luke has invited him to the play, and he's going to the after-party at Jeffrey's with all of us. I just wanted you to know that he's eager to meet you."

"So I can feel really relaxed while I watch my daughter's debut on the English stage?"

"Mom, don't be silly. It'll be fun. Besides, you'll have Kit right there with you."

That, I didn't tell her, was part of what had me worried.

***

"So what do we think?" Kit asked as we walked along the high street.

Emily had finally been forced to cease her sales pitch so she could get to rehearsal on time, and Kit and I had finally set off on our shopping excursion. "About what?" I asked.

"Take your pick. The script. Your blind date. DC Downey's revelation about Devon's motive—"

"It's not a blind date. Or any kind of date. I made that clear to Emily. I can't stop her from inviting whomever she wants, but if he comes thinking I'm there for him, he'll have another think coming. And it's none of my business that Devon Scoffing had a reason to . . . well, there *is* no reason to commit murder. But either way, that is none of my business. And I don't give a flip about the script."

"First, plenty of people find a reason to commit murder. And second, if you don't give a flip about the script, why did you hide it, for crying out loud?" Kit stopped in the middle of the sidewalk and looked at me.

I paused too. "I don't know. Isn't that what you were telling me to do?"

"I didn't say a word."

"No, but your look did. You know it did."

She sighed, admitting her part in it.

"Why, Kit? Why did you think we should hide it?"

"I don't know." She resumed walking, and I quickly caught up. "It just seemed like . . . like . . . it might be important, or incriminating . . . I don't know."

"Well, we better think about it. You're right. It might be important to the . . . investigation."

"Ya think?" It wasn't her sarcastic *ya think*. She was seriously wondering what I thought.

"I don't know."

A few minutes later we approached The Lady of Shalott, and my thought process was broken. "I'm hungry," I said. "Let's stop for lunch."

"But shouldn't we shop a bit first?"

"Why?"

She followed me through the door of the pub, and we both stopped in our tracks just inside. The place was empty except for Pinky behind the bar.

And the woman in his arms.

They didn't seem to notice us, in spite of the tinkle of the bell above the door that should have announced our presence.

She was small and blond. And when she pulled away from Pinky and looked our way, I saw that she was also curvy and pretty.

"What the hell," Kit murmured, softly enough, I hoped, that only I could hear.

I cleared my throat loudly, until Pinky also turned in our direction. I was shocked to hear him burst into laughter instead of a string of excuses and apologies. Didn't he *care* that we'd just seen him cheating on his wife?

"Ladies," he said, "come on in." He motioned for us to join them, and we stepped away from the front door. "Sit down. I'll take your order. But first," he added, "meet The Duchess."

***

"Well, that was a shock," I said, when we were safely out on the sidewalk an hour later, ready to finally do some shopping.

"I know, right? Didn't you picture The Duchess as a female Pinky?"

"At best." I laughed. At least our lunchtime with Pinky and his bride had proved to be the comic relief needed to lighten my mood. But as we made our way toward Knit One, Purl Two, my irritated thoughts of Emily's scheme and my dark thoughts of Devon Scoffing soon replaced the repartee between Pinky and The Duchess that I'd so enjoyed.

My bad feelings were banished again, however, when just as we reached the knitting shop, my phone rang. I saw that it was my boss, so I told Kit to go ahead and start shopping without me. I'd join her as soon as I finished talking to Tom.

"Yeah, spare me," she said, as she opened the door and entered the store.

I sighed, even though I wasn't surprised. It was the very reason I didn't want to talk until she was out of hearing range. I didn't want to be distracted by the disparaging looks and comments she couldn't seem to resist throwing Tom's way.

Of course he was no better when it came to her. I was used to it, because their relationship hadn't changed since we'd all been in high school. But it didn't mean I felt comfortable when I was thrust between the two of them, in person or via phone calls.

And we had all already processed the fact that Kit and I were on our trip to England largely due to the big bonus I'd received from Tom. Things had quickly returned to normal among us, no matter how grateful we all felt.

"Val? You there?"

"Yes, I am. Where are you?" I didn't ask it literally; I didn't need to know where he was. And I didn't care. I just like throwing things back at him.

"On my way to the James house. Can't wait to experience a dinner there without your nut-job friend."

"Tom, don't be tiresome." I wanted to tell him I had bigger worries than his opinion of Kit. But I didn't want him involved. I never know how he might react.

He ignored my comment. "And of course some poker. It's all about the poker. And you'll never guess who else is joining us there."

"Cool Hand Luke?"

"No, smart one; it's your pal Culotta."

"He's your pal, not mine," I said, but I felt palpitations in my chest at the thought of the Downers Grove detective and all his gorgeousness. Never mind that our history together was like a ride on the American Eagle roller coaster at Six Flags Great America.

I felt irritated all over again at Emily's quest to fix me up.

"I think I'm losing you, Tom. Tom? Tom?" And I hung up to the sound of his protest that he could hear *me* just fine.

When I joined Kit in the knitting shop, not only was she holding the most god-awful sweater I'd ever laid eyes on, she was standing at the cash register purchasing it. I didn't want to insult the shop owner by critiquing Kit's choice out loud, so I merely tapped my friend on the shoulder and proceeded to bug my eyes out as I looked at the sweater and then in her eyes and then back at the sweater, surely body language for *why the hell are you buying* that *one?* It was a putrid shade of chartreuse with a golf green knitted in the middle of both the front and back. A red flag with a blue number one was stitched atop the front green, and a purple flag with a gold number eighteen decorated the back one. Although I admired the intricate knitting pattern, the total effect couldn't have been more garish.

"You're buying that for Larry?" I tried to sound neutral.

But Kit didn't seem to worry about the shop owner's—or her own husband's—feelings. "I told you I was irritated with him," she said.

***

We did a bit more window shopping, but we both seemed to have lost our urge to actually buy anything. So we returned to our cottage, took naps, and then decided to do what we figured English people do after nap time. We were going to have a spot of tea and some digestive biscuits.

I reached for the porcelain teapot dotted with tiny pink flowers and dropped in two bags of Typhoo tea. Meanwhile, Kit picked up the teakettle as soon as it began whistling and poured the boiling water into the pot. I didn't know why we'd need them, but I decided to place spoons on our saucers, next to the delicate teacups. And when I opened the drawer to grab two, I immediately spotted them.

Six spoons once again nestled together in the drawer. I was certain there were now six because I counted them twice.

CHAPTER ELEVEN

Before I could fully grasp the fact that there were once again six spoons, a light tapping on the front door captured my attention.

Tossing the spoons in the drawer, I hurried to see who had come calling. It was a young woman, nineteen or twenty, who looked vaguely familiar. Tall and pretty, she had glossy brown hair falling over her shoulders, and a sweet heart-shaped face.

"Hi," I said, as she smiled back at me, displaying even, sparkling-white teeth.

"Hi," she said. "I'm Pippa. From Knit One, Purl Two." I noticed the inflection in her voice as she went up a notch at the end of each sentence, making it sound like a question.

"Yes," I said, answering her. "I recognize you now, Pippa."

She gave another smile. "You and your friend were in the shop this afternoon?" Again, a question.

"Yes."

"My mum owns the shop. Your friend bought a sweater earlier—"

"Right. Come in, Pippa. I love your name, by the way."

"Thanks." She stepped into the hallway, and then I led her to the living room. At the same time, Kit joined us from the kitchen.

"This is Pippa, from Knit One, Purl Two," I said to Kit. "You haven't come to take back the sweater, have you?" I turned toward Pippa and ushered her farther into the room. "Or did Kit forget to pay?"

"Oh no." Pippa dug into the pocket of her jeans. "In fact, you left your credit card in the shop," she now addressed Kit. "Mum asked me to return it."

"How kind." Kit took the Amex Gold Card Pippa offered. "I'd be in deep doo-doo if I lost this little baby." She kissed the card, and we all three laughed.

"How did you know where to find us?" I took a seat on the couch and gestured for Pippa to do the same.

"Everyone knows who you are. You're quite the celebrities around here. This is such a small village, and news travels fast. May I ask where in America you are from?"

"Chicago area," I said.

"I'm going to Virginia in the autumn, to attend college."

"That's great," Kit said. "Can I fix you a cup of tea?"

"Yes, that would be ever so lovely." Pippa smiled.

***

Sitting across the table, in the same spot DC Downey had occupied earlier, Pippa asked, "How are you enjoying your holiday, Ms. . . ."

"I'm Kit, and this is Val." Kit took the chocolate-covered cookies that had escaped the police officer's ravenous appetite and fanned them out on a plate in front of the young woman. "And we love it here."

"You were in London for a few days, right?" Pippa took a cookie and nibbled the end.

I wondered briefly how she knew, then remembered what she'd just said; the population of Little Dipping did indeed seem to know everything.

"London's cool." Pippa nodded, and she got no argument from us.

I noticed she was wearing a hand-knitted sweater, pale blue, with the words KEEP CALM AND DON'T FORGET TO FLOSS knitted into it with white stitches.

When she saw me eyeing it, she looked down and laughed. "Sorry about this; my dad's a dentist, and Mum knitted it for me. She insists I wear something she made whenever I help her in the shop."

"It's cute," I said, and compared to the hideous item Kit had purchased, it was Chanel.

"So, what a terrible thing . . . about Vera Wingate," Kit changed the subject abruptly, digging right in.

"It's so sad," I added. "We met her only a couple of times, but she seemed very nice."

"Yes, she is . . . was." Pippa stopped to take a sip of her tea.

"I don't guess you have many murders here in your little village," Kit said.

"Oh no . . . only the other one, of course."

"Other one?" Kit looked intently at our guest.

"Yes. The other woman. Perhaps you didn't hear. A lady was murdered about two years ago. It was awful. She was also stabbed." Pippa visibly shuddered. "The police never did find out who did it."

"Oh my goodness," I said. "That's horrible. Where did they find her body?"

Pippa looked at us both, her brown eyes wide. "They found her body here. In this cottage. I guess Vera didn't mention it?"

"Wait a minute," I said. "What do you mean? Why would Vera mention anything?"

"Didn't you know? Vera Wingate owned this cottage. In fact, she owned several on this street."

"We got it from a real estate agent," I said. But Emily had taken care of the rental, and the truth was, I didn't actually know who she had rented it from.

"I expect the agent didn't mention who owned it. It's got rather a bad reputation, what with the murder and all. But it is lovely." She looked around the small kitchen, her gaze taking in its whitewashed stone walls and the heavy dark beams that ran across the ceiling.

"Yes," we both agreed, as Kit poured more tea from the pot.

***

"*I come to wive it wealthily in Padua; If wealthily, then happily*—Jeffrey, this bloody costume is too tight. I can hardly raise my arms." Petruchio, also known as Ernie Limestone, looked down to the row of seats closest to the front of the stage, searching for the director.

"Oh, *please*," Jeffrey yelled back. "I've told you a thousand times that we'll get the bloody costume adjusted before Saturday. Would you mind just getting on with it?"

Ernie/Petruchio, who Emily had told me owned a butcher shop in the next village, sighed deeply and returned to his character. "*If wealthily, then happily in Padua.*"

"Thank heavens for that," I heard Jeffrey grumble loudly from his seat three rows ahead of us.

Two seats down from him sat Emily. She turned and gave me a raised-eyebrows smile, her lips pursed, and I was stunned by how lovely she looked in her costume. She was wearing a wig of luxurious long black hair, with a smattering of tendrils outlining her face. A headband of tiny flowers covered the crown of her head. Her red velvet bodice was laced over a fluffy white tunic, cut low enough to reveal a hint of cleavage. When she stood and stretched her arms, I admired the long full skirt, gathered at her tiny waist. She looked as comfortable as if she dressed that way every day.

I turned my attention back to the stage and the not-so-comfortable butcher. As the scene ended, Jeffrey jumped up from his seat. "Okay, okay, people." He clapped his hands. "You all need to pick up the pace; I'd really like our first dress rehearsal to be finished *before* opening night—if you can manage it. Deidre, what is that expression on your face?" He snapped his fingers at Deidre, who, I had learned, ran the Books on Wheels traveling library. "You look like you just stepped in a pile of dog . . . Fred, are you sure you don't have that wig on backwards? It looks awkward."

I was realizing that Jeffrey's style of directing was to never give a compliment, but rather to find flaws wherever he could. He waved to the gang of disgruntled actors on the stage and dismissed them for a five-minute break. Then he turned around and faced the back of the theater before exiting his row and heading in our direction.

"Dear American ladies," he greeted us.

"Hi," we said in unison.

He inched his way down the row in front of us and took a seat, turning to face us. "So, what do you think?"

"Terrific," I said.

"Illuminating," Kit added.

He began speaking in a hushed voice. "I wonder if you'd be interested in doing me an enormous favor." He didn't wait to get a response, but leaned closer toward us. "Here's the thing. Two cast members are not going to make it to the weekend performances. One blasted woman has a wisdom tooth being pulled tomorrow. She assures me she'll be ready for next week, but . . ." He waved a hand in the air, indicating she was dead to him no matter when she showed up or how many wisdom teeth she had pulled. "And another one has a grandbaby scheduled to be born on Saturday morning. She has begged me for the weekend off so she can visit it. Ugh! Amateurs! So, what I propose is that you two ladies fill in on Saturday night and Sunday afternoon.

Obviously, these are not speaking roles, just townspeople meandering around the stage taking up space. Might be fun for you. You could come along to tomorrow night's final rehearsal and—"

"We'll do it!" Kit yelled so loudly I had to actually put my hand on her arm to shush her.

"That'll help me out a lot." He smiled. "There's nothing to it, really; as I said, it's mainly milling about the stage looking all Italian and Elizabethan at the same time. If that's even possible."

"We'll do it," Kit said again, this time in a normal voice. "What about costumes?" She was so into it and sounded so authoritative, I thought her next move might be to employ an agent and start negotiating a contract.

"Emily can take you to see Macie tomorrow; she does our costumes. You can get fitted, and I'm sure she'll have no problem adjusting what we have on hand. I lack one noblewoman and one commoner."

"We'll do it," Kit said for the third time, nodding seriously, and I inwardly groaned.

I didn't need a crystal ball to predict who would be the commoner.

***

As we walked home, Kit was clearly channeling *A Star is Born*. "I've always wanted to be on the stage," she said dreamily.

"Really? Well, this could be your big break, Kitty Kat. It's obvious a noblewoman is the role you were born to play."

"It'll be fun. Wait until I tell Larry." She laughed and linked her arm through mine. As long as we'd been friends, we'd never spent any time walking arm in arm, the way we had seen plenty of women do in England. Of course I don't think we'd spent as much time walking anywhere as we had here.

"Well, it might make up for that awful sweater you bought him," I mumbled. If she heard me, she didn't comment. In her mind, she was already accepting a Tony Award.

As we turned the corner onto Magpie Lane, she suddenly stopped, dragging me backward. She held out a finger and pointed down the lane, past our cottage to Vera's. The police were gone from her front door, but we could see a dim light in the window facing the street. "C'mon." Kit grabbed my arm and pulled me past our own front door. "Let's see who's there."

We came to a halt outside Vera's place and opened the squeaky gate that led to her tiny front yard. As we did so, I realized the light emanating from the front room was not from an electric bulb, but rather a flashlight. Its owner swept the light across the room inside and then the light disappeared.

"Here," Kit whispered, moving swiftly to a space in the hedgerow that ran along the fence just inside the tiny yard. Then she crouched down and beckoned me to follow.

"What are you doing?" I whispered back, taking up the space beside her. She had patted the ground as if offering me a seat on a couch. "Kit, this is ridiculous."

"Shush." She put a finger to her lips. "Let's see who's in there."

"Aargh. This is stupid; really, we—" And then I shut up as Vera's front door opened and a figure silently appeared, closing the door after stepping out and then running past us and into the street.

Kit nudged me. "Oh my," she said. "Did you see who that was?"

CHAPTER TWELVE

What do we do?" I asked.

"What do you mean, what do we do?" Like me, Kit was no longer whispering.

"Well, we saw her in there. We let her run right past us. We need to tell someone."

Kit started to respond just as the front door of the cottage opened again. She clamped her jaws shut, and we both remained mute as we watched Devon Scoffing scurry past us, following in his daughter's footsteps.

Then Kit spoke. "What the—"

"What the, indeed."

We both looked at the cottage in silence for a few moments, waiting for someone else to exit. Then, as if concluding the parade was over, Kit stood up. I followed suit, although not nearly so smoothly. I'd been crouched long enough to grow stiff, so my return to a standing position was slow. I held my hand on my lower back, wondering how my friend stays so limber. "Kit, wait up," I said, as I realized she'd taken a few steps toward our cottage. "What are we going to do?"

"I'm thinking, I'm thinking." She continued walking briskly. "First, we're going to have a drink. And I don't mean sherry."

***

"We have to tell someone," I repeated my earlier directive, although I was aware that I said it tentatively, sounding like our new friend Pippa. What I meant, of course, was *DO we have to tell someone?* We had taken our spots on either end of the couch, and we'd been sipping our wine in silence. But I figured Kit had had enough time to think by now. We needed to *act.*

"Who would we tell?" she asked.

"Well, the police? Or at least Claire Scoffing? Shouldn't she know that her ex-husband was breaking his restraining order?"

"And that's our business how?"

"Oh yeah, like you ever worry about something being your business or not." I didn't say it meanly. I was simply stating a fact. "Really, Kit, we have to tell *someone.*"

"No, we do not. What did we see? A father and a daughter obviously having had a visit. Restraining orders aren't always fair in custody battles, ya know. Maybe they were visiting the only way they can."

"Yeah, but in the house of the dead woman who had turned him in?" I felt myself starting to agree with Kit. Maybe we should keep out of it, given the demise of this last person who had tattled on Devon Scoffing.

"Probably the one place no one would suspect them of meeting, Vera Wingate's cottage."

Even though I didn't have the energy—or will—to fight Kit on this, I thought I should try one more time. "We could get in trouble if we don't report—"

"Who knows we saw them? Only us. At least let's sleep on it," she added.

We sipped in silence a while longer before I asked her, "Why are you irritated with Larry?"

"Humph. Let me count the ways." She chuckled.

"So nothing serious," I said, feeling relief that my best friends remained contentedly married. Someone had to.

"I didn't say that." She took a drink of her wine.

"Well, what then?" I sat up straighter, concerned yet glad for a distraction from what I thought of as the Ivy/Devon quandary.

"He's talking about retiring."

"Larry? Retire? But he's so young!"

"Exactly. Too young to be home with me all day every day, that's for sure."

"Can he afford to?"

"*He* thinks he can. *I* don't. I'm not ready to sell our house and live like paupers, when he's perfectly capable—"

"Well, he's an accountant and financial planner. I'm sure he's figured—"

"I don't see why on earth he'd want to retire."

"Maybe he's sick of the pressure. Maybe he's not feeling that great. Maybe he wants to spend his time—"

"On the golf course. Or in front of his TV or computer."

"So?"

She looked at me as if I were speaking a foreign language, and I decided maybe I just couldn't relate to her feelings about a husband retiring. I, after all, no longer had a husband.

"You guys will work out what's best. You always do." I reached to her end of the couch and patted her knee.

"Humph." She looked deep in thought as she sipped her wine, and I supposed she was conjuring up all sorts of irritating scenarios of their life in retirement. So I was shocked when she asked, "How the hell did that script get into this cottage? And what's up with that bell disappearing and reappearing? And the spoon that went missing?"

"Oh yeah, about that." I told her how I'd found the sixth spoon back in the drawer with the others just before Pippa arrived.

"Someone is obviously coming and going from *our* cottage. Do you think it's Devon and Ivy?"

"Well, I think Ivy is a prime suspect. But *why*? She's just a child."

"A very precocious child."

"A very annoying child."

"Val, that's mean."

"It's not mean, it's true."

Kit shook her head in disagreement. I knew she had a soft spot for Ivy, and nothing we'd seen or suspected had hardened that.

***

Not surprisingly, I didn't sleep well that night. I found myself wondering about the murder that had taken place in the very cottage—maybe in the very room—I was trying to sleep in. And only two years ago. I wondered if Emily had known about it before she rented it for us. And I wondered if it should make any difference.

I kept picturing Ivy running—escaping?—out of Vera's cottage, followed by her father. Had Ivy been there with him of her own volition?

I knew that come morning, whether Kit liked it or not, we had to tell someone *something*.

But the morning brought other distractions and worries, and I quite forgot about Ivy, Devon, and yes, the woman murdered in our cottage. The show, it seemed, must go on, and that meant Kit and I had to be properly costumed.

We were awakened by Emily's rapping on our door at six o'clock, hours before her preferred wake-up time, I knew. Only the fact that I was in England and my body clock was in utter disarray accounted for the fact that *I* was still sleeping at that hour. But I was, and so it took a few minutes before I realized the sound I had incorporated into my dream as that of my super back home finally fixing my loose molding was actually someone at our door in Little Dipping.

By the time I descended the stairs, Emily was inside our living room. "How did you get in, Em?"

"There's a key under the rock by the stoop. Didn't I tell you that?"

"No, as a matter of fact you didn't. Who else knows?"

She shrugged. "Not sure. Why?"

"Well, I just—never mind." I could tell by her face—and the hour—that she was here on business, and I decided it didn't matter who knew about the key. I'd just see to it that it got brought inside and kept away from any unwanted visitors. The kind that withdrew and deposited objects like so many bank transactions.

"Is Kit awake?" my daughter asked, and before I could answer, Kit appeared on the stairs. She sleepily made her way down, a black silk kimono wrapped around her slim body and a sleep mask embroidered with the words *Queen Sleeping* pushed up to her forehead.

"Yes, I am, honey. What time are we meeting with the costume designer?" She suddenly sounded as infused with energy as if she'd drunk two lattes—with extra shots of espresso.

"Um," my daughter stalled, and I knew she probably dreaded reminding Kit that the costume designer was actually a local homemaker donating her time to alter a dress from the Goodwill for her to wear. Or the English equivalent of all that. "We have a seven o'clock appointment with Macie Brown, who lives in the next lane," Emily said.

I smiled inwardly at how British my daughter sounded, but Kit muttered a disappointed, "Oh." I knew she'd rather be driving into London for some haute couture.

I glanced at my watch and said, "We'll hurry and throw something on, Emily. We can make seven easily."

"Is there coffee?" Kit asked, no longer sounding already fortified.

"No," I said. "And I don't want to mess with that caffy-affy thing when we're in a hurry." I knew I sounded rather grumpy. I-haven't-had-my-coffee-yet grumpy, to be precise.

"Cafetière," Kit corrected, sounding, to my ear, even grumpier.

"No worries," Emily assured us. "We'll pop into Brew Ha Ha; it's on the corner on our way there. The coffee is very good."

"So Macie lives in that direction?" I asked, feeling disappointed that we wouldn't be walking by Vera's house. I was morbidly curious, and eager to see if someone *else* would come running out as we passed by. Feeling more like Kit than myself, I vowed to walk by there when we were done with our fittings.

Emily nodded and yawned before plopping down on the couch to wait for us. I realized she probably hadn't had any coffee yet herself.

***

Paper cups filled with the hot beverages of our choice in hand, and at least three sips under our belts, we exited the coffee shop knowing we were going to arrive at Macie's a few minutes late but feeling, at last, close to normal, if not cheerful. At least *I* couldn't claim to feel cheerful yet.

I felt slightly annoyed, in fact, that Emily and Kit seemed awfully lighthearted, given all that had gone on recently. And two years ago. Which reminded me . . .

"Em," I said, "did you know there was another murder in Little Dipping, a couple of years ago? And right in the Gaston cottage, of all places?" I shuddered, and a little coffee spilled out of my cup.

"You're kidding me," she said. Then, after a minute of utter silence that I dared Kit with a glare to break, my daughter added, "So that's why I got it so cheap. I thought my agent acted a little weird. And I'd heard it hadn't been rented for a long while. Oh, Mom. And Kit. I'm so sorry."

"Who cares?" Kit said. "I'm just glad you got a discount, sweetie." She chuckled.

"Don't worry, honey," I added. "It's a lovely place, and that . . . unfortunate incident has nothing to do with us. Or the cottage, I'm sure."

"Yes, I'm sure too," Kit said, but I could tell she was not.

"I don't know," Emily said warily—and more honestly.

We walked along the sidewalk, sipping in silence. And then Emily spoke again. "OMG. So *that's* what she meant."

I was certain I'd just been entertaining the same thought. "You mean Claire Scoffing acting surprised that we'd rented the Gaston cottage?"

"No. Well, that too, of course. But no. Doreen said something to me that made no sense. Until now."

CHAPTER THIRTEEN

Yoo-hoo, ladies!"

Before I had a chance to question Emily about what Doreen had said, my thoughts were interrupted by a woman standing at the gate of her cottage. She held out a hand in greeting but didn't wait for me to take it. Instead, she moved both arms in a sweeping gesture, ushering us inside her home. Rather like a flight attendant indicating the emergency exits.

The center of Macie Brown's living room housed an old Singer sewing machine, complete with foot pedal. Bolts of fabric and sewing notions took up the couch and two fat armchairs, and assorted finished garments hung from a picture rail that ran the circumference of the small room.

"Please make yourselves at home," she said. "I'm Macie. How are you, Emily? Do sit—just move some of that stuff. You must be Emily's mum. I see the resemblance. Do you want a cuppa—oh, I see you have some. This is very last-minute, but don't worry; I'll fix you up in a jiffy. Emily, was that bodice comfortable? Because I can take it in if you want me to. She's got such a lovely figure . . ." Macie paused to catch her breath, looking at me for confirmation of Emily's fine frame.

"Hello, Macie," I spoke quickly, before she could begin talking again. "Yes, I'm Val Pankowski, Emily's mom, and this is our friend Kit James. This is so nice of you." I felt I had to hurry, before my words were eaten up by another stream of her yammering.

"It's nothing. I'm used to last-minute fittings; Jeffrey keeps me on my toes. I once had to dress Buffalo Bill and two cowboys in an hour for *Annie Get Your Gun*. Outbreak of Spanish flu in the village, and the cast was dropping like flies."

She flapped a pudgy hand in the air, then pulled a square of paper out of the pocket of her skirt and studied it. "So, we need a noblewoman and a peasant—"

"Actually, it's supposed to be a commoner, not a peasant," I said, already resigned to my role but eager not to be downgraded before I'd even begun.

"Right." Macie nodded, still scrutinizing the piece of paper. "You're the peasant—er, commoner—then?" She looked up at me, but she wasn't questioning my assigned role.

"Exactly." Kit was gazing across the room, eyeing a green velvet gown hanging from the back of the living room door. "This is quite magnificent." She took a step over a large plastic container of hats, most of them with feathers. Caressing the hem of the green costume, she asked, "Did you make this, Macie?"

"Ah well, it started out as Maid Marian for Jeffrey's *Robin Hood*—"

"You are a genius," my pal said.

Macie touched the tape measure hanging around her neck, as if to make sure it was still there. She was a short woman and pleasantly plump, as plump people like to say. Her gray hair looked quite fetching twisted up into some kind of intricate knot on the top of her head. "Here, why don't you try it on?" She nimbly hopscotched her way across the room, avoiding the debris littering the floor, and took the gown from its perch.

Seeing it up close, I was impressed by the fine stitching and realized it was actually two pieces: a full skirt and a cropped jacket.

She handed it to Kit and then bent down to the container holding some hats and pulled one out. It was the same shade of green, with a magnificent feather sweeping across its crown. "This will be perfect with your lovely auburn hair. Emily, show Kit into the bedroom, will you, and help her change, and let's see . . ." She began tapping her lip while studying me. "Peasant—ooh, sorry; I mean commoner. Where did I put that?"

"Didn't you already have the costume for the lady who was supposed to be in the play?" I asked.

"Yes, love, I did. But she's a lot smaller than you."

Just what every woman wants to hear, I thought.

"I'll have to find something else," Macie continued. "Don't worry; I've got all sorts of odds and sods around here. And it's only for a couple of nights, right? I expect Jeffrey wants you to stick to the back of the stage. Hmm . . . let's see." She cast her eyes around the room and then pulled a large cardboard box out from behind the couch. "This is the stuff I used for *Les Miz* a few years back. I bet I can find something in here. French peasants shouldn't be too different from Italians, eh?"

"Commoner," I reminded her wearily, but I had a feeling I should just accept the relegation and go with it.

"Right . . . bingo!" She had opened the flaps of the box and pulled out a long piece of something or other. It was muddy brown, or maybe dishwater gray. "This will do nicely," she said. "Look! It's even got a hood."

At that precise moment Kit emerged from the bedroom in the green velvet number, looking a bit like Scarlett O'Hara on her way to meet Rhett (after doing her thing with the drapes). She was wearing black leather gloves and had somehow appropriated a small riding crop. With the hat and its feather perched on her head, she swayed into the room, stepping carefully over a stack of magazines.

Macie dropped the ghastly robe, or whatever the hell it was, and clapped her hands together in delight. "Oh, Kit, you were *made* to wear that. You look magnificent. She looks magnificent, doesn't she, girls?"

I nodded in agreement, and I could see Emily's eyes light up with joy.

"Here, Val." Macie bent down. "Try this on." In what was clearly an afterthought, she handed me a bunch of fabric that I had merely to slip on over my head. Trappist monk came to mind.

***

"Shall I pour?" Kit picked up the teapot.

Emily had left us to run back to the theater. Macie had made tea, and Kit and I joined her at the kitchen table, where she was busy securing the gold braiding that wrapped around the shoulders of Kit's velvet jacket.

Apparently, my hooded garment needed no such embellishments.

"Yes, please." Macie didn't look up, but instead took a pin from the pincushion she wore on her wrist. "So, how are you liking the Gaston cottage? I heard it was refurbished after . . . well, after the . . ."

"The murder?" Kit poured milk into the teacups from a jug shaped, appropriately, like a cow. I watched the milk gush from the cow's mouth.

Macie looked up. "Yes. You know about that? It was awful. First murder we had here, that I know of. And now poor Vera."

She stopped to give a shudder, her double chin shaking slightly. Then she put the end of a piece of thread to her lips, licked it, and held it up to the eye of a needle.

"Who was the murdered woman?" Kit was still wearing her feathered hat, along with a plaid robe Macie had supplied. "Do you know?"

"Oh yes," Macie said, after successfully threading the needle on her first attempt. She began putting impossibly tiny stitches into the shoulder of the jacket. We waited for her to continue, but for the first time since we had arrived, she seemed at a loss for words.

I glanced at Kit, but she also remained silent. "So, Macie," I said. "Who was——?"

"Her name was Belinda Bailey. She was young . . . in her thirties; these days that seems young to me. She was a good friend of Vera Wingate's, so poor Vera was devastated. But who would have thought the same thing would happen . . . She was a pretty girl; she had been doing research at the university—Sussex University, that is. She was very bright. Medical research, I believe it was. I had heard that Vera was funding her . . ."

She stopped talking and took up a pair of tiny scissors and snipped the end of the thread attached to the braid. "There, that should hold it." She laid the jacket out flat and gave it a once-over, seeming satisfied. "Are you excited for tomorrow's performance? I was in one of Jeffrey's plays once. I was the cook in an Agatha Christie thingy; it was a lot of fun, but I told him afterwards I'd stick to the costumes, thank you very much——"

"And they never found out who killed Belinda?" Thank goodness Kit interrupted her.

"Nooooo. But we all had our suspicions."

"Such as?" I asked, before Macie could go off on another tangent.

"I don't like to say, and I certainly don't like gossip, especially village gossip. It spreads quicker than wildfire in Little Dipping. But there were rumors and . . ."

"And?" Kit and I said in unison.

"All I will say is that Belinda was seen hanging around with . . ."

It was infuriating, but she stopped talking. Kit and I were left with our mouths open, staring at her.

"With who?" Kit asked.

"With whom?" I flashed my friend an apologetic look. I hadn't meant to respond with a spoken autocorrect.

"Devon Scoffing, if you must know. Of course he never would have won husband of the year. And I suspect— no, I'm certain—he only ever married Claire because she was . . . you know . . ."

"Pregnant with Ivy?"

"Right. But I'll give him his due; he adores that girl . . . when he isn't banged up inside, that is."

"Macie." Kit poured more tea from the pot. "We understand that Devon was just released from prison a month ago."

"Right. He was in for receiving stolen goods, although he claims he was framed. Fitted up by the police, if you can imagine. Anyhow, he was sent down. But I hear he's back in Little Dipping. Claire has a restraining order, but they're as useless as the paper they're written on. I assume they are written on paper, right? Although these days, who knows? Maybe they just text it to you."

***

Kit and I took our time walking home. My outfit was stashed in the bottom of a brown paper bag, but Kit's fabulous gown was on a hanger with a large sheet of clear plastic covering it. She was still wearing her hat with the feather.

"Who'da thunk we'd come to England and end up on the stage," she said happily.

And I was happy for her. I figured I could make it through two performances, lurking at the back of the stage doing whatever the hell Jeffrey directed.

"So," she changed the subject, "are we thinking that Devon Scoffing murdered Belinda Bailey?"

"Maybe Claire Scoffing did it," I said, reaching our gate and opening it for the noblewoman to precede me. "Maybe she was jealous."

"Maybe Vera did it."

"Why would she do it?"

"Maybe she was jealous too."

***

At five o'clock Kit and I drove to the theater for the dress rehearsal. Kit had insisted we wear our costumes for the short journey, and just like the noblewoman she had become, once we got out of the car, she glided along looking so very, very pleased with herself.

I slunk along behind her, holding my hooded getup a few inches off the ground. It was way too long, but Macie hadn't offered to alter it for me.

There were several cars parked in the lot, and we wedged our way in between a dark sedan and a Mini Cooper.

"Look!" Kit tried to find my arm in the billowing fabric of my costume. "There, over there, in that BMW. I think it's Jeffrey and . . . someone else." She stopped on the pretense of adjusting her hat and feather. "See? Over there?"

I followed her gaze and did indeed see Jeffrey with a woman seated beside him. It appeared she was crying; her head was bent forward, and her long dark hair fell over her face.

"It's Doreen," I whispered when the woman raised her head. "She seems upset."

"C'mon." Before I could stop her, Kit headed over to the car, bent down, and tapped on the window with her crop. "Hi, Jeffrey," she said as the window slowly lowered. "One noblewoman and one peasant at your service."

I didn't bother correcting her because the passenger door flew open and Doreen darted out, running through the parking lot and disappearing from sight. I was impressed that she could do it in her ridiculously high heels.

"Ladies." Jeffrey emerged from his vehicle, ignoring his fleeing passenger. "I would hardly have recognized you. What a bang-up job our Macie did on you two."

He hit a button on his key fob, and we heard the sound of his door locking.

"So, are you ready for your close-up?" He laughed, and with an arm around each of our shoulders, led us toward the theater's stage door. "Little Dipping today, Broadway tomorrow, eh?"

"Was that Doreen?" Kit turned her head in the direction of his car. "Is she okay? She looked a little upset."

"Nothing to be alarmed about. Dramatics. Even worse, *amateur* dramatics. Now, let's go put on a show."

***

"*Townspeople.* Where are my townspeople?" Jeffrey stood in the aisle by the front row, clapping his hands loudly. "Okay. So, we're milling, we're chatting, we're doing what bloody townspeople do."

I mingled with the other twelve or so residents of Padua in an attempt to depict life in the Italian town back in the day. My main problem was that I was one of only a few commoners/peasants, and it was difficult striking up a conversation with my betters.

Kit, who was stunning in the green velvet she was born to wear, was also apparently in the role she was born to play. I watched her from my place as far back on the stage as I could get without actually disappearing into the scenery. She was now in deep talks with a guy dressed in some sort of military uniform. Waving the crop in the air, although there was no horse in sight, she occasionally punctuated her fake words by slapping her left palm with her horsey prop. In general, I had to admit she was very good, although I didn't think I should tell her. It was going to be hard enough just to get her to remove her feathered hat before she went to bed.

"Okay, people, listen." Jeffrey ran up the four steps to the stage and indicated we should all gather around him. "Here's what I need," he said.

Kit was the first at his side, eagerly looking for direction while the rest of us trudged toward our director like Renaissance zombies.

"I want all of you to watch this lady." He took Kit's gloved hand and raised it high, like she was a boxer and he was declaring her the winner. "She is the perfect noblewoman."

"Ah *shit*," I heard a muffled sound from the townsperson standing next to me. As commoners go, his costume was the closest to mine in total shabbiness.

I looked at him and raised my eyebrows, silently demanding an explanation.

He lowered his head and spoke in a hoarse whisper. "That damn woman has stepped on my foot three times and pushed me out of the way twice. If someone doesn't take that bloody riding crop off her—"

"Yes," I had to agree. "She's an absolute menace. Bloody amateur!"

CHAPTER FOURTEEN

Emily rode home with us after rehearsal. I'd been surprised she was willing to leave the theater as quickly as I'd insisted Kit and I depart. And that hadn't been easy, removing Kit from her moment of glory.

Jeffrey had invited us to the pub with some of the cast members, but I'd told him we had other plans. It was a lie, but I'd felt suddenly claustrophobic in my robe and wanted more than anything to get back to our cottage to don my Cubs T-shirt and enjoy a bowl of cereal. An episode of *Law & Order* would be the perfect nightcap.

But I could tell immediately that something was up with Emily, something she had to tell me, however much she dreaded it. "Mom," she said in that tone that warned me, as soon as she climbed into the back seat and before she even shut the door.

"Yeah, Em?" I shut my own door and turned in the seat so I could see her. Suddenly I went cold with fear. My robe couldn't counteract the chill that came with my sudden gut feeling for what Emily had to tell me. "Em? Did you talk to Grandma? Is William okay?"

"Huh?" she said, and just that quickly my chill stopped.

Obviously, William was okay. Or if he wasn't, Emily didn't know any more than I did. "What, Em? What were you going to tell me?" She wiggled in her seat, but as much as I wanted to watch her body language, my neck was getting a crick in it. I turned to face the front, but my attention remained in the back. I pictured her still squirming, and that image matched the strain in her voice when she finally spoke.

"Mom, about tomorrow night."

Oh brother. Here it comes, I thought. *Some info about my "date," no doubt.* I remained silent, not willing to make it easier on her. What *had* she been thinking?

"You should know . . . um . . . there's—"

"Did you see our scenes, Emily?" Kit asked, as if no one else had been speaking. She was obviously still in her own little world of theater, oblivious to the conversation Emily and I were having trouble starting.

"For heaven's sake, she was five feet away on the same stage," I said, hating the irritation I heard in my voice. "How do you think she would have missed it?"

"Yes," Emily said. "You were both great. You looked beautiful, Kit. You did too, Mom."

"Kit, we were in the middle of an important discussion." I waved away Emily's compliment. But perhaps she *couldn't* see us. If she thought I looked beautiful, she should get her eyes checked. "Would you forget about your starring role long enough to let us finish?"

The mere thought of having to make small talk with the guy from Luke's work, maybe while still wearing my tacky robe, was annoying me almost as much as Emily's inability to just spill out whatever it was she was trying to tell me. Did she feel she had to warn me what to say, or what not to say? Humph. Kit was more apt to need her direction. Or David.

Well, at least I won't have to endure my date around him, I thought, *since he's too busy to come to his daughter's play.* And then I thought, *Oh no! Maybe that's changed. Maybe he* is *coming.* "Emily, is this about your father?"

"How did you know?" I could feel her leaning forward, and by now we were at her cottage.

"Kit, can you park for a minute?" I turned to face Emily.

"Why don't you guys just come in?" my daughter asked.

"Yeah, let's toast to our new roles," Kit said.

I started to tell them I longed more for a peaceful hour in my own home away from home before grabbing a good night's sleep, but then I reminded myself I was with *Emily.* In *England.* I had to savor every minute, annoyed or not. No, I *wanted* to savor every minute.

"Sure," I said. "But Emily, for Pete's sake, tell me what you wanted to tell me."

"Let's go inside." She was already halfway up the walk, and Kit and I could barely hear her as we followed.

"Hi, girls." My son-in-law looked up from his laptop to greet us. "You all ready for opening night? Those costumes are great. Kit, you look magnificent."

His smile slowly faded as he looked at us. "But why the long faces?"

"Long faces?" Kit looked at him as if he'd said the world was flat. "Are you kidding? Tonight was wonderful, and tomorrow night will be even better." She actually squealed in delight.

"I meant my wife and her mum," Luke said, exhibiting the conversion to Britspeak I had been noticing. I'd thought it was so cute, but now I thought of his British coworker—or boss, or whatever the hell the guy was—and found it less so.

"Oh," Kit said. She looked at Emily and then at me and probably recalled my harsh words to her in the car before repeating, "Oh."

"I guess you told her," Luke said, with what sounded like a note of sympathy.

"No, she hasn't told me. Will you just do so now, Emily?" Then I softened, remembering once again how short my time with her was. "Honey, is everything okay?"

Somehow I knew it wasn't. But somehow I also knew it was bad news for *me*, not her.

I just didn't realize *how* bad.

"Mom, Dad's coming tomorrow night, after all, and he's bringing Heidi." She sighed, as if a big load had been lifted. And no doubt it had.

But now *I* wore it. *Crap.* So that's why she'd arranged the date for me. She didn't want me to be a single around David and his date. Or rather his fiancée. "How long have you known this?" I asked, as if it mattered. But I was curious as to whether I was right about her motivation.

"Not long. But when he found out he *could* come opening night, well, I guess he just assumed I was inviting Heidi too; but you know, Mom, if I'd thought he would bring her—"

"Oh, Emily, you don't need to worry," I said. "I'm fine with him bringing Heidi." From where she stood behind my daughter, Kit gave me a *who are you kidding* look. But it was quickly followed by a look of empathy and respect. She knew it was just the mother in me speaking. And she was conveying with her expression that she'd make sure I made it through.

"Really, Mom?"

"Really, Em. Now where's our wine? How can we toast without wine?"

"Wine, schmine," Emily said, giddy with relief. "Luke, get the champagne."

"I thought we were saving it for opening night?" But he headed to the refrigerator, as if acknowledging that his wife knew best.

Emily put her arm through mine and led us over to where Kit stood. She linked her other arm through everyone's favorite noblewoman and said, "No, I want to drink to Mom and Kit. Just Mom and Kit."

***

Kit and I insisted one glass of champagne was our limit, as much as we—at least she—would have liked to sit all night and chat with Luke and the now-relaxed Emily. Unfortunately, I did still wear the load Emily had bestowed upon me and could think of little else except how much I wanted opening night to be over so I could genuinely savor my time with Emily. One inane thought did break through my worry as the four of us sat around their kitchen table, about how kitchens on both sides of the Atlantic seem to be more popular gathering spots than living rooms, family rooms, or sitting rooms.

I was about to suggest to Kit that we make a move to our own cottage. After all, Emily no doubt wanted a good night's sleep in preparation for her role, too, even though Kit might think it less important than her own part. *Ha ha*, I was thinking, when I heard Kit speak. I immediately paid attention, given the weight in her tone of voice.

"Emily, what was it Doreen said?"

"How would Emily know—" I stopped when I realized she wasn't talking about the scene with Jeffrey and Doreen in the car. *Scene? Had I really thought the word* scene *again?* I was getting as bad as Kit with the theater jargon. "Oh yeah, Em, you said you understood what Doreen had been talking about. You told us last night that suddenly it made sense, what Doreen had said to you. What did she say to you?"

"Yeah, what?" Kit echoed.

Emily shuddered, as if she'd just watched the scary climax of a horror movie. "She said Vera got what she deserved, being murdered. That she'd been given fair warning two years ago. Surely it's the murder in the Gaston cottage she was referring to, right?"

***

"I *told* you we should have reported them." I was angry. And scared. Angry because I was scared. Kit and I were finally turning onto our street, our cottage in sight. The Gaston cottage.

After Emily had shared Doreen's ominous declaration, the four of us had sat for another ten or fifteen minutes trying to return to talk of the impending opening night, as if silently agreeing we didn't want to end our conversation on the topic of murder. When it became apparent that the joy in our gathering had been killed, however, we had all grown quiet.

Finally, Kit and I made good on our decision to leave.

The silence had continued as we drove the short distance to our cottage, but not an awkward silence; Kit and I don't do awkward silences with each other.

"Stop!" I screeched, when we were only a few doors away.

Kit slammed on the brakes. "Wha—"

"Shhh," I ordered my friend, but of course it was too late.

Whoever it was who had been stooped down by our front door stood up and then bolted off, not even glancing in our direction. Not even allowing me a look at him. Or her.

"Well, go on then! Hurry!" I almost said *duh*, as if Kit should have known that once we'd been discovered, we should forget trying to go unnoticed and just work on getting a better look. But before she could get the car farther down the street in the direction he'd run, he was out of sight. "Never mind," I said. "He probably cut through some yards."

"Gardens," Kit gave me the correct British label for the grass surrounding a cottage.

I gave her a *who the hell cares* look, which of course she couldn't see in the dark.

"You didn't make any move to call anyone this morning, either, ya know," she said, as she parked and turned off the car's engine.

Of course I knew. It was as much my fault as hers that we hadn't reported seeing Devon and Ivy Scoffing running away from Vera's cottage the night before. There was a good chance, I felt sure, that our sighting of an intruder in front of our own cottage just now was related. A good chance that it was Devon Scoffing.

But why? What had he been doing stooped down in front of our door? Had he thought we were in bed for the night? Had he been planning to break in? And why? To steal a spoon? Or to murder us in our beds?

When we got out of the car and walked up to our cottage, it was no surprise—but disturbing nonetheless—that we saw the rock by our front door overturned and out of its resting spot.

"He was looking for our key," I said to Kit. "OMG. He was looking for our key."

"Ya think?"

***

"Ivy!" I looked at my watch. "What are you doing here so early?" I'd heard her knock at the door as soon as I finished fumbling through the process of making coffee.

"You're up, aren't you?" she asked, as she walked under my arm that held the door open, making her way to the couch and sitting down by the end table—and the bell.

"Ivy, did you know there used to be a key under the rock?"

She looked down at her shoes. "Is Kit awake?" She raised her head and smiled. "I wanted to tell you guys to break your legs tonight. Then I'm gonna go tell Emily."

"Kit's asleep; Emily probably is too. It's not even seven yet." I decided to ask her something I thought she might answer. "Ivy, about Doreen."

115

Her smile morphed into pursed lips, and a frown appeared above her eyes. "What about her?"

"Well, do you like her?"

"You already asked me that." She eyed me suspiciously. "And anyway, I have to like her. She's my sister."

Her expression as she paused promised more, and so I remained silent.

"I used to *really* like her," she said at last. "I *loved* her." Again a pause, and she seemed to be thinking back in time.

How far back can you think? I wondered. *You're only eight.* "What changed? What made you, um, mad at her?" I was having trouble deciding just what emotion she was feeling. I figured she was having the same trouble.

She sighed and crossed her legs, as if to warn me to *get ready.* "Promise you won't tell anyone. But Doreen used to help me be with my dad. He doesn't have any . . . rights . . . yeah, rights. He's not allowed to come near me. But how can someone tell me I can't see my own dad? So Doreen would find a way for Daddy and me to get together. Someplace we could meet without Mum knowing."

"Like where would you meet?" I asked, thinking, *Little Dipping isn't that big. Not big enough to hide in.*

She looked at me rather defiantly, I thought, before answering. "Right here."

"Here? In this cottage?" I shrieked.

"Yes," she said, her look daring me to object.

"So you had to stop when we rented it?" My mind was spinning, trying to match possible explanations with recent events.

"No, we'd already stopped because suddenly Doreen wouldn't help us. She wouldn't be the, uh, messenger?" Again Ivy seemed uncertain of her word choice.

"So Doreen had arranged your meetings by passing a message back and forth? By telling your father when you'd be . . . here?"

"Yeah, sort of. But then she told me I couldn't see him anymore. She told me to stay away from him. Or else."

CHAPTER FIFTEEN

Good morning, Ivy," Kit said. She was smiling as she came into the kitchen, where our young guest was now seated at the table. She removed the sleep mask from the top of her head, and Ivy quickly reached for it. She examined it carefully and then slipped it over her ginger curls.

"Why d'you wear this thing?" she asked.

"For fun." Kit poured herself some coffee from the cafetière. "I hate this bloody contraption," she said. "I'm gonna buy us a normal coffee maker."

I smiled, glad she finally admitted it was a nuisance. "Ivy came to tell us to be sure to break our legs tonight," I said.

Kit laughed as she took a seat on the same side of the table as her little friend. "That was sweet of you," she said, taking a sip of her coffee.

"So, Ivy." I sat down across from them. "You didn't answer before. Did you know there was a key to this cottage under the rock?"

"Of course. Everyone knows that. This cottage is famous because of the murder. You do know about the murder—I mean the *other* murder—right? A lady was stabbed twenty times with a big dagger." Ivy held out her hands to demonstrate how big the dagger had been. As she spoke, the weapon increased in size, reminding me of a fisherman explaining the size of his latest catch.

"That must have been scary for you," Kit said. "I mean, living so close."

"Nah, I'm not scared. Oh, maybe I was then, because I was only six, but now I'm older and stuff. Got any cake?"

I went to the fridge and took out the treacle tart that Kit had purchased from Marbles exclusively for our little visitor. "Will this do you?" I asked her.

She nodded and took a sip of milk from the glass I had set before her, leaving a bubbly white moustache under her nose.

"So," I said, cutting her a slice of the tart, "did you know the lady who was . . ."

"Stabbed with the big dagger?"

"Right. Did you know her, Ivy?"

"Her name was Belinda." She took the napkin Kit offered and wiped her mouth. "My dad knew her. But my mum didn't like her." She shook her head. "Ooooh no, she didn't like her one bit."

"Ivy," I said calmly, "are you making that up, because you were only six—"

"Six years, Val, not six *months*," Kit clarified for me. "Of course she can remember." She put an arm protectively around the child. I felt like a policeman interrogating a suspect, but Kit continued my line of questioning for me. "What did your mom say about her, darling?"

"I gotta go," Ivy said. "Can I use your toilet first?"

"Yes," I said, feeling frustrated, "the bathroom's upstairs."

"Yeah, I know *that*." Ivy jumped up. "I'll be right back."

118

We listened to her clomp up the stairs as we drank our coffee in silence for a couple of minutes. Then Kit spoke. "I suppose we should report last night's visitor to the police."

"Yeah," I said. "We could head down to the station now, and then go out for breakfast. But are you sure you don't want to rehearse some more?" I smiled a little.

"I don't think it's *me* who needs rehearsing, ya know. Jeffrey seemed impressed with—"

"I'm off, then." Ivy stood at the kitchen entrance. "Can I keep this, Kit?" She was holding the sleep mask, her fingers toying with the words *Queen Sleeping*. "It's so pretty."

"Of course you can." Kit smiled. "It's all yours, honey. Will you be at the play tonight?"

"Yeah. Front row. Look for me." And then she turned and was gone.

***

"We could just *call* the police," I yelled to Kit from my bedroom next door to hers.

"Yeah, but by the time we figure out how to get the number, it might be quicker to just go there. Besides, I'd kinda like to see what the police station—"

"Is that someone knocking at our door?" I went out to the small landing and leaned over the railing. "I think it is."

"Are you dressed?" I heard Kit ask me. "Go see who it is. I'll be down in a minute."

I ran as fast as I dared down the narrow staircase and opened the door to a tall thin blond woman in her midthirties. Her silvery hair reached just below her chin, and she was wearing a slim-fitting gray jacket and matching pants. The simple blue shirt under her jacket was the same color as her eyes: cornflower blue.

"Hello?" I said.

She half smiled and quickly held out a leather cardholder. "I'm DI Tromball, Chichester Police. May I come in and have a word?"

"Of course." I opened the door and then took the cardholder. I saw that she was indeed Detective Inspector Evelyn Tromball. "This is weird. We were just going to the police station."

"Is that right?" DI Tromball squeezed past me and went straight into the living room.

"Kit!" I yelled up the stairs. "The police are here."

"Just me." DI Tromball turned around, after surveilling the room. "I'm making inquiries about the Vera Wingate murder. Chichester is taking over. I'd like a word with you. You are Valerie Pankowski, right?"

I nodded.

"Hi," Kit said, coming into the room. "How can we help? Ya know, we already spoke to Inspector Downey—"

"*Constable* Downey," the DI said, taking a small leatherbound notebook from the pocket inside her jacket. She flipped it open, and her lips formed an amused smile. "You are Katherine James, I expect?"

"That's me."

"So, let's see . . ." She flipped some pages of her notebook. "Apparently, you offered Detective Constable some cake."

A slim shiver of fear ran through me. Was that considered bribing a police officer over here? I quickly dismissed the notion as ridiculous, although the English did seem to spend an inordinate amount of time drinking tea and eating cake. *Or was that just us?* "Yes," I replied, not the least bit guiltily.

DI Tromball's expression seemed to confirm we were in the clear. "He says you met Vera Wingate only a couple of times . . . didn't know her well at all. Hmm . . ." She flipped a page of the notebook. "Did you know that Ms. Wingate owned this cottage?"

"No," I said quickly. "At least we didn't find that out until Pippa—a young girl from a shop in the village—just happened to mention it. My daughter made the rental arrangements for us—"

"Were you aware that a young woman was murdered here two years ago?"

"Not at the time we rented it." Kit came farther into the room and confronted DI Tromball. "We just learned that—"

"Did you know Belinda Bailey?"

"Of course not," Kit said. "How could we?"

"But you apparently did know the victim's name." DI Tromball sounded far from satisfied. "Mind if I have a look around?"

"Well, if you want to," I said. "But I don't . . ."

DI Tromball moved between us and out into the hallway and down to the kitchen.

"You're from Illinois, yeah?" she said with her back to us, after we had followed her into the kitchen.

Kit looked surprised. "How the hell do you—"

"Just making routine inquiries." Her half smile appeared again.

"Downers Grove, to be exact," I said. "Look, we're just here on vacation. My daughter—"

"Emily," DI Tromball said.

"Right. Emily. She's in England for a year or so with her husband—"

"Luke." Tromball flipped the page of her notebook. "Did you know that Belinda Bailey was American?"

"How the hell do you think we would know that?" Kit asked. "We'd never heard of Belinda Bailey until—"

"She was from California; Monterey, I believe," the DI said, ignoring Kit and addressing me. "Same state your daughter and her husband live in, right?"

"Well, yes," I said, "but believe me, neither Luke nor Emily knew Belinda. Look, Inspector, what's going on here?"

"Just thought it might interest you to know that one of your countrywomen was murdered, in this very cottage." Tromball said it as casually as if she were informing us that the Boston Red Sox were a shoo-in for a pennant this year.

"And you never found the killer?" Kit took a seat at the table.

"No one was ever charged," came the response. If you could call that a response. DI Tromball snapped her notebook shut and returned it to her jacket pocket. "I'm looking forward to seeing Emily in the play this evening," she said, this time a full smile lighting up her face. She was handsome, rather than pretty, but that didn't imply she was anything less than feminine. In a *Xena: Warrior Princess* kind of way. She headed down the hallway to the front door, and we followed her. When she stopped, she turned to face us. "Why were you planning to go to the station?"

"We saw someone attempting to break in here last night," Kit said, just as Tromball opened the front door and took in the overturned rock, where the key had been hidden. "He—or she—ran away before we could see who it was. We just saw this person crouching by the doorway."

"So they never came inside, as far as you can tell?"

"No. But it was frightening."

"I'm sure." Tromball nodded, looking at the lock on the door. "Use this." She indicated the chain lock, which we had hardly noticed, much less used. "If you see anything unusual again, ring 999. It was probably kids. The crime rate here is pretty low, but two rich Americans might attract—"

"We are hardly rich, Inspector Tromball." I took some pleasure interrupting *her* for a change.

"Yeah, well, your intruder might not know that." Her smile was unpleasant now, as she handed me a business card. "So, that's it, that's all you wanted to report?"

"Well," I began, but Kit spoke louder.

"Isn't that enough?" she asked, avoiding my stare.

"Of course. Just ring us if anything else happens." Our intruder seemed low on DI Tromball's caseload.

"We will," Kit said.

"Okay, well, you ladies have a nice day and break a leg tonight," she said, and then she headed down the small pathway to our front gate.

Kit slammed the door behind her. It had sounded like the inspector was literally ordering us to break a limb. "What the hell was that all about?" Kit leaned her back against the closed door. "Now I feel like I need to take another shower."

"Kit, why didn't you want her to know we'd also seen Ivy and her dad? Hadn't we planned to report that too? There is a restraining order on Devon—"

"Yeah, I know. But I think we should stay out of it. Let's not make trouble for the kid."

***

"Look out! Yanks in the house!" Pinky bellowed from behind the bar, following it with his customary gale of laughter.

It had been almost time for lunch when we were finally ready to leave the house, after our visit from DI Tromball, and so we'd decided to eat at the pub. Gammon steaks with peas and chips were the special of the day.

"How's the theater world?" He put two glasses of pinot on the bar in front of us.

"So you know we are actually performing tonight?" Kit handed him a fifty-pound note.

He turned to put the money in the cash register and then handed Kit some change. "Hmm. Noblewoman and farmworker." He scratched his bald head. "Let me guess who is who. You are clearly the noblewoman." He pointed to Kit. "So, you must be the farm—"

"Commoner," I corrected him in a huff. But then I realized I rather liked my character having an actual profession.

"So you have the harder role then, eh?" Pinky seemed to confirm my assessment.

"Meaning?" I picked up my wineglass.

"Anyone can pull off being a noblewoman, but a farm—sorry, commoner—takes real acting skills. The

Duchess is giving me the night off, so I'll give you my review tomorrow."

"Great," I said. "Kit, let's grab a table."

We turned to the back of the pub. There was an elderly man doing a crossword puzzle at one table, a black Labrador sitting quietly at his feet. At the next table sat a young girl, her head bent down and her dark hair falling over her face as she tapped into her smartphone.

"Look," Kit whispered. "That's Doreen."

As we neared her table, she looked up.

Kit set down her glass. "Mind if we join you?" She busied herself pulling out two chairs.

"Er . . . I'm actually waiting for someone," Doreen told us.

"We'll move as soon as he arrives," my friend assured her.

"How do you know it's a he?" Doreen brushed back her hair, tucking it behind her ears. I hadn't realized how lovely she was, with her blue eyes fringed in dark lashes. She appeared to be wearing just a hint of makeup, or it was artfully applied. A touch of pink blush on her cheeks and glossy natural lips.

"So, will you be at the play tonight?" Kit asked, ignoring Doreen's question.

"Maybe. Not sure, really, since I don't have a role anymore." She said it wistfully, and not unkindly, but I remembered how she had snubbed us at the theater.

"Hmm." Kit took a sip of wine. "I hope you don't blame Emily for that, because ya know, if you had been here—"

"No, no." Doreen waved a hand in the air; her fingernails were capped with green nail polish. It looked good and matched her green sleeveless dress, which was linen, very simple, and no doubt expensive. "I'm glad Emily got the role. She's a much better actress than me, and I don't blame her for anything. I'll definitely stop by the theater before showtime and wish her luck."

"That would be nice," I said. "Your little sister was at our house this morning; she came to tell us to break our legs."

Doreen laughed, and I noticed her face showed great affection at the mention of Ivy. "She's rather taken with you two." She sipped from a Coke in front of her. "I hope she isn't a nuisance."

"Heavens no, we adore her, don't we, Val?"

I nodded in agreement. "She sure has a lot to say."

"If she gets to be a pest, just send her packing. And remember, she's the best storyteller in the village, but anything she tells you should be cut in half, and then half again, and you might be within a hundred miles of the truth." Doreen gave a sweet laugh, and I was impressed by the elegance she exuded. There was something about her; I wasn't sure what it was. Maybe it was the elusive "it" factor that is not easily defined. But even though she was young, I felt anyone around her would want to impress her and make her like them.

Then I remembered her crying the night before in Jeffrey's car. "We saw you last night, before the rehearsal. You seemed upset. I hope I'm not speaking out of turn, but were you okay? I was worried it was about, you know, Emily getting the lead." I couldn't believe this was coming from me, especially since it wasn't even true. Emily was the last person I had been thinking about when I'd seen Doreen crying.

"Oh, *that.*" She dismissed it with another wave of her hand. "I was being stupid." Just then her phone pinged, announcing an incoming text. Glancing at the screen, she pulled the phone down to her lap, below the table and out of our sight. "Sorry," she said. "Gotta go. I might see you later at the theater. In case I don't, have a good show!"

She squeezed between our table and the black dog to get out, stopping to pat the Labrador's head. "Good boy, Rory." The old man beside him looked up from the crossword puzzle and gave Doreen a little wave.

"Wow, talk about a change of attitude," I said to Kit, as soon as Doreen was out of earshot. "She seemed really nice just now."

"Hmm. I don't trust her."

"Gammon steaks." Pinky stood behind us, holding two plates. "One for you, m'lady," he said with great flourish, carefully placing one dish in front of Kit. Then he addressed me. "And one for you . . . whatever you are." He swiftly dropped the second plate before me.

"You'll be singing a different tune when the commoners revolt, Pinky," I said, latching on to his infectious humor and laughing with him.

"Oh, as far as I'm concerned," he replied, giving me a wink, "the commoners are revolting enough already." And then he exploded into more laughter.

***

We finished our juicy steaks and one more glass of wine. By the time we were ready to leave, the pub had filled up with its lunchtime crowd. As we pressed our way out through the throng of people, we heard several good-luck wishes for tonight's performance. All from people we didn't know.

Little Dipping really was a friendly village—except for the two murders, of course.

I linked my arm through Kit's, and we moseyed home. "Are you nervous?" she asked, swinging her arm and mine too.

"Nervous? Of course not. Why would I be nervous? All I have to do is mill about the stage and not trip over my robe."

"I meant about your *date*."

Oh crap! I had forgotten that entirely, probably due to the two glasses of wine. And I wasn't sure what was worse: the date or David and Heidi. "I'll just have to get through it, Kit."

"Of course you will; it's gonna be fun. And if you need me to have Heidi clapped in irons or thrown into a dungeon, just give me a nod."

"So, this is you in character, right?"

"Yeah. See how I did that? I just slipped into noble mode."

"Ah, you are gooooood."

***

"It's gone!" I heard Kit scream from her bedroom. "How can it be gone? I put it right there."

I raced into her room from mine. It was half an hour before we were due at the theater, and we had been packing up our stuff. I'd refused to wear my robe on the way there, and so we planned to transport everything we needed in the car.

"What's gone? What are you talking about?"

"My riding crop thingy. It's gone. I left it here on the dresser, along with my hat and gloves. It was right here."

"Okay. Well, calm down, noblewoman. We'll find it. It's gotta be somewhere ... unless ..." I immediately formed a picture of Ivy when she had needed to use the bathroom. "Was it here when we got back from the pub?"

"I don't know. For crying out loud, I wasn't checking for it. You don't think ..."

"That Ivy took it? Yes, I most certainly do."

"No, not *her*. I mean, while we were out, did someone break in and take it?"

"Right, that makes perfect sense. Someone breaks in and steals a riding crop that probably isn't even a real riding crop, but rather just a prop—"

"How do you know it's not real?" Kit looked genuinely upset.

"I don't know; I just assumed. Oh, for heaven's sake, let's just look. You probably flung it across the room when you were so busy swishing it about."

We did a quick search, since time was now getting away from us. I checked the wardrobe that looked about five hundred years old. And Kit began pulling out drawers from the dresser. Equally as old. She knelt down on her knees and pulled out the bottom drawer, which was completely empty. When she tried to shove it back in, it got stuck.

"What the hell?" she said, sounding irritated.

"Look, it's not here; but since you're such a fantastic actress, I'm sure you can improvise."

"No. I mean something is making the drawer stick. I haven't even opened it since we got here." She gave the drawer a big tug and pulled it all the way out. "There's nothing back there," she said, peering into the spot the drawer had occupied.

"Kit, we don't have time to mess with this. We have to leave for the theater."

"Okay, okay." She tried to slide the drawer back. "Something is making it . . ." She pulled it all the way out again and turned it over.

There was a brown envelope, twelve by twelve, taped to the bottom. Still on her knees, she pulled it away from the wooden underside of the drawer.

"So," she said, "what do we have here?"

CHAPTER SIXTEEN

The good news and the bad news was that I was too nervous onstage to worry about my date *or* David and Heidikins. I hadn't expected any stage fright, given my minor part in the play. So minor that had I not shown up, no one would have been the wiser, except perhaps Luke's boss, and then not until the after-party.

Apparently, my date had been so looking forward to our meeting. Quote unquote.

But I didn't know that until after I'd suffered through my time onstage, the butterflies in my stomach practically lifting me half a foot in the air, as if I were moving about on a hoverboard. Not that I was gliding. No, it was more of a robotic lurch, so stiff had I grown with fear. Who knew that I, the mother of an actress, was obviously born to do anything *but* act. Comforted only by the realization that no one had been paying any attention to me—all accolades were bestowed upon Emily and Kit after our final bows—I made my way to the dressing room to change. I for one was not going to be attending any post-opening celebration in costume.

I was already in my street clothes—or rather my simple LBD—by the time Kit swept into the room that served as both costume storage and a place to change said costumes, with only racks of clothes to serve as "curtains" and provide a little privacy.

"Val! Why did you disappear so quickly? Luke's looking for you. He wants to introduce you to—"

"Yeah, I'm sure he does." I made my way to one of the mirrors that had been hung around the room with more attention to function than form, continuing to rub a makeup-remover wipe across my face as I went. When I looked at my reflection, I realized I still had enough foundation on to serve my purposes and more than enough mascara. I added a touch of lipstick and told Kit I'd wait for her in the lobby. "Might as well get it over with."

Not sure if the "it" was meeting my date or Heidi, I pushed my way through the other performers coming toward me to the dressing area as I headed to the theater entrance.

An attractive couple standing by the front door caught my eye, the man tall, dark, and handsome and the young woman with him equally cliché in her willowy blondness. Before I could ponder long on why I hadn't noticed *them* around the village—they weren't the sort one could miss—I noticed David standing nearby. He was looking at them also, but more in irritation than admiration. Puzzled, I moved my gaze in search of who might be Heidi, and then it dawned on me. *She* was the willowy blond.

But only after I'd been introduced to her did I realize that it was my date she'd been cozying up to.

Now *I* felt irritated. But at what, or whom?

It didn't matter because it didn't last. I was soon too busy being charmed by Sean Meacham's good looks, British accent, and sharp wit. Take *that*, David and Heidi.

***

"Sorry," Luke said, joining Sean and me by the punch bowl. We were at Jeffrey's house, for the highly anticipated (by some) after-party. "Didn't mean to ditch you two, but being married to the star of the show has its responsibilities." He sounded giddy with pride.

"No problem, old man." Sean patted my son-in-law, a good two decades his junior, on the back. "We're getting along brilliantly, aren't we, Valerie?"

"Yes, Luke, no worries. You go follow your star." I smiled and hoped dear Luke would understand all I wanted to convey. *Thanks for the gift of this amazing man; now leave us alone.*

But apparently, he was as obtuse as the other men in my life—my boss, Tom Haskins, and (in my dreams) my sometimes almost-boyfriend back home, Detective Dennis Culotta. (I knew *potential* boyfriend was more accurate, but whatever. And man! There needs to be a better word than *boyfriend* for those of us over thirty or forty or certainly fifty.) Instead of rejoining my daughter, Luke brought up the subject of some computer glitch at work.

Work!

"I had an idea," I heard him say, and then I zoned out.

And of course, what else would I do then but look for David and Heidi? My ears still burned when I recalled his introduction. "Heidi Kellogg, this is my ex," he had said, his adoring eyes remaining on her face the entire time. And who could blame him? She had the pale-blue eyes of a Siamese cat and skin as velvety-looking and clear as a baby's. And she looked like she was about thirteen.

"Valerie Pankowski," I'd supplied the name David had apparently forgotten.

That's when Sean had come to my rescue. "Valerie Pankowski!" he said, showing all the enthusiasm David had lacked. "I'm Sean Meacham. Your blind date." His eyes twinkled as he said the words with alacrity, as if we were about to embark on a great adventure together.

Oh, how I hoped he was right.

Take that, *David and Heidi*, I thought, in what was to be my mantra for the night.

Still, as I watched them now from across the room, I felt . . . something. Something not good. I supposed when you vow *till death do us part* with someone, it never feels good to see him with another woman.

" . . . right, Val?"

I pulled my eyes off my ex and his fiancée and looked at Luke. "I'm sorry. What did you say?"

"I said there's something magical about Little Dipping. A bit of paradise. Except of course—"

"Yes," Sean said. "Sorry you have to be here when there's such a gruesome situation." He looked shocked, as if he couldn't quite believe we were really discussing murder in Little Dipping. Without actually saying the words, of course. I wondered if that was British manners or just human nature. "I feel the need to apologize," he added.

"Nonsense," I said. "The murders aren't *your* fault." Oops. I hoped I hadn't committed an egregious faux pas, using the word *murders* so carelessly. I didn't want him to think me an ugly American.

But then he said it himself. *"Murders?* Have there been more than one?"

I felt great relief when Luke immediately explained about the two-year-old unsolved case.

"Nasty." Sean shook his head.

My neck was starting to hurt from looking up at him. The two or three inches he had over the other men in my life were having a negative as well as positive effect on me. Maybe if I took a step back. But when I moved my right foot behind me to do just that, it tripped up my best friend, literally.

"Kit!" I bent down to help her up. "Oh my gosh, I'm so, so sorry."

She laughed. Nothing was going to spoil her successful opening night. "No worries. I don't think it was you; I think it was this riding crop. It keeps getting underfoot. I've almost fallen several times. Glad it was only you I finally landed by."

"*Only* me. Thanks for—hey, where did you find your riding crop?"

"Yeah, funniest thing. It was on one of the chairs. I saw it as soon as we entered the theater. Didn't I tell you?"

"No," I said, but I knew that when we'd entered, I'd been focused on my fear. In fact, I'd been gripped with terror that went far beyond what I was sure was normal stage fright from the moment I set foot on the outside steps upon arrival. Now I felt a sense of peace at just the realization that it was *over*. Until tomorrow's performance. Ugh. Well, maybe it would turn out that only the first night would be so terrifying. "How did your riding—"

"Sheesh. Who knows?" Kit said. "And who cares? Aren't you going to introduce me to our new friend?"

I smiled at how she included herself before she'd even met Sean. Kit and I do share everything, but I knew I'd be drawing the line when it came to my *new friend,* as she called him. Well, she could share the *friend* part, but if it turned into something more . . .

***

I saw Kit turn her head my way when I giggled for the umpteenth time at one of Sean's wry comments. My pal's eyebrows arched, half in an *I can't believe you're giggling again* look and half in a *good for you, girlfriend* look. I preferred the latter half.

We were still at Jeffrey's, now seated around his dining room table. There wasn't a free chair in the place, nor enough wiggle room to make it to the loo, so jam-packed was his home with cast members and their proud families. A sense of euphoria permeated his abode, and I was surprised that not *everyone* was giggling. Then again, not everyone could hear my Mr. Meacham, as I had been playfully calling him.

"Well then, Mr. Meacham, if you find Simon Cowell so offensive, why do you sing the praises of Ricky Gervais?"

I thought he sounded like *both* of them when he talked, but he assured me there was a great difference in their "ahccents."

"It seems to me," he continued, "that Simon is mean to the little guys, the aspiring performers. Ricky picks on people his own size."

Ah, so my Mr. Meacham had wisdom as well as wit. I liked that.

I also liked the freshness he carried off with charm, the cheekiness that didn't preclude kindness or good manners. He was no Dennis Culotta; he wasn't even a Tom Haskins. (*Or did I mean that the other way around?* I wondered.) But maybe, just maybe, he might be someone even better than either of them. Or at least someone special in my life. For a while, anyway.

Well, I wasn't going to find that out on our first "date," if you could call being surrounded by my BFF, my ex, his fiancée, my son-in-law, my daughter, and the population of an Italian Renaissance village a date. Still, when he gave me a peck on the cheek as we said good-bye at Jeffrey's front door, I thought it felt a bit like a date.

I even promised him a second one when he asked me to dinner the next night. Just the two of us. "I promise I don't bite. Not on the second date, anyway," he said, and then he trotted down the path to his red MG.

***

"Inspector Tromball!" I rubbed my eyes. "What time is it?" I looked at my watch but couldn't see the hands. I'd left my reading glasses on my nightstand when I hurried out of my bedroom and down the stairs to answer the loud knock at our door. "Is everything okay?"

"Detective Inspector, and not really," she said. *There have been two murders,* she didn't add, but I assumed—hoped—that's what she meant. I hoped there was nothing *new* that was bad. "I have a few more questions for you. And your friend."

I opened the door farther and backed up to let her pass, tugging at my T-shirt to try to get more coverage. I felt naked compared to her completely clothed body, only her hands and her head showing any skin.

"Is your friend here?" she asked, standing in front of the couch, ignoring or not noticing my motion for her to have a seat. Instead, she took out her notebook and appeared to flip to a clean page. Then she withdrew a pen from the same place inside her jacket.

I sat down on the end of the couch, but when I realized it hiked my T-shirt up even farther, I stood again. "Um, I'll go check." *And grab a robe*, I thought.

Pulling the bottom edges of my T-shirt down and close to my thighs as I climbed the stairs—feeling certain the good inspector could view things too private for her eyes and desperately hoping she was looking at her friggin' notebook—I hurried to my room. After belting my robe around me, I listened at Kit's door. No sound.

I descended the stairs feeling much more comfortable than I had on my way up and told the DI that Kit was not yet awake. "I hate to get her up any earlier than she has to," I said. "She'll want to be fresh for her performance this afternoon."

"What about you? Didn't I see you in the play too?"

Crap. I'd hoped I'd gone unnoticed, knowing how stiff and unnatural I must have appeared. "Well, I couldn't sleep. And besides, my part is—"

"What kept you from sleeping? Not a guilty conscience, I hope." Her half smile appeared, but I didn't read any warmth in it.

"What in the world do you mean by that?" I tightened the belt on my robe so hard it hurt.

"Joking. I was joking. Haven't you heard of the British wit?" She scribbled something in her notebook and then sat down on the couch. Just when I'd been hoping she'd leave. Maybe she read my thoughts because she looked up and said, "Do you mind if I wait for your friend to wake up?"

"Suit yourself." I went to the kitchen to make some coffee, but I noticed my hands were shaking as I put the scoop into the coffee canister.

"I should tell you—oh, sorry; did I scare you?" Tromball's voice coming from right behind me had made me jump, causing coffee grounds to fly over the counter and onto the floor.

"Well, yes; I didn't hear you come in."

"Sorry," she said, but she sounded anything but. "I just wanted to tell you that we found something besides the California connection."

I stared at her dumbly as I reached for the dishcloth to wipe up my mess. "The California connection?"

"You know, your daughter and son-in-law coming from California, and the young lady murdered in this cottage also from there?" Her tone implied *duh*.

"You do know, don't you, that Monterey is a good five and a half hours north of Los Angeles, where my Luke and Emily live?" *I* knew because I'd googled it on my smartphone as soon as she'd left after her *last* visit.

"Yeah. As I was saying, the California connection isn't the only thing that is troubling."

"What's troubling?" Kit stepped into the kitchen.

My relief was audible as I let out a huge sigh. Kit would know how to handle this. I smiled at my friend, never having felt more grateful for her.

"What's troubling?" she repeated, and she was definitely using her *I'm in charge* voice.

136

CHAPTER SEVENTEEN

Detective Inspector Tromball reached into the pocket of her jacket and pulled out a photograph.

"Do you recognize this woman?" She handed the picture to me.

Without my reading glasses, I was forced to squint and hold it at arm's length, but I could make out a woman who appeared to be in her early thirties. She was wearing what looked like a short white tennis dress and had dark hair, oversize sunglasses, and a wide smile. "Who is this? Is it Belinda, the woman—"

"So you recognize her?"

"No, not at all. Kit, have you ever seen this woman before?"

I handed the picture to Kit, who took her glasses out of her robe pocket and scrutinized the image. "Nope. No clue." She handed it back to Tromball. "Sorry," she said, removing her glasses. "Who is she?"

Tromball returned the picture to her jacket pocket. "Never seen her before?"

"No." Then I said again, with emphasis, "No. Why do you think we—"

"Just checking." Tromball turned and proceeded down the hallway to the front door. "I won't keep you. Enjoy the rest of your day."

We hurried after the policewoman, Kit passing her in the hallway. "You mentioned something else was troubling you, besides the *California connection*, Inspector." My friend used air quotes to convey how ludicrous she found the so-called connection. "Wanna clue us in?"

Stepping outside, Tromball stopped and faced us. "Nothing important. It can wait." She gave her menacing half smile and hurried off.

We watched her as she opened our gate and stepped onto the sidewalk. I saw no car and briefly wondered if she traveled on foot.

"Geez," Kit said, as soon as she closed the front door. "What is up with that woman? She's really starting to piss me off."

I returned to the kitchen, with Kit following me, and began wiping up coffee grounds from the floor. "You didn't recognize the woman in the picture, did you?"

"Hell no, did you?"

I turned on the faucet and washed the grounds off my hands. "No. Well, I don't think so. Did she look familiar to you?"

"Familiar? No. Not at all. Should she?"

"No." I resumed the task of putting coffee grounds into the cafetière. "This thing really is a pain. Wanna run down to Brew Ha Ha? Their coffee was really good, right?"

Twenty minutes later we were seated at a high table by the window of our new favorite coffee shop. We watched a man we had seen before hurry past, wearing a three-piece suit and trailing a dachshund on a leash. He was followed by a slow-moving elderly lady wearing an elegant turban. And then came seventysomething identical twins marching arm in arm and wearing matching beehive hairdos and striped sweaters.

"Are we going to church?" Kit asked. "We could make the ten o'clock service if we hurry." She clutched her coffee cup in both hands, elbows on the high table.

"Yeah, we could do that. By the way, where did you put the envelope?"

"Ah." Kit put down her cup and pulled her purse onto her lap. "I've got it in here. I'm not letting this baby out of my clutches." She reached in for the brown envelope and put it on the table between us. "I don't know if it's important, but the way things have a habit of disappearing from the damn cottage, I think we should be careful."

I smiled, even though what she said was true and made me a little uneasy. I reached over and opened the envelope that was too large for its contents. Removing the small white piece of cardboard inside, I once again studied the tiny pressed flower that was attached to it, preserved by a piece of clear cellophane. "What do you think it is?"

"Seriously?" Kit asked.

"Okay, I know what it is, obviously. But it's curious, right? I mean, it's sweet to think of some starry-eyed girl wanting to press a flower for a memento, but to hide it so carefully? I just wonder who did it." She nodded in agreement as I added, "I think I'd like one of those pastries before we go; want one?"

***

We had to be at the theater by noon for the two o'clock matinee performance. Sean Meacham was picking me up at the cottage at seven, and I was grateful that I would have time to go home and change.

"Are you sad this will be your last performance?" I asked Kit, as we drove to the theater.

"No," my pal replied, but she sounded wistful. "You?"

"Gosh, no. I'm looking forward to seeing the production with the rest of the audience. We are going Wednesday, right?"

"Doesn't that depend on how full your dance card is? Ya know, with your new boyfriend and all."

I turned to catch her expression, but she was carefully watching the road ahead. Truthfully, I was a teensy bit concerned about my date this evening . . . well, not so much the date, as leaving Kit on her own. I was reverting to our teenage years, when one of us (usually her) had a boy in the picture, leaving the other one (usually me) to fend for herself. "Kit, are you sure you don't mind my going . . ."

"Out with Mr. Meacham?" she finished my question for me, but kept her hands gripped on the steering wheel, her eyes on the road.

"Yes, exactly. Because—"

"Oh, honey." She turned her head toward me. "I am thrilled for you. Finally . . . *finally* you meet a guy who appears—on the surface, anyway—to be good enough for you. I want you to go, have fun, enjoy yourself."

"What will you do?"

"Truthfully, I will be glad to get rid of you. I plan to have a long, hot bubble bath, and then I might experiment in the kitchen and make us something fabulous."

I sighed in relief. Thank goodness. And even though I was not in any way looking forward to the next few hours and the dreaded play, I was looking forward to seeing Sean Meacham again.

***

And place your hands below your husband's foot:
In token of which duty, if he please,
My hand is ready; may it do him ease.

From the side of the stage, out of sight of the audience, I listened in awe to Emily's final monologue of the play, Kate paying tribute to her husband and showing obedience.

As Ivy said, she was brilliant, even if I didn't quite agree with the sentiment.

Glancing out to the onlookers in the front rows of the theater, I caught sight of Doreen. She looked intent, eyes glued to the stage, and when Emily's final lines were spoken, she jumped up and clapped loudly. "Bravo!" I heard her yell, as her enthusiasm fired up the rest of the audience. Within seconds they were all on their feet, and I was never more proud of my daughter.

Amid the cheers of the audience, Emily and her leading man took several bows, with Ernie/Petrucchio extending an arm in deference to her. She took a solo bow and then reached for his hand to join her. Just then a small figure clutching a large bouquet of flowers trotted up the side stairs to the stage. As I watched Ivy hand the spray of roses to Emily, I was reminded why my daughter loves doing what she does.

Back in the makeshift dressing room, there were hugs and kisses and even a little praise from Jeffrey. "Well done, people. Damn good job. But Sandy, remember there are audience members at the back of the theater, and if they haven't already fallen asleep, they might like to hear what you have to say. And Pete, I don't think Nikes were on offer in Padua; I could clearly see them. What happened to your boots?"

"Sorry, Jeffrey. I left them at home and didn't have time to go back and get them."

"Do me a favor and just sleep in them from now on, will you?" He clapped some more. "So, people, I'll see you all on Wednesday. Don't be late." Jeffrey then moved through his cast, shaking hands and smiling with satisfaction.

"American ladies," he said when he reached Kit and me. "Can't tell you how grateful I am for your help. The two performers will be back on Wednesday, barring any more babies being born or teeth falling out, but I'd be grateful if you didn't stray too far, just in case." He winked and gave us each a kiss on the cheek.

"So . . ." I turned to Kit, who was carefully removing her feathered cap. "Back to normal."

"Yeah." She looked a little sad. "I enjoyed it; it was really fun. Do we have an amateur theater group in Downers Grove, I wonder?"

If we do, I thought, but didn't say, *God help them.*

***

"I need something to wear," I yelled down the stairs to Kit and Ivy.

Our little friend had followed us back from the theater and now made herself comfortable on the couch. I had packed only one dressy outfit, my LBD, and Sean Meacham had seen it, but I was confident Kit had something I could borrow.

I heard her, followed by Ivy, run up the stairs to my room.

"Where's he taking you?" Ivy flung herself on my bed and stretched out, feet crossed, arms behind her head. I was often struck by her mature poses, or did all kids do that? I couldn't remember.

"No idea," I said, "but everything else I have is too casual."

Kit, who had already hurried off to her own room, returned with a stack of clothes on hangers. "Okay," she said, "let's see what we have here." She laid the clothes down on the bed by Ivy's feet.

I'm a few sizes larger than Kit—more than I care to admit—but I could see she had selected several long, loose tops, any of which would look good over slim black pants. I picked up a glorious turquoise-and-pink garment and held it up to my body. It had a simple neckline and three-quarter-length sleeves. "This will do nicely," I said.

"Yeah, I think that will fit you," Ivy chimed in. "But remember, neither a borrower nor a lender be." She had jumped off my bed to follow Kit, and left the room briefly.

Now she stood at the doorway, teetering on a pair of Kit's black high heels.

"Huh?" I said. "Where did you—"

"It's from a Shakespeare play," Ivy said, "but I don't know which one. He wrote a lot of plays."

"Yes, but—"

"Face it, the child is a bloody genius," Kit cut in, taking her phone out of her pocket and pulling up Google. "It's from *Hamlet*. Polonius said it." Kit looked as proud as any parent as she stepped back to capture Ivy's image on her phone's camera. "Here," she said, tossing her a long strand of pearls she'd worn that day. "Put these on."

Ivy wrapped the beads several times around her neck, the end loop still reaching below her waist. Then she posed, looking way too seductive for her years, with one hand on her hip, the other on the door frame.

Two things came to mind. First, I had so many similar pictures of Emily through the years, dramatically posing in various grown-up outfits.

And second, judging by the look of pure pleasure on Kit's face, my friend was having as much fun playing dress-up with Ivy as the little girl was.

Now Ivy hurried off to Kit's room and returned wearing my pal's silk kimono. She had also helped herself to some dark-red lipstick.

"You two better behave while I'm gone," I said, joining in their mirth.

"Oooooh." Ivy put her hand up to cover her mouth in an exaggerated fashion. "You mean when you are out with your booooyfriend?"

"That's right," I agreed. "My boyfriend. And you better watch it, missy. He don't take kindly to back talk."

She plunked down on the end of my bed, her thin legs hanging over the edge, the high heels still balanced on her tiny feet. "He's quite handsome, like my dad."

"How do you know that, sweetheart?" Kit asked, as she took more pictures.

"I saw you with him at the theater last night. He's got a very small car. Hope you can fit in it."

"I'll manage," I said. "Now why don't you two get out of here and let me get ready."

"Yeah," Ivy jumped off the bed. As Kit took her hand and led her out of the room, I heard Ivy ask if we had any cake.

**

"Your son-in-law is a brilliant asset for us," Sean said, taking the wine bottle from the silver bucket next to our table and topping off both of our glasses.

"Yes. He's a good guy," I agreed. We were in a restaurant, seated by a window with a view of a lush garden lit by discreet lights hidden in the trees.

"And your daughter . . . she's an amazing Kate."

"Kate? Oh, you mean in the play. Yes, she is, isn't she? I'm very proud of her. You don't happen to have any connections in Hollywood, do you? I always feel she's on the verge of a big break."

"Sorry, my only connections are in the technical world. But it must be hard for an actress like Emily to get recognition. Unfortunately, I don't think Little Dipping has much in that way to offer her."

"Ah well, she's having fun. And that's what counts."

A waiter came to clear away our dishes, and from his back pocket he produced a small laminated sheet describing the desserts. Sean chose a profiterole, and I ordered sticky pudding with toffee sauce. It sounded hideously fattening, but I had long since given up counting calories while in England.

Our conversation flowed easily. Sean, I learned, was fifty-six and had been divorced six years. He had two grown sons, both in college—or as he said it, *at university*—and he had no contact with their mother. My earlier nervousness now gone, I found myself comfortable with this man. The butterflies I had always experienced when in the company of Dennis Culotta, the only man in my life I considered datable, were not evident.

Strangely, I missed them.

After our dessert, we carried our drinks to the bar area, where we found a table. There was a young man playing the piano and singing American ballads. When he began to sing the Sinatra classic "The Way You Look Tonight," Sean reached across the table for my hand, then led me to the tiny dance floor in front of the piano.

Being in his arms was nice. I hadn't been held by a man in such a manner for a long time, and I felt myself relax even more. It wasn't that either one of us was a great dancer, or needed to be. We just kind of shuffled around, along with two other couples, one a lot older that looked like they belonged on *Dancing with the Stars*, and a younger couple who shuffled like we did.

When the song ended and another ballad began, Sean moved his head back to look at my face, without letting go of his grip on my waist. "Again?" he asked.

"Sure." I leaned back into him. But all I could think was, *Why hadn't Dennis Culotta and I ever gone dancing?* And then I thought, *The heart wants what it wants.*

The heart doesn't know what it wants, Valerie.

Yikes; where had my mother come from?

***

Back on Magpie Lane, Sean maneuvered the tiny car (way too tiny for my taste, not to mention my rear end) into a parking space near our cottage. Then he turned off the ignition and twisted slightly so that he was leaning against the door, facing me.

"Thank you for a lovely evening, Sean," I said.

He smiled. "Can we do it again?"

"Absolutely." I sounded way more enthusiastic than I felt. What was wrong with me? How often did I get to spend a perfectly charming evening, with a perfectly charming man? *Oh yeah*, I reminded myself, *that would be never.* I leaned over and gave Sean a kiss on the cheek and then quickly turned toward my door to exit the car. Not easy, by the way. I wasn't used to such a low, small vehicle, and I can only say that I was glad Sean wasn't actually witnessing the debacle from the street.

I ran the few steps to our cottage, hearing the MG's engine start up, and then banged on the front door. The light was still on in the living room, so I didn't bother digging my key out of my purse. Sure enough, Kit opened the door right away, glass of wine in hand.

"Hi," I said breathlessly. "I'm glad you're awake. Need to talk."

"Valerie." She smiled. It was her hostess smile, the one I'd seen many times when she was entertaining her husband's clients. "We have a visitor." Her eyes widened, and her smile grew bigger.

As I entered the room, I saw a woman seated on our couch, a glass of wine in her hand, too, but no corresponding smile on her face.

"Claire," I said, surprised that I even remembered who she was.

"Right," Kit said. "Ivy's Mom has come to call."

CHAPTER EIGHTEEN

I glanced at my watch, not caring that it probably looked rude. Like *what are you doing here at this late hour?* Which is precisely what I meant to convey. I wasn't in the mood to talk to Ivy's mom. I was in the mood to talk to Kit.

About Sean, about Dennis, about anything but what Ivy's mom was here to discuss.

And that's *before* I knew what that was.

Once I learned her topic of choice, I *really* had no interest in joining the conversation. It was just too scary.

Kit disappeared before I even took a seat on the couch, but she returned before I noticed her absence, handing me a glass of wine. "You're gonna need this, girlfriend," she said as she glared at Claire Scoffing.

"What your friend is trying to warn you about," Claire said, "is that you might find what I have to say disturbing. But I thought you'd want to hear it." She looked at Kit as if to say *don't kill the messenger.*

I set the wine down on the table in front of me. I wanted to be clearheaded for whatever it was Claire had to say, and the wine I'd had with dinner was probably already more than I needed. "What is it?" I asked, looking her straight in the eye, daring her to ruin my night, let alone my trip abroad.

"As I was telling your friend, I don't think you should be staying in this cottage."

I didn't like the way she was dragging out the drama. Kit likes drama herself, but she knows how to get to the point. "What is she talking about, Kit?" I turned and looked at my friend as if Claire Scoffing had been speaking a foreign language.

"I don't know. She was just starting to explain when we heard you out front. So please don't hesitate any longer, Claire." Kit joined me on the couch. "Say what you came to say. At this late hour," she added, looking at her own watch.

"Yes, forgive me for coming so late," Claire said, sounding more sarcastic than sorry. "Some things can't wait for a convenient time. And this is one of them."

"What the hell is the *this* you refer to?" Kit stood up, and for a moment I was afraid for Claire. But then I remembered it was *Kit* I was watching approach our new acquaintance, not some character in a crime show.

"*This* is the fact that I don't think it is safe for you to be in the Gaston cottage." Claire set her own glass on the end table, as if she had more important things to do than sip wine.

"You mean because someone was murdered here? Two years ago?" I asked, wondering why Claire was so concerned for our welfare.

"No, not because Belinda . . . because someone was murdered here, as you so callously put it," she scoffed. Yes, Claire Scoffing scoffed.

How appropriate, I thought.

And then she continued. "Because this is not a safe place to be. And because my daughter Ivy seems hell-bent

148

on visiting you. I'd rather she visit someplace that isn't dangerous."

"Explain," Kit insisted.

Claire sighed. "The one you really need to speak to is my daughter," she said.

"We just talked to Ivy this afternoon," Kit said, and for the first time I noticed she had a smudge on her cheek that looked like flour, like the flour I now saw on the apron she was wearing and that I was also just seeing.

So she really *had* wanted to bake while I was gone. I sniffed the air for a hint of what it might be. Not that I was hungry. Not exactly. Although I *had* eaten like a bird on my date with Sean. I'd opted for pushing my food around on the plate over worrying about what might be stuck in the new spaces that age had created among my teeth. But I had devoured my dessert, hoping it didn't stick to anything, despite its name.

" . . . right, Val?"

"Huh?" I asked, still unable to pinpoint the source of the aroma I was now aware of. "Are you baking something?"

"Oh, for crying out loud," Kit said. "I *was* baking something, yes. Before Claire arrived. Will you just focus?"

"What?" I asked.

"I said will—"

"No, I mean what were you baking?"

"Val." Now she looked more upset with me than she was with Claire.

"Sorry. What were you asking me?" I felt as sheepish as I sounded. I blamed the wine for my being so easily distracted.

"I was telling Claire that we had a visit from Ivy just before you went on your apparently dreamy date."

"And that's precisely what I'm worried about," Claire said. "Ivy won't stay away from this place as long as you're here. I don't know what it is about you Americans, but you seem—"

149

"Just tell us what is dangerous about it," I said. I didn't want to hear what she was going to say about us Americans, for fear it was something worse than just the fact that Ivy seemed enamored of us.

Claire stood up and said, "I hope you will forgive me, but please follow."

And to my astonishment—and Kit's, judging from her suddenly wide-open but silent mouth—Claire walked to the stairs and began to climb them.

We hurried behind her, me wondering if Kit was going to stop her, and when she didn't, wondering why not.

I was glad Claire entered Kit's room. I knew it would be as tidy as everything else in her life always is. Mine, not so much. A couple of last-minute glitches with my makeup and choice of jewelry had found me tearing through my bags and tossing things around that I never took the time to make right.

We were barely in the room when we realized what Claire was doing. She'd opened the bottom dresser drawer and was rubbing her hands underneath it. Obviously looking for the envelope that was now in Kit's handbag, the envelope with the pressed flower. "Why, that little liar," she said.

"Wait. You mean *Ivy*?" I asked. She was the only little person I'd met since we'd arrived.

"No. I mean Doreen. I told you that you should talk to Doreen. It looks like I need to talk to her myself. The liar."

Kit pushed past me and went farther into her bedroom. "That's no way for a mother to talk—"

"Don't tell me how I should talk. How would *you* talk if your precious Emily lied to *you*?" she asked. If looks could kill, Kit would be dead.

"Emily's not *her* daughter; she's mine," I said, as if that mattered.

Claire seemed to agree that it was irrelevant. "Whatever," she mumbled.

"Let's go downstairs," Kit said. "We need to talk."

***

"Well, that wasn't draining," I said an hour later, after Claire Scoffing had finally left our cottage and I'd put an ice cube in my wine, ready to finally enjoy it. Or try to.

"Exhausting." Kit had freshened her own glass and sat down on the other end of the couch from me.

"What do you make of it? Do you believe her?"

"Maybe. She knows something, obviously. She knew where that envelope had been hidden."

"Yeah; do you think we should have told her the truth when she asked if we'd found something there?"

"No. Not yet, anyway. Not until we talk to Doreen."

"Well, that might be hard. Her mom says she's disappeared again, remember?"

Kit looked at me as if I'd just accused her of forgetting her own name. "Like I'm going to forget that? But ya know, everyone has told us Doreen always comes back."

"Yeah, but now that I know why she leaves, and where she goes, I'm not so sure we can count on that." I put my barely touched wine down on the end table. It had no appeal all of a sudden. "I'm going to bed," I said. "I think we need to sleep on all of this."

"And then?" Kit asked, her tone implying sleep would be of absolutely no help.

"And then . . . and then I have no idea."

"Luckily for you, I *do* have an idea."

Why was I not surprised?

***

Kit *always* has an idea. Some are better than others. This one didn't seem half-bad, even though it had us waking before the first noisy nuthatches could be heard. And even though I was more scared than I had been on the stage. Now I found myself wishing for the safety of my role as an

English commoner. Better than my current one as sidekick to a sleuthing American "nut job," as my boss likes to call her. But Kit does some of her best sleuthing in nut-job mode. So I agreed to cooperate.

We'd driven about ten minutes out of Little Dipping when I saw it. "There it is, Kit. Coventry Lane."

She braked as fast as she quietly could. "Some lane. I think they should call it Coventry Dirt Path. These Brits."

"Like we Americans don't embellish." As a Realtor, I've had to apologize to countless clients for the exaggerated claims implied by both street and subdivision names, including many that all but guaranteed a veritable *English* experience. *The Isle of Scilly* and *Stonehenge Court*, for example, promised so much, while yielding no more than a string of starter homes and a pothole-riddled road, respectively.

After Kit negotiated the turn, we bumped along the narrow "lane" before we spotted the house Claire had told us about: Doreen's refuge, an old cottage in disrepair that had been in her father's family for centuries. Apparently, Doreen had pilfered and copied a key she'd found lying around at his home, and no one knew she came here until Claire had dragged it out of her after her last disappearance.

"I'm still not sure why we're coming to call at this hour," I said, afraid of the dark—and so much more.

"The element of surprise, Valley Girl. The element of surprise. And according to her mom, she's apt to be outta here any time now."

"Yeah, but wouldn't that be just to go back to Little Dipping? Isn't that what Claire said has always happened?"

"Yes, that's been her history—but not necessarily her future. Ya know, something tells me she'll be much more forthcoming if we take her by surprise here at Alistair's old cottage than if we question her back in the village."

"You mean grill her."

"If we have to, yes. We'll grill her like Larry's famous barbecued chicken, if we have to. We're going to get to the bottom of . . . something."

***

The nuthatches were still singing their earnest morning song when we drove back to our cottage.

We'd taken Doreen by surprise, all right. And she'd spilled her guts, all right. But now what did we do with the information? On the one hand, it might not be *that* big a deal. On the other hand, it might be deadly.

Just when I'd been about to declare that we must have been given bad information, since the cottage remained as quiet as a tomb in spite of our increasingly louder knocks, Doreen had finally opened the front door to us. Well, sort of. At least as far as the chain lock allowed. When she saw it was us, she undid the chain and swung the door all the way open.

"What are you ladies doing here?" Her voice was raspy from sleep. Or maybe from disuse. Did she *talk* to anyone when she was out here?

"We have some questions for you," the ever-direct Kit said. "Let us in. Please."

I didn't feel we had the right to be so demanding, and I'd told Kit that on our drive out. She, on the other hand, said it was the cottage *we* were renting that was involved, so we had *every* right.

Doreen headed into the kitchen, Kit and I following behind like ducklings imprinting on her. We watched as she fiddled with her own cafetière, and I noticed she was much better at it than we were. But what was *up* with these things and the Brits? Wasn't life complicated enough?

Finally, she spoke. "I'm guessing you've been putting two and two together—"

"Nah, you're giving us too much credit." Kit pulled out a kitchen chair and sat down at the table. "Your mother paid us a visit."

We watched as Doreen tried to process the implication of this.

Then she spoke. "My mother . . . but she . . . she doesn't—"

"It seems Ivy's been telling her things." I had joined Kit at the table. "And Devon told Ivy—"

"Devon!" Doreen spat the name. "Like anyone should believe *him*."

"Tell us what you know," Kit said. "We can believe *you*, can't we?"

Doreen remained silent while she finished preparing the coffee. Then she walked over to the table and took a third chair. She sighed deeply before telling us what she knew. And what she didn't.

Shortly after the restraining order that was meant to keep Devon from Ivy, Doreen had sympathized with both of them and at Devon's behest had cooperated in a scheme that found the three of them entering our cottage. "That part was a piece of cake," Doreen said, and I found myself wondering if that was a British saying that had made its way to the United States, or the other way around.

"It was just common knowledge that there was a key to the place under the rock. Or so Devon told me. We used the cottage as a place Devon and Ivy could meet. I love Ivy! And I knew how I would hate not to see my own father, so it seemed only right . . . my mother can be quite . . . *vindictive*, I think is the word my father uses, and it captures it quite well. Oh, I love her, and she can be—"

"So you helped Ivy see her father at the Gaston cottage?" Kit was in no mood to hear good things about Claire Scoffing.

"Yes. And we developed a system, a code, whereby moving certain things around in the cottage would indicate a meeting for that day."

"What things?" Kit asked, sounding like a prosecutor about to nail a witness.

"Oh, there's a bell on the end table—"

"Ahhh," I said, and I figured my whole head had no doubt lit up like a spotlight.

"No kidding," Kit said. "That might explain a few things. Except . . ."

"Except what?" I asked. We watched as Doreen brought cups and then the cafetière to the table, pouring our coffee before continuing.

"Except we're still finding things missing. How d'you explain that?"

Doreen laughed a little, nodding her head. "Does this happen after Ivy has paid you a visit?"

"Yes," I said, hoping it *was* only Ivy doing it.

Doreen added some sugar to her coffee cup and stirred it slowly, her laugh replaced by an affectionate grin. "Ivy loved that game. It wasn't really even necessary, but she had a lot of fun with it, so we kept it up. My guess would be that your missing items are all down to her."

"Just for fun," I added.

"Yes. She's very naughty."

"What happened after we rented the cottage? How did you arrange for Ivy and Devon to meet then?" I questioned further.

"And where?" Kit added.

"Actually," Doreen said, her elbows on the table, her coffee cup up to her lips, "I'd already told Devon and Ivy they should quit meeting. I just wasn't comfortable anymore."

"Why? Because you thought Devon might have had something to do with Belinda's murder?"

"Yes." She nodded in confirmation. "Maybe Devon did kill Belinda. And now Vera."

CHAPTER NINETEEN

We were back home in our own cottage, drinking tea and eating French toast. The sun had just appeared in the gray sky, but it was weak. And it was still early.

"So, what do you think?" I asked Kit.

"About what in particular? My head is about to explode. But first, tell me about your date."

"It was fine." It seemed like days had gone by, instead of just hours. "This is really good French toast, Kit. By the way, what did you bake last night?"

"A Battenberg cake; it's in the fridge. I got the recipe from Google. And what do you mean by fine? Was everything ok?"

"Yes, he's a very nice man." I took a big bite of the toast. "But more important, what do you think about Claire and Doreen's stories? Do you buy them?"

"Yes, parts of them, at least. I mean, it makes sense, in a villagey sort of way, that Doreen would disappear out there to stay at her father's cottage from time to time. Who would want to live with a mother like hers? And since her father's place is so conveniently empty ... I know I'd take advantage of it. I can only wonder why she let Claire drag it out of her."

"But what about the part that she's out there *this time* because she's afraid—"

"It's all too easy to believe, seeing as how we're sitting in the spot where someone was murdered two years ago, and now there's been another—"

"Yeah, I guess that makes just about anything believable. But I don't trust Claire." I stirred my tea and raised the cup to my lips, contemplating their stories again. "I wonder why they tell us *anything*. I mean, it's not like we're the police, for Pete's sake."

Kit stared off into space for a few seconds and then she spoke slowly. "Ya know, this damn cottage is too involved to suit me."

I involuntarily looked around the small kitchen, and a shudder took over my body. "You're giving me the creeps." Then I tried to laugh it off.

"Think about it." Her eyes once again focused on me. "Everything seems to stem from this place. Why does Ivy spend so much time here—"

"That's easy; it's because of you. She clearly adores you."

"That may be true," Kit agreed immodestly. "But even I can concede that it's not quite normal for a kid to want to spend time with someone so much older. Even if that older person is really cool."

She stopped for a second and gave a little laugh. "But I'm convinced the mystery has to do with this cottage. Specifically, with Belinda Bailey."

"Okay, what do we know about her?"

"Let's see. She was from California, in her thirties, and doing some sort of medical research at the university here. Apparently, she was a good friend of Vera Wingate's, and

Vera was either renting this cottage to her or letting her live here free."

"And don't forget the two big rumors. Vera may have been funding her education."

"Right. And what's the other one?"

"She may have been having a fling with Devon Scoffing."

"Oh yeah. So, poor Belinda gets herself stabbed two years ago, and Inspector Trombone—"

"Tromball."

"Whatever. Inspector Tromball is still hot on the case."

"Yep, that sounds about right. Seems like it all starts with Belinda."

"Okay, I guess we really don't know all that much. So now tell me about Sean Meacham."

I gave a recap of my evening. Nice man, good manners, attractive, witty. On paper, he was pretty much perfect.

"So what's the problem?" Kit asked.

"No problem; why do you think there's a problem?"

"Because you act like you were at an accounting conference instead of out to dinner with a nice guy." Kit always equates boredom with accounting, with no deference to her accountant husband, who is not in the least boring.

"No, not at all. Why would you say that? I had a very nice time."

"And are you seeing him again? Please tell me you're seeing him again. Because I think—"

"I said I'd call him, okay? Good grief, it's not like anything can come of it."

I had a sudden flashback to when I was sixteen and my mother was trying to sell me on Leonard Brick, whose father was her chiropractor.

Me: Mom, he looks like Pee-Wee Herman.

Mom: I don't know who that is, but he sounds nice.

Me: Leonard is weird, Mom.

Mom: Okay, he's a little different. But there's a good chance he'll grow out of those tics.

"Val, are you listening? Why do you say nothing can come of it?"

"A million reasons."

"Give me one. And it better be good."

"I'll give you a big one."

"Let's have it," she said.

"The Atlantic Ocean. Is that big enough for you?"

***

Emily called my phone just as we entered The Lady of Shalott. "Helloooooo, Kitty," Pinky yelled from the bar at the same time I said my own hello to Emily.

"How long have you been waiting to say *that*?" I heard Kit ask as she took a stool.

"Since the day we met, of course." Pinky laughed. "Glad to see you ladies back again, but I'm going to have to start charging you rent for those stools." He gave another laugh as he took the small towel draped over his shoulder and wiped the bar area in front of us. "What can I get you?"

I heard Kit order the special of the day, which was toad in the hole with gravy. I pointed a finger at the blackboard behind him and nodded, giving him a thumbs-up, as I continued talking to my daughter.

She, of course, also wanted to know all about my evening with Sean. "So did you make plans to have another night out?"

"Emily, I'll call him, or he'll call me."

"He's nice, though, right? I mean, I don't know him very well, but Luke seems to really like him."

"He's very nice." I was getting tired of talking about Sean Meacham. "Look, I better go; we're getting lunch. When will we see you guys? Wanna have dinner tonight?"

"How about tomorrow?"

"Well, tonight might be better—"

"No, Mom. Can't tonight. Tomorrow, okay? Gotta go. Love you."

I returned the phone to my purse, a little surprised at Emily's abrupt good-bye.

"That kid," I said to Kit. "I hope she's not going to hound me about Sean."

"Maybe she wants you to put in a good word for Luke with his boss." Kit dug in her wallet and put a twenty-pound note on the bar.

Pinky snatched it up, then held it above his head and pointed it toward a light fixture. "Hmm. This real?"

"You tell me," she said. "You gave it to me last time I was in here."

This set off a belly laugh from him. "No flies on this one, eh?" he said, addressing me and pointing at Kit with his thumb.

We took up our drinks, Diet Coke for me, bitter lemon for Kit, both with one solitary ice cube floating helplessly in the glass.

"Let's sit over here," I said, and we moved farther into the pub, looking for an empty table among the lunchtime diners.

"We better be quick, before my ice cube melts." Kit looked down into her glass.

"Please don't make a fuss." I was still cringing from the debate Kit had gotten into with the British Airways crew member who had served us drinks on our flight over. "It's their culture, and a lot of people don't care for a barrel of ice with every drink."

"Ice is culture? Give me a break. And anyway, shouldn't that mean more ice for the rest of us?" She took a seat. "Oh hell, is that bloody Tromball over there?"

I looked in the direction she indicated and did indeed see DI Tromball sitting alone at a table. She was wearing pants and a jacket again, this time in navy blue, with a white shirt. She had her head bent, studying her smartphone; in front of her on the table was a half-empty beer mug. "Gee, can cops have lunch in a pub?"

"Why not?" Kit asked.

"Seems like that shouldn't be allowed," I said, getting comfy in my seat just as Pinky approached us with two plates.

"Toad in the hole, ladies." He placed the dishes before us. "Compliments of The Duchess."

"Looks delicious." I unwrapped my cutlery from its paper napkin. "What exactly is—"

"Sausages in a Yorkshire pudding batter, right, Pink?" Kit answered, looking at him for confirmation.

"That's what we're telling people." He gave his mischievous wink and returned to the bar.

Kit cut a slice of her food and took a bite. "Mmm, not bad. Very simple, of course. I should make this."

I took a bite too. "You could make this in your sleep." Kit is an amazing cook. She defines herself as a gourmet, although I'm not sure what that actually means. I just know she loves to try new recipes and amaze us with her prowess. "But it's really good." I nodded in agreement.

"So, Chichester this afternoon?"

"Yes." I nodded. I was excited to drive into the nearest large city, which Emily assured me had many fascinating points of interest, not the least of which was its 900-year-old cathedral. "We won't be seeing the kids tonight, so no need to rush back."

"Maybe we'll bump into Sean Meacham. That's where Luke's office is, right?"

"*Maybeee*," I said, a wicked smile on my lips, not because I felt wicked, but because I knew it would drive Kit crazy.

"How was your lunch?"

Kit and I looked up at the same time to see DI Tromball standing before us. She was putting her phone into her pocket, and I noticed she didn't carry a purse. I wondered how women do that. Where do they put all their stuff? My amount of personal paraphernalia is in direct correlation to the size of the purse I happen to be lugging around. The bigger the purse, the more I carry with me.

161

"Fine." Kit looked at me. "Val, we should get going now."

"Somewhere nice?" Tromball asked, not moving.

"Why don't you put a tail on us? Then you'll know." Kit removed her purse (about one-tenth the size of mine) from the back of her chair.

"If we were in an American cop show, I probably would. But we don't waste police resources on that kind of thing. Have a nice day, ladies, as you Yanks say." She turned and left us, reaching for her phone as she went.

"She gives me the creeps," Kit said, as soon as the DI was gone.

"I know. Let's forget her and have a nice afternoon sightseeing."

"Right." Kit stood, looking in the direction of the bar. "One thing I have to do first."

She headed through the crowd of customers to the bar, with me following. When she got there, she leaned forward and waved at Pinky. "Is The Duchess busy?" she asked, speaking loudly over the noise of the crowd.

"She's probably watching *Coronation Street*; she records it, if you can believe that."

"I wondered if I could talk to her for a few minutes."

"Don't see why not. As long as you don't complain about the food."

"On the contrary, I want to ask about an ingredient."

For some reason, this caused a big laugh. But he turned his head and yelled, "Duchess! We need you out here, love."

"What is it?" came the slightly irritated reply, followed by The Duchess herself. She was about the same age as her husband, midforties perhaps, and I noticed the top of her blond do didn't quite reach his shoulder. I also noticed she wore way more makeup than her delicate face needed, but it didn't hide her pretty features.

"Our American friends here want a word about the food." He put his arm around her, which forced him to bend slightly.

"Oh," The Duchess said, a wide grin forming on her pink lips. "What can I do for you ladies? I hope my husband has been behaving himself."

"First, I want to compliment you on your cooking," Kit said. "It's one of my hobbies—cooking, that is. I wondered if I could pick your brain a little."

The Duchess motioned for us to follow as she started down toward the end of the bar where there were no customers. We all heard Pinky mutter, "Hope you brought a shovel."

"Cheeky devil." She leaned her elbows on the bar, which was a stretch for her.

"We're staying at the Gaston cottage," Kit said.

I had no idea where this was going.

"Yes, I know," The Duchess said. "How is it? There's some bad history with that place. Oh, I don't mean to ruin your holiday; it was a long time ago."

"Yes," Kit said. "Two years, right?"

"Right. Belinda Bailey. Lovely young woman. Medical researcher at Sussex."

"Do you know what kind of research she was doing?"

"I believe it was something to do with a new drug. But it was all very hush-hush." As she said it, she leaned forward some more, and I imagined that her feet might have left the floor on the other side of the bar.

"Well, we heard that Vera Wingate was funding her," I said.

"Only as far as her room and board and living expenses, I'm sure. I expect the university paid for the study she was working on, but I don't know how those things work."

"I wonder what the relationship was between Vera and Belinda." Kit's face took on a perplexed look. "Do you know? I mean, it was very generous of Vera, don't you think?"

"Vera could be a very generous lady, when it suited her." The Duchess put a hand to one side of her mouth, implying she was about to share a big secret. "She had a lot of money."

Just then Pinky's voice rang out. "Duchess, we need you down at this end."

"Oops; looks like I gotta go. What was it you wanted to know about the cooking?" She gave us a radiant smile.

"Ah," Kit said. "I just wondered if there were organic eggs in your Yorkshire batter."

The Duchess giggled. "Hmm. If they were supposed to be organic, someone forgot to tell the chicken."

CHAPTER TWENTY

Speaking of medical research, any word on your stepdaddy?" Kit pulled her visor down in a vain attempt to shield her eyes from the sun that had finally broken free of the clouds. I knew the sunglasses she had on at the moment were more about looks than protection.

"Huh? Oh, you mean the tests he's having. No, and I really do need to call my mom. Seems she's talking to everyone but me. I mean, David! Why would she call *him*? I think I'll try while we're in Chichester. I'll probably get a better connection."

"Yeah, my cell service in Little Dipping is sporadic too." She cupped her right hand at her temple in a further attempt to block the brightness. "I thought England was supposed to be so cloudy."

"You sound disappointed." I chuckled. I'd never known Kit to avoid or be annoyed by the sun. Thus her collection of sunglasses that is outdone only by her assortment of flip-flop magnets covering her refrigerator door.

"Me? Disappointed? No, I'm loving everything about this trip. Especially our little murder mystery." She cackled. "Val?" She turned her head to look at me, no doubt wondering why I didn't scold her. She knows how I hate when she tries to make something a bigger deal than it is. And murder is a plenty big deal, with no help from Kit.

I waved my hand at her head, a signal for her to keep her eyes on the road. She obeyed, but asked, "What's up? What are you thinking about?"

"William. I do hope he's okay. You never know when people are in their eighties . . . my mom would be devastated—"

"He's not dead, ya know. We'll call your mom as soon as we stop, make sure he's all right."

I nodded. "Thanks, Kitty Kat."

And then my phone chose that particular time to work perfectly well. When I heard it ring, I had to dig it out of my purse. I hadn't planned to use it during our drive. *Crap.* My boss. Since I was trapped in the car, Kit would have to be part of the conversation, and I dreaded the sarcastic observations I'd have to hear from her, even if I could keep Tom from knowing about her presence and thus avoid his exacerbating the situation. I decided maybe I just wouldn't answer.

"Answer it," Kit said. "Who is it?"

She'd be able to tell if I lied to her, and just saying his name would trigger in her a monologue on his deficiencies, so I gave up any notion of maintaining the peace. "Hey, Tom," I said into my phone.

"You've been gone too long."

"Wha—"

"I should never have agreed to give you this much time off. We need you here, Kiddo. *I* need you."

Words I'd never heard. Forgetting about my stepfather, I asked, "Are you okay? Is everything all right?"

"No, it's not all right. Perry screwed up at least two listings, and Billie's cat died."

"Oh no, poor Aerosmith—"

"Aerosmith? Why are you talking to Tom about Aerosmith?" Kit looked over at me.

"Who the hell is Aerosmith?" Tom barked into my ear.

"Is he reliving his youth?" Kit returned her eyes to the road ahead.

"Geez, guys. Aerosmith is . . . er, apparently *was* . . . Billie's cat," I said into the air, so both of them could hear me. "Poor Billie."

"Poor Billie? What about me? What about Haskins Realty? You know we can't run this place without her."

That I know. I've often wondered how we ever did get along without her. She's only in her twenties, so Haskins Realty existed long before she was hired. It existed long before *I* started there, and I know that the years I worked without her were nowhere nearly as smooth as the ones she's been in charge of, with her organizational skills that are surpassed only by her coffee-making ones. "How much work has she missed?" I asked.

"Billie? Miss work? You know better than that. She hasn't missed a day, but she mopes around here like—" He stopped to grope for an adequate comparison, but apparently could find none. "Do you know she made a whole pot of coffee without putting any grounds in?"

"Of course I don't know that, Tom. I'm in England, and we have our own set of—"

"Gotta go. But come home earlier if you can."

"Of course I can't. In fact—"

But he'd hung up. *Oh well,* I decided. *Probably not the best time to ask if I could stay longer.* But I knew I wouldn't be leaving England until I was sure things were safe for Emily in Little Dipping. And right now I wasn't sure they were safe for anyone.

"That was short," Kit said.

"Yeah, he had to go."

167

"Of course. Tom always has such pressing matters. So why did he bother to call you, then?"

"He wants . . . he wanted to tell us to have a good time."

***

"Mom!" I said. Kit and I had returned to the coffee shop that had been our first stop in Chichester. It was the third time we'd been there in as many hours and the third time I'd tried getting ahold of her. This time with success.

"Valerie? Is that you? Where are you?"

Since I'm not Buddy, your son, surely I'm the only other human being on earth who would call you Mom, I thought. But I said, "I'm in England, Mom." Was she losing her mind? She *was* in her seventies, and that wasn't too young for—

"I know you're in England, for Pete's sake. With that Katherine." She paused, no doubt to make sure I had time to register her disapproval. "I meant *where* in England."

"That doesn't matter, Mom. What is going on? Is William okay?"

Silence. And then the soft sound of stifled crying.

"Mom!"

"What's wrong?" Kit returned to our table with coffee and a Cornish pasty for each of us.

I shook my head at her, hoping to convey that I didn't know yet. "What's going on, Mom? Is William okay?" I asked again.

"This is why I didn't want to call you. I knew I'd break down hearing your voice." She sniffed twice and then continued. "William Stuckey has . . . you know, that thing they used to call senility. Not dementia. Or I guess it's a type of dementia. You know—"

"Alzheimer's, Mom?" I felt shocked, but I immediately recalled a handful of stories my mother had shared in her phone calls the past half year or so. Funny little tales of William losing his keys, only to find them in their refrigerator; of William sending the payment for his water bill to the electric company; of William getting dressed for church on a Thursday.

"Alzheimer's?" Kit echoed me, and I glared at her, sending all my fears and horror her way. Isn't that what friends are for? "Sorry," she whispered, patting my shoulder in comfort.

I smiled, knowing once again I would rely largely on her to get me through something awful. "Are they sure, Mom?"

"Well, they said they were." She sniffed. And then I heard her say, in what I felt was a too-harsh tone, given the circumstances, "Not now, William Stuckey. I am on the phone."

I marveled at my mom's persistence in calling her husband by his first and last names. So Jane Austen-y of her. "Look, Mom, I'll be home soon. We'll take William to a neurologist in Chicago. We'll figure this all out. Are you okay until then? Do you need me to come home right now?" But what I thought was, *I can't come home right now. I can't leave Emily in the middle of this mess.*

"No, Valerie. You don't need to come home. Mary and Scott are here."

Good. I was off the hook. William's kids could handle things from their father's perspective, and I'd be home to help my mom and him by the time she'd need me. Not that I knew just what all a diagnosis of Alzheimer's entails.

"Well, know that I'm thinking of you every single second, Mom. And praying for both you and William. Will you please keep me posted?" *Instead of talking to everyone* but *me*, I thought. *David! For Pete's sake, why had she called* David?

I realized she'd hung up, and I hoped she'd heard my last words. It was a new habit of hers, hanging up when she figured our conversation was over, without a good-bye. *Maybe* she *has Alzheimer's*, I finished my earlier thought. I looked at my friend, feeling grateful we were both still so young, and determined that we were going to enjoy each moment of our trip as it came. Who knew *what* the future held, for us as well as for my mom and William.

Kit looked at me quizzically.

"You know as much as I do," I said. "Let's focus on things here. We'll deal with things in America when we return to America."

But in spite of my determination, my heart felt heavy.

We left Chichester far sooner than we'd intended, no purchases made, nor any sightings of Sean Meacham. No doubt about it: the phone call to my mom had put a big damper on our outing. A bigger damper, even, than what awaited us upon our return to Little Dipping.

***

"Let's stop by Emily's first," I said, as we approached the edge of the village. "She sounded weird when I talked to her. I want to make sure everything's okay. Maybe she knows more about William than my mom is telling me." I was newly obsessed with William, although it had to vie for my attention with the murders that likely had to do with my current living quarters, not to mention the possibility that the recent one could even have to do with Emily.

Maybe it was because I was hearing David's voice in my head saying *there you go again, Valerie, making something out of nothing; you'd think a murder has to do with Emily just because it occurred in the same country she's in.* Or maybe it was because David and Heidi had never been far from my thoughts since I'd first heard of her. Not that I cared. But for whatever reason, I didn't register shock or even surprise when we knocked on Emily's door and immediately let ourselves in. No, it took a minute to sink in that the living room was filled with people. Well, six people, anyway. Emily and Luke (no surprise) and (big surprise) David and Heidi and a strange couple about my age.

I immediately felt wretched that I'd put Emily in an awkward situation. "Wha—"

But Kit spoke right over me. "What the—"

If I'd been able to think, I would have been relieved that Emily interrupted her before she could finish with the eff word. I knew that's where she was headed.

"Mom!"

"Kit!" Luke said, as if to take the focus off me. "Come in, come in." He grabbed a kitchen chair and set it next to the one he'd vacated. He motioned for us to sit.

But we stayed by the front door, still not having closed it. I cleared my throat and tried not to faint. "I'm sorry we interrupted—"

"Mom, don't be silly," Emily said, looking extremely uncomfortable, no doubt feeling guilty about her earlier declaration that she couldn't see us this evening. "Come in. Meet Harry and Debbie. Heidi's parents."

But of course. Heidi's parents. I looked at them—really looked at them—for the first time. And right after I registered their Hollywood attractiveness (tall stature, big blue eyes, and thick blond hair—both of them), I noted their tight smiles. My guess was they were none too happy about their baby girl planning to marry a Yank who was probably older than they were.

Harry and Debbie rose at last, and I finally found my voice. "Nice to meet you, Darry and Hebbie, I mean Harry and Debbie." Oh great. The ex-wife acting like a fool. I fought the urge to assure them I hadn't even been drinking.

"This is my mom, Valerie," Emily was saying. "And her best friend, my Auntie Kit."

I appreciated the reminder that I wasn't alone in being an outsider, that I had Kit at my back, literally and figuratively.

"Sorry, but ya know we really can't stay," my pal said. Then she took my arm. "We'll talk to you in the morning, Emily."

I was vaguely aware of Heidi's parents uttering some unenthusiastic niceties as Kit turned me around and ushered me out the door.

We walked to our car in silence and didn't speak until we arrived at our cottage and settled on the couch with glasses of sherry that she'd poured.

And even then we didn't speak. Instead, I burst into loud laughter, and when Kit deemed it safe, she joined me. "Did you see David's face?" I asked, trying to catch my breath.

"Did you see *Heidi's*?" Kit responded.

And then we laughed some more. We laughed until I cried.

***

DI Tromball woke us up the next morning. My eyes were still puffy from crying, in spite of—or maybe because of—the fact that we'd gone to bed early and I'd had a good twelve hours of sleep. Of course that sleep had been interrupted by bouts of wakefulness, during which I relived the few minutes I'd spent humiliating myself at Emily and Luke's, as well as way too many horrible experiences from my failed marriage.

I don't know who I expected would be on the other side of our front door when I opened it in response to the loud knocking. Emily? David? Ivy? Certainly not DI Tromball. It had taken me so long to fully awaken and make my way down the stairs that I was surprised anyone was still there at all.

As soon as I saw who it was, I felt irritated that Kit hadn't heard the knocking and come to the door. She would be able to handle this so much better than I. For lack of anything better, I said, "Good morning."

"May I come in." DI Tromball said it like an order, not a question. And it didn't go unnoticed by me that she hadn't even returned my greeting.

Now what? I wondered.

CHAPTER TWENTY-ONE

Without waiting for my response, Tromball stepped inside. She was again wearing a simple pantsuit, only this time in brown, with a pink shirt underneath. As she moved past me, she took her leather-bound notepad from an inside jacket pocket.

"Is your roommate around?" She stopped at the bottom of the stairs and looked up.

"Kit!" I called, as Tromball headed into the kitchen. "We have a visitor."

"Is it Ivy?" Kit called back.

"Think taller."

"Ah geez," I heard her response, followed shortly by her footsteps on the stairs.

I joined Tromball in the kitchen and took a seat at the table, purposely not offering to make coffee. She leaned her tall frame back against the counter, checking her notes, and then took something from the pocket of her pants. As soon as Kit entered the room, Tromball stopped leaning. From my vantage point, I realized again how tall she was.

"What now?" Kit asked, taking a seat on the same side of the table as me, just as Tromball slapped a photograph down in front of us. Then she placed her hands, fingers splayed, on either side of the picture and leaned in toward us.

Kit and I stared at the photo. It was a headshot of Devon Scoffing—not his best picture, and judging from the background, it seemed to have been taken by a police photographer.

I thought how Doreen had told us he might have murdered both Belinda and Vera. It seemed Vera, who was close to Belinda, hadn't liked Devon and had put pressure on her to break up with him. Whether due to that pressure or something else, Belinda had done just that. Devon blamed Vera, just as he blamed her for his stint in jail. Doreen thought those were reasons enough to suspect Devon of killing them both.

"This," the DI said, "is what is still troubling me. Why didn't you tell me you know this bloke?" Still leaning on the table, she hovered over the photograph, as if ready to pounce.

"Who is it? He looks a bit like that actor on *Modern Family*." Kit put her glasses on and peered down at the snapshot.

"It doesn't look anything like him," I said, picking up the photo and holding it at arm's length. "Is it Damian Lewis? The guy from *Homeland*?"

"No." Kit took the picture from me. "Same red hair, yes, but otherwise totally different." She moved the picture closer to her face. "I know," she proclaimed loudly. "It's Benedict Cumberbatch, right?"

"He doesn't have red hair, does he?" I looked at her.

"Ya know," she said, "it's a little bit—"

"Stop!" Tromball snatched the photograph away from Kit and stood to her full height, tucking her pink shirt into her pants with one hand, although it hardly needed any more tucking. "I'm not sure if you realize that lying to the police is a serious offense, so I'll ask you again. Do you know who the man in this photograph is?"

"Prince Harry?" Kit asked, just before my swift kick to her shin. "Ow, that hurts, Val."

"Be serious," I said under my breath.

"Er, excuse me, he's the only other redheaded Englishman I can think of."

Tromball glared at us, then folded her arms across her chest, looking a little bit like a North Korean prison guard. Kit and I both placed our hands in our laps and looked down at the table like good North Korean prisoners.

"Red Skelton?" I heard her whisper.

"Shirley MacLaine?" I heard myself whisper back.

"It's Devon Scoffing. And you two were seen conversing with him at The Lady of Shalott on Wednesday evening. Remember him now?"

"Riiiight . . ." Kit raised her index finger in the air. "Now I remember. Gee, this guy doesn't look anything like Benedict Cumberbatch."

"How is he known to you?" Tromball was again consulting her notepad, flipping the pages. "What was your business with him?"

"With Benedict?" Kit looked perplexed for a few seconds. "Oh, you mean with Devon Scoffing. We had no business with him. We were simply sitting in the pub talking to Alistair Carlisle, and Devon came over to our table. Thirty seconds later we left. End of story."

"And that's the only time you've ever seen him?"

"I *did* watch an episode of *Sherlock* . . . oh, sorry; *again* you mean Devon Scoffing. Yes, that's the only time we've ever seen him."

I felt Kit's grip on my knee under the table. "Right." I looked up at Tromball. "That's the only time."

***

"Should we have mentioned seeing Devon leaving Vera's cottage with Ivy?" I asked.

We were at Brew Ha Ha, enjoying chocolate croissants with our coffee.

"Definitely not," Kit said.

"But what if Devon's guilty of . . . something . . . I mean Doreen thinks . . . surely we don't want him hanging around Ivy if—"

"Ya know, first of all, we don't really know for sure it was Devon we saw at our cottage. Let's leave it to Inspector Tremble to figure it out."

"Tromball. And second?"

"I'm pretty certain Devon is nothing more than a father who wants to spend time with his kid."

"*Really*? And what makes you so certain of that?" I used my napkin to wipe some delicious melted chocolate from my top lip.

"For one thing, who'd want to upset Claire Scoffing? Devon's ex-wife is far scarier than he is."

I wasn't convinced by Kit's reasoning, but at that moment my phone rang and I recognized the number as belonging to Sean Meacham. I hit the button to decline, hoping Kit didn't notice.

But she seemed too busy waving at someone who was at the counter paying her check. "Hi, Macie!" Kit called. "Over here."

Macie Brown turned in our direction. "Oh, hi." She took her change from the cashier and headed toward our table. "How are you, Kit? Or should I say *m'lady*?" She giggled and put her hand to her chest, displaying the pincushion still attached to her wrist. "Your performance was so *good*." She gazed up to the ceiling as she said it, and I wondered if she'd attended the wrong play.

"Thank you," Kit said, as modest as ever, which is to say not at all. "I'm eager to see how my replacement does tomorrow night."

"Er . . . replacement? I think *you* were the replacement," I said, but Macie made a shooing gesture, waving her pincushion in our faces.

"Oh, you don't have to worry about Christelle," she said. "She doesn't have your . . . er . . . flair, Kit. Although she tries; I'll give her that."

"I'm sure she will be great," I said, feeling the need to defend the unfortunate Christelle, as Macie sat down in the empty chair at our table.

"Her name's not even Christelle," she said. "It's really Carol, but she likes to Frenchify things. When she started going out with Jeffrey, she took on all sorts of airs and graces."

"Jeffrey?" I asked. "When did she go out with him?"

"Hmm, let's see." Macie put a plump elbow on the table and placed her wobbly chin in the palm of her hand. "It was *A Midsummer Night's Dream*, two years ago. She was a fairy. Very light on her feet."

Kit raised her eyebrows. "Our Jeffrey seems to like the ladies."

"Yes, he likes the ladies, all right, Doreen being his most recent."

"What about Belinda Bailey? Did she catch Jeffrey's eye?"

"Probably. But she was the studious type. Know what I mean?"

"Right, a student at the university," I confirmed.

"Yes." Macie nodded. "And besides, like I told you, if the rumors were true, Belinda only had eyes for one bloke."

"Devon Scoffing," I said.

"Yep." She nodded.

Just then my phone rang, and I again recognized Sean Meacham's phone number.

"Your new boyfriend is very persistent; you should take it." Kit had her eyes fixed on my cell.

"How do you know who it is? Oh, don't even bother answering." I picked up the phone and rose from my seat, going out into the high street. Across the road I could see Pippa standing in the doorway of Knit One, Purl Two. She waved at me and yelled *hiya*. I thought again how nice it was to be in this small village for such a short time and have made so many acquaintances.

"Hi, Pippa," I shouted across to her, as my phone stopped ringing. My preference was to just review any voice mails later. But the realization that I would eventually have to deal with Sean prompted me to hit his number and call back.

"Valerie! I don't believe it. You returned my call."

What kind of man answers his phone on the first ring?

CHAPTER TWENTY-TWO

Oh . . . um . . . Sean. Of course. Why wouldn't I return your call?"

"You tell me." I heard him laugh. "I've been feeling ignored."

Well, I *feel* stifled. That's what I was thinking. What I said, sounding innocent, I hoped, was, "What do you mean? I really don't have very good phone service here—if you've been trying to call." *Aargh.* Because I'm such a bad liar, I wondered for the millionth time why I even bother to try.

"So, before we get disconnected, let me ask you this: can we have dinner tonight?"

Why did I hate how eager he sounded? There'd been a time I would have killed to have a handsome man like Sean—a Brit, no less—eager to have dinner with me. But something was preventing any enthusiasm on my part. "Sorry, tonight won't work. The play, you know."

"I thought the play wasn't going to resume until tomorrow night." He sounded as suspicious as Tromball.

"Well, there's a lot to do, um, preparing . . . helping Emily prepare—"

"Look, if you don't want to have dinner, that's fine."

Oh no. Was I going to get Luke fired? I hadn't meant to humiliate this very nice man, and I certainly didn't want him to take the rejection out on Luke.

But I'd underestimated him. And his ego. "We can do something besides dinner. Let's do something touristy. I'll show you some sights as only a true Englishman can. I've got just the thing. How about Thursday, day or night?"

I thought of Luke and his job again. Surely by Thursday I could come around to feeling excited about—or at least interested in—such a date. Or I could come up with a good excuse to cancel it by then. "Sure. Thursday."

"I'll pick you up at noon." And then he hung up. Or did I *really* have a bad connection again?

By the time I returned to our table in the coffee shop, Macie had left it for another one, where three women sat, all talking at the same time. Some customs know no boundaries, and apparently a group of women talking at the same time and all knowing what the others are saying is the same practice everywhere.

I rejoined Kit, plopping down into the empty chair and sighing loudly, waiting for her to ask *why* so I could complain about Sean. I knew of course that she would just remind me how happy I should be to have the attention of such a debonair man. But she didn't seem to even notice me, so engrossed was she with her phone. "Whatcha doing?" I asked, feeling irritated that she deemed it more important than me and the problem that had triggered my sigh.

"I'm trying to find that flower," she said.

"What flower?" Now I really felt irritated, but I knew it was probably mostly at myself, for being too big a wimp to just tell Sean *no*. Isn't that what we're supposed to do? *Just say no?*

"*Our* flower. The one in the envelope. The envelope that's now in *your* purse. You do still have it, don't you?"

I'd put the flower in my bag when Kit had switched to a smaller purse, and I wasn't even sure where it was now. I'd transferred contents to and from my suitcase several times, trying to lighten my load so I could carry only the necessities when we walked anywhere. I reached down by my feet and groped in my purse. "Yeah, I have it. Why?" I picked up the coffee cup I'd abandoned long enough ago to guarantee its contents would be lukewarm.

"Because I'm pretty sure it's not just a memento."

I couldn't disagree with that. "So, what are you thinking?" I set my coffee back down, wondering if it would be weird if I asked our waitress to microwave it for me.

Kit's serious visage broke into a grin. "I'm surprised you can't read my thoughts, Valley Girl."

"I guess I'm slipping. Please enlighten me."

She returned to the subject at hand. "I've been mulling this over from the time we first found that flower. But I know how you hate when I make a big deal—"

"Like that ever stops you."

"Anyhoo, I wondered why anyone, presumably Belinda, but not necessarily, would go to all that trouble to hide a pressed flower that reminded her of a walk in the woods or whatever. And why Claire and Doreen knew about it. And why Claire insisted she knew only of its supposed whereabouts, not *why* it was there. Hah!" She thrust her phone at me. "Read this."

I groped in my purse again but couldn't find my reading glasses. So I fanned my fingers apart on her phone screen, trying to enlarge the words yet keep them together enough to make sense of the text. I saw *modern medicine* and *phytochemicals* and *pharmaceuticals*, and in the strange way we do, I knew what she was getting at. "Kit, you don't think that—"

"I most certainly do. Look at this." She grabbed the phone away from me, flicked the screen with her index finger a few times, and handed it back. "Our flower," she announced.

And sure enough. There it was. The same pressed flower that lay in the envelope I had stashed in my purse. A valerian. And the few words I could readily make out under the picture were intriguing, if not ominous. *Sedative. Psychological. Medicinal.*

***

"Sean tells me you two have a date Thursday." Luke beamed as he sliced into one of the haddock fish cakes on his plate.

I squirmed a little in my seat as I dished up a healthy dollop of Kit's homemade dill-and-lemon mayonnaise. "Well," I said, "we *are* talking about doing a little sightseeing together. No big deal." I dabbed a small chunk of fish cake into the mayo and took a bite. "Kit! This is amazing. You've really outdone yourself."

"Not so sure that's how he looks at it," Luke said. Still beaming. "I think you've got yourself an admirer, Val."

"Kit, did you tell Em and Luke that Larry's considering retirement?" I changed the subject again. I'd never thought of my son-in-law as stubborn before. I guessed matchmaking brought that out in him.

"Really?" Emily said. "That's wonderful. I think it's great when people can retire while they're still young and enjoy—"

"He's not retiring," Kit said, as if Larry were not part of the decision and she'd made up her mind. And his too. She set her fork down as if she'd lost her appetite. "For that very reason. He's too young."

"I don't know," I said, and the truth was, at the moment I didn't really care. I was just glad we'd changed the subject from my "date." "Larry's provided very well for you for decades. And he's a smart moneyman, so I'm sure he's figured out how to do this without you guys having to give up anything. Seems he should be able to do what he wants with his remaining—"

"Oh, for crying out loud. He's not going anywhere for a long time." Kit sounded as if it would be she who decided when he went anywhere.

"I'm just saying, he's always supported you in anything you wanted to do . . . for the most part," I added, remembering times when he'd unsuccessfully tried to talk his wife out of what he considered a harebrained idea. But that came with the territory that was our dear Kit and didn't really count. "If you want my opinion, I think he deserves *your* support."

"As a matter of fact, I do not want your opinion."

I knew my plan had backfired when Luke changed the subject again. Clearly uncomfortable with what he no doubt thought was tension between Kit and me, proving he did not understand our friendship, he asked, "Where do you think Sean will take you?"

"Are you nervous to go on tomorrow night, Em?" I asked. "Or is it old hat by now?" I looked at my daughter, willing her to go along with my latest change of subject and leave stupid Sean in the dust. I knew I was being totally irrational, resisting a romance with such an eligible bachelor, since I had only two other men even remotely in my life: the boss with whom I was way too comfortable to be romantically involved and the police detective who was far too elusive to ever be more than an off-and-on flirtation.

"Not really. Oh, I think a little nervousness is good, and I have that," Emily said, as if nervousness were something that could be controlled and she was retaining just enough for it to be beneficial, like a chemist concocting just the perfect formula. She took a bite of fish. "Wow, Kit. This is awesome."

"Well, I don't know how you do it," I said, shivering at the memory of my own time on the stage.

"I can't imagine *not* doing it," Emily said with a smile.

By the time we'd finished our brandy snaps and retired to the living room for a nightcap of sherry, I'd completely forgotten about Sean and the murders. But suddenly, the cozy feeling I'd been enjoying evaporated, as I recalled that a woman might have been murdered *in this very room*.

And I thought I had a good idea who had done it.

***

"Why do you think it was Claire Scoffing?" Kit asked.

I'd waited, of course, until the others had left before sharing my thoughts with my pal. We were now in the bathroom removing our makeup and brushing our teeth.

"I didn't say I thought she was the murderer. I said I *had* thought she was. And that's because she was jealous, I'm sure, of Belinda having a fling with Devon."

"But what about Vera? Why would Claire kill Vera?"

"I figured Vera somehow knew Claire had killed Belinda. I don't think Vera missed much about what went on in this cottage, or anywhere else. Including murder. So I thought it very likely that whoever killed Belinda eventually had to kill Vera."

"You say you *thought*."

"Yeah; but that flower business you found . . . well, the more I think about that, I guess I'm not so sure it was Claire who done it, er, who did it."

CHAPTER TWENTY-THREE

Mom!"

"Valerie? It's me, and I'm in America. I'm using William Stuckey's phone. This is called FaceTime."

"Yes, I can see. Is everything okay?" I tried to keep the panic out of my voice, knowing how much my mother hates using smartphones. But surely she'd use a telegram—if they still existed—to deliver bad news.

"Can you see me?" she continued. "I can see you perfectly. Why aren't you wearing makeup? You should never—"

"Mom, it's two twenty in the morning. I was in bed, asleep." I glanced at the clock on my nightstand. Her distorted image filled the small screen, and the tip of her nose appeared to be pressed against the glass.

"Well, for heaven's sake," came her reply, displaying not only her displeasure with time zones, but also a good view of her dentures.

"Mom, you don't have to hold the phone so close." I reached for my glasses, although I hardly needed them. She moved the phone a little too far away from her face, so now I had a great view of the light that hung above her kitchen table. "Okay, that's better. Is everything okay there?" I asked.

"What?" Apparently, moving the phone two feet from her face had rendered her deaf.

"I asked if everything's okay," I said, more loudly this time.

"Well, there's no need to shout, Valerie. And yes. Everything is okay. That's why I'm FaceTiming with you, so you will know. William Stuckey had a checkup today. The doctor gave him some pills—*William Stuckey*? Where are you?"

I waited patiently while moving with my mother through her house, ending at the armchair in her living room. I could see her husband was sitting on the couch, although he wasn't visible behind the *Chicago Sun-Times*.

"Heeeere's William Stuckey," my mom said. She sounded like a host on an evening talk show introducing a new guest. Like I'd never even met the man and was about to discover his latest movie role. The image on the phone swept from her face to the carpet, the ceiling, and then a bowl of oranges on the coffee table.

Finally, William put down his paper and took the phone from her hands. A huge smile spread across his handsome face. "How are you . . . dear?" he asked me.

I didn't quite know what to expect—maybe my stepfather wrapped in a shawl, sitting in a wheelchair and talking to an imaginary pet parrot? But he looked as dapper and elegant as ever. "I'm fine, William. How are you?"

"As you can see, not quite in my dotage yet. Sorry about this. Minnie Ebert let the cat out of the bag, so to speak, at church on Sunday. Apparently, she has a nephew in Australia she uses FaceTime with, so naturally when Jean heard—"

"She had to try it. Got it. And I'm glad she did. It's good to see you looking so well."

"How are you?"

"Wonderful, William. And are you okay?"

"Yes, I am." Suddenly the screen's image changed: more ceiling shots, a view of some pink fluffy slippers, and then my mother's face.

"Valerie, I wanted to warn you not to drive in the fog, because—"

"Mom, we haven't had any fog—"

"Because I know it's always foggy in England. Isn't that right, William Stuckey?" The screen image swung wildly back to her husband, who had returned to reading his newspaper.

"If you say so, Jean." I heard him chuckle. "You know, it's very early in the morning there; why don't we let . . . um . . . your daughter get some rest."

Back to Mom. "All right. Go back to sleep, Valerie."

"Valerie," I heard William say in the background, as if he were just remembering my name. Or was that my imagination?

"And don't forget to moisturize," my mom continued, jerking my thoughts back to her. "Your skin looks very dry. You're not a teenager any—"

"Mom, I'm losing you; your image is fading. Thanks for calling; so glad William is doing well," I said, but I felt a little sick to my stomach. Had his eyes looked a bit more vacant than when I'd last seen him? "Byeeee, Mom; love you. Byeee . . ." I switched my phone off, grateful to whoever had invented FaceTime; but *come on*, they shouldn't let just *anyone* use it.

Unable to go back to sleep, I read an old *People* magazine I'd brought with me from the plane. Reese Witherspoon and her look-alike daughter seemed to be the main story.

An hour later I descended into the kitchen to tackle the cafetière. But suddenly I couldn't be bothered and chose to make a nice English pot of tea instead.

An hour or so after that, when Kit still hadn't emerged, I decided to slip out to Brew Ha Ha for some apricot croissants. I thought it would be a nice way to reciprocate for her haddock fish cakes, even if my efforts weren't homemade.

Although it was still early, the coffee shop was quite full. I stood in line behind a man wearing a cloth cap and a heavy leather jacket. When his order of six coffees in a cardboard holder was handed to him, he smiled and tipped his cap. Such a genteel gesture from such a burly bloke. *Bloke?* I smiled, realizing what a Brit I was becoming.

"Valerie," I heard a call from behind me and turned to see Doreen's father sitting in the back of the shop with an open laptop on the table in front of him.

"Hi, Alistair." I turned back and placed my order with the girl behind the counter.

"Come join me," he called.

I looked in his direction again, as he waved toward the three empty seats at his table. I didn't want to join him. His obvious flirtation made me uncomfortable, especially since I had a feeling he directed it at too many women. "Okay," I heard myself say, to my own surprise. And then I asked my server to add a latte to my order.

"I'll bring it over," the young girl said.

Alistair Carlisle was looking good. He still had his half-grown beard (or was it fully grown to his specifications?), and his hair was slightly damp, as though he'd just stepped out of the shower.

"How's it going?" He smiled, showing perfect white teeth.

"Good. I had a very early call from the States this morning and couldn't get back to sleep, so I thought I'd surprise Kit with some of the to-die-for croissants they have here." My mouth watered just thinking of them.

"Yeah, I know what you mean," he replied, although I could see from the plate by his laptop that he had a half-eaten slice of unbuttered toast. Was that why he appeared so slim and why I was wearing jogging pants with an elastic waistband?

"How's Doreen?" I asked.

"She's great. Looking into applying to uni."

"Uni?"

He laughed a little. "University. She's a smart girl, so she'll probably have her choice. I suggested she take a gap year, but she wants to get started."

"Is she planning to go somewhere local?"

"I wish. She's thinking of Edinburgh. A bit too far away for my liking, but it probably would be good for her to get away from here. Either way, I'll back her decision."

"She's lucky to have such a supportive father," I said, but what I was thinking was, *I'm sure you* do *want her to get out of here and away from Jeffrey.* I had to agree he was too old for Doreen. I took the coffee cup the server brought over, along with the bag of croissants. Their aroma was tempting, but I resisted.

"Yeah, well, she needs at least one parent who's on her side, right?"

"Right." I nodded, taking a sip of coffee.

"You're divorced from Emily's father, I understand. Sorry if that's too personal."

"No, it's not a secret."

"And you and your ex make it work?"

"Yeah, we do, although it seems my ex-husband is planning to get married again."

"Is that not cool?"

"Oh, I don't care. Emily's a grown woman." I sipped some more coffee, wondering why this topic was making me uncomfortable.

"So." Alistair also seemed to want a change of subject. I liked him for that. "How's everything at the Gaston cottage?"

"It's great. We love it. I'm going to miss it when we leave."

"Yeah, it is a brilliant cottage; I've always liked it. It's just a shame it has such a notorious history."

"You mean, of course, Belinda Bailey. Yeah, we had no idea—"

"Right. You'd think Vera Gaston would have mentioned it when she rented it, but I don't suppose—"

"*Gaston?* You mean Vera Wingate, right?"

"Oh, right. Sorry. Wingate. Gaston was Vera's maiden name. That cottage has been in her family for generations. Unfortunately, Belinda wasn't the only death they had there. Several of Vera's family members passed away there too. But not as sinister as Belinda's death; there was a hereditary disease in the Gaston family."

"Really? What exactly was it?"

"Not sure, but some ghastly incurable thing. Don't worry; it's not infectious." He laughed and patted my arm, his hand lingering just a little too long. I pulled away, and he took a bite of his dry toast. "You and your friend are quite safe. I mean, you haven't come across anything nefarious, have you?"

He chewed on his toast, and suddenly I was uneasy with the way he was staring so intently at me. "How do you mean?"

"Nothing, really. It's just that the police never did find the culprit in poor Belinda's case, and she did live in that cottage for some time." He waved his hand in front of his face. "I'm being dramatic—too much Agatha Christie, I expect. I was just wondering if you came across some hidden panels behind the bookcase, or a secret tunnel." He gave a chuckle, but I wondered if he knew about the flower too. *Did everyone?*

"No, nothing so exciting," I said, not really convinced I meant it.

"Say, I was wondering. Would you like to—"

I stood and grabbed my bag of apricot goodies. "Better get back; Kit should be awake by now."

CHAPTER TWENTY-FOUR

Kit was not only awake, she had covered the dining room table with a full English breakfast fit for a queen: eggs, back bacon, sausage, fried bread, beans, tomatoes, roasted mushrooms, and potato cakes. And of course a pot of tea.

And she also had a breakfast guest: Ivy.

"Where've you been?" my pal asked. "Your breakfast is going to get cold." She reached across the table and removed a frying-pan lid she had placed over a brimming plate of food.

"Well, I guess I got us some breakfast dessert." I joined them and put the sack from Brew Ha Ha in the center of the table. "Apricot croissants," I announced.

"My favorite," Ivy squealed.

I felt a ripple of relief. In the few moments I'd been in the room, I'd sensed more than thought that Ivy was not acting like herself. Quiet. And serious-looking. And I wasn't in the mood for anything else serious to enter our vacation lives. So I was as surprised as Kit and Ivy when I heard myself say, "Ivy, what were you and your father doing inside Vera's cottage last week?" Just saying the words *last week*— and it *had* been almost a week—made me shocked that I hadn't asked the question sooner.

Ivy looked as if she'd been caught stealing from an offering plate. "We weren't in—"

"We saw you." I immediately regretted not listening to what lie she would have fabricated.

"Val, this is not the time—"

"Kit, I think it is. I think it's way past time." I felt my chest about to explode with the gravity and confusion of our situation.

"My dad said not to tell anyone. He said they wouldn't understand, that they'd think it was bad, what he did."

I looked at Kit, willing her to ask the right question, since we both knew she had Ivy's trust and I did not.

Kit threw me an irritated look, but then she spoke. "Ivy, what is it your dad did? We won't think it's bad."

I assumed she had her fingers crossed under the table.

"He was just searching for proof. That's all he was doing."

"Proof of what, sweetie?" Kit asked, and I was amazed to be seeing this kinder, gentler version of my friend. I mean, *I* know you catch more flies with honey than with vinegar, but I've told Kit that a million times to no avail. Or so I'd thought.

"Proof of his . . . innovation."

"Proof of his *what*?" Kit's normal tone was poking through.

"Innovation. No, not innovation. Um, proof that he wasn't guilty."

"Oh, *innocence*," Kit said. "Proof of his innocence."

Ivy nodded.

After a pause that grew uncomfortable for me, I asked, "Innocent of what?" I caught a glare from Kit. *Well, you should have asked her that yourself,* my look shot back.

Now tears were trickling down Ivy's cheeks, and Kit did what I wished I'd felt comfortable doing. She knelt down beside our young friend and put her arms around her. "It's okay, sweetheart," she said, as she patted Ivy's back. And in spite of her urging, "You can tell us," I knew her consolation was heartfelt. So what if we got the bonus of a little information to offset our ignorance.

"He said he was only trying to find out who killed Brown Owl. He said people were going to say *he* did it, and he didn't. My daddy wouldn't kill anyone!"

That's not what your sister thinks, I didn't say. If it were anyone but Ivy, I knew Kit *would* have said that. "What did he think he'd find in Vera's cottage that would prove he didn't kill her?" I asked, ignoring Kit's look of dismay. I'd waited long enough before asking what she should have followed up with.

Ivy looked puzzled, as if she didn't understand herself what was meant by her answer. "He said something about medical reporting. No, not reporting. Research. That's what he said. He was looking for some reports on medical research. But my mom said . . ." She started sobbing now. Big, wracking sobs, shaking her tiny body.

"So you told your mom what your dad said?" Kit finally held up her end of our interrogation.

After her sobs dwindled to slight gasps, Ivy answered. "Yes. I had to. She was saying such bad things about my dad."

My heart ached, as I realized that my Emily was caught between her own divorced parents. Like Ivy. Emily was older, so she didn't show her feelings as clearly. But I knew it was hurtful to her nonetheless to feel caught in the middle. Ever. About anything. I vowed she'd never have to feel that way again. And I knew it would take all the willpower I could muster to keep that vow.

I gave Kit a chance to ask first, but if she didn't hurry, I was going to have to. "Ivy," she said gently, and I knew she regretted even the hint of pitting Ivy against her parents.

It's okay, I wanted to urge her on, *we have to know. We have to ask.*

As usual, we were on the same wavelength. "What did your mom say when you told her?" she asked.

"Oh, she never believes anything good I say about Daddy. She said he's a liar and she could prove it."

"Did she?" Kit asked. "Did she prove it to you?"

More sobs. And then, "Yes."

***

Kit flopped down on the couch, towel drying her hair so vigorously I feared I'd see a bald spot when she stopped. Her brow was furrowed, and she seemed unaware of my presence in the chair only a few feet from her.

"You okay?" I asked.

She put the turquoise towel in her lap, and I was relieved to see there was no bald patch on her head. Her auburn hair was as thick as ever. "Yeah, I'm okay; I'm just not sure what to make of Ivy's story."

"You think it was just that? A story? She always has been a little dramatic."

Kit gave a humorless chuckle. "Yeah. No kidding. She should have been cast in the lead instead of either Doreen or Emily. No offense."

"Kit. None taken." *Was she serious? Like I'd be offended that she joked about Ivy deserving the lead over my Emily?*

"I know." Now her chuckle was more lighthearted. "This whole thing has my thinking so topsy-turvy, I forgot for a minute that Ivy's a decade too young for the part."

"Well, she does seem awfully mature at times," I tried to soften my pal's chagrin.

"Okay. So what did she tell us, really, about her dad supposedly lying? According to her mom."

"Well, those are your key words: *according to her mom.* I don't think her mom can see straight, she's still so in the throes of her obviously bitter divorce from Devon."

"But what exactly did she offer for proof?" Kit asked.

"You're right. It wasn't much."

"It wasn't *anything*. Only a young girl like Ivy would trust that her mom was onto something. It was *nonsense*."

Ivy had told us that Claire's so-called proof was the fact that the police would have gone over Vera's cottage with a fine-tooth comb and that her daddy had no reason whatsoever to believe that there would still be anything important to find. "He was just up to no good," Ivy told us her mother had said. "He was probably *planting* something, not looking for it," Claire had told her young daughter about Devon.

"That is a possibility," I said to my friend now. "But planting *what*? And *why*?"

"I think it's more likely he *was* looking for something, like he told Ivy. And let's face it, the police might never have found something like the envelope we discovered."

I shuddered at the thought—and at our continued ignorance—of what *that* was about. "I still think we should go to Detective Tromball with *all* of this. She might know something that could make it all come together." What I really wanted was to be shed of "all of this" so I could just enjoy my visit with Emily—before I had to return home to the troubles that awaited. I thought of poor William and what my poor mother might be facing.

"Not yet," Kit said. "Now let's forget about this for a while. Let's find something for you to wear on your sightseeing date tomorrow."

And with that she hopped up from the couch and fairly sprinted up the stairs. She still held the towel behind her back, making it look for all the world as if she had a turquoise terry-cloth tail.

Little did we know that before tomorrow was over, a sightseeing date would be the least of our worries.

CHAPTER TWENTY-FIVE

Valerie?"

I instantly stopped applying my CoverGirl lipstick (Garnet Flame). To my left I saw the bathroom door was open and a tall blond woman had stepped in.

"Hiya," Heidi said. "I thought that was you."

Crap.

I had, of course, noticed David and his fiancée at the back of the theater when Kit and I made our way to the small area just outside the main doors where the audience had collected. We'd headed over to Luke, who was standing alone waiting for his wife. He and Emily were planning to go to the pub with Jeffrey and the rest of the cast for a celebratory drink.

When I spotted David and Heidi heading in our direction, I immediately told Kit I'd meet her at the car. Then I ducked into the tiny bathroom, where I planned to wait out their departure.

So much for my best-laid plan. "Hi, Heidi," I said, feeling defeated. And also foolish, since it sounded like I was announcing a kids' television show. *Hi, Heidi.*

She took the two steps necessary to stand beside me at the sink, as I stuffed my lipstick into my purse. The bathroom was so small, I would literally have to either push her into the stall or ram her into the sink if she didn't let me pass. She was taller than me, but I had a good ten (okay, more like twenty) pounds on her.

"Did you enjoy the play?" She turned sideways to face me.

"Yes." I also turned, facing her, but it was a little too close for my comfort. "I didn't realize you and David would be here tonight."

"Right. Last-minute thing. David wanted to see Emily again."

"Okaaay," I said, as if I'd just reluctantly granted the man permission to see his own daughter. "Well, it was nice seeing you." I amazed both myself and Heidi at this obvious lie.

Up close, I took some satisfaction in noting she wasn't as young-looking as I'd first thought. She was very pretty, no doubt about it, and a good twenty years younger than me (and her intended), but she was wearing a lot of makeup. Heavy, dark eye shadow, brows that were more powder than actual brows, and lips that were heavily lined in a shade darker than her lipstick. For some reason, all this made me happy.

I picked up my purse from the counter and heaved the strap onto my shoulder. She, I noticed, had a tiny clutch purse, even smaller than Kit's, and by comparison, I felt like I was toting around a backpack. "Well, I guess I'll be going—"

"I wonder if I could just have a word." She put a hand on my arm, her left hand, the one with the engagement ring, the one with the diamond that was at least four times bigger than the half carat the cheap bastard had given me.

197

"Oh . . . er . . . Kit is waiting . . . and I . . . I need to go . . ."

"Valerie. Val. I know this is awkward. I never wanted us to meet like this. Dave didn't even tell me we would be meeting the other day until the very last minute."

Dave? I wondered for a second who this Dave was, and then of course realized she was referring to David, the diamond king.

"It's okay," I said. Although really, it wasn't okay.

She leaned back against the sink, crossing her arms over her chest. "Look. I know how you feel; I really do. I was married before, and I would have murdered my first husband if he'd put me in this uncomfortable situation." She looked down at her feet. They were small and encased in black suede pumps with high heels. Very sexy.

"So this isn't your first . . ."

"Marriage? Hell no. I was married for seven years. My husband was a total tosser."

I wasn't sure what that meant, but it didn't sound good. "Well, I hope you and *Dave* are very happy."

She laughed. "Yeah, if you say so." She nodded her head. "He's not a bad chap, but I expect you know that. You had some good years, right?"

I found myself nodding too. "Some," was all I could agree to.

"I just want you to know I adore Emily."

Really? Who doesn't? That was like admitting to adoring Christmas, or birthday presents, or three-and-a-half-carat diamonds.

"Well, I hope you will be very happy," I said again. How many times did I have to say it before she stepped aside and let me out of the bathroom?

"My kids love him too." Her arms were still crossed, her head still bent down toward her feet.

Whoa. Wait a minute. Kids? "You have children?" I asked sweetly. *Please, have at least six, with a couple of them in prison and a baby with permanent colic.*

"Yeah. Two, a boy and a girl. Six and four. Dave is great with them, but I expect you know what an amazing father he is . . . despite everything."

I smiled—a huge, genuine smile—and looked toward the mirror, running my fingers through my hair. "Heidi, seriously, I hope you—and your children—will be very happy." Third time a charm. "Now, I really must go." Okay, so her children were past the colic stage and not yet old enough for incarceration, but there was time.

"Are you going to the pub?" she asked.

"No, Kit and I have other plans. But you enjoy."

Heidi leaned in toward the sink, giving me room to squeeze behind her. There was just enough space for me to swing the door open without having her topple forward. I looked at her face in the mirror and noted the smile she gave me. It seemed real, no sign of meanness, but her words were buzzing in my head. "You said *despite everything*." I closed the door behind me and took a step toward her. "You may know, or not know, or even care, but he cheated on me. Repeatedly."

She didn't take her eyes off her image in the mirror, but she nodded her head slowly, like this wasn't news. "He hurt you," she said, after a few seconds. It was not a question.

I nodded, then smiled. "Good luck, Heidi." I didn't add that I thought she would need it, because I didn't think she would. Heidi was the type of woman who made her own rules, unlike the woman I had been. I had a sudden feeling of elation, like I'd just returned a defective product to the manufacturer, and it was no longer my problem.

It felt good, and now I wanted a drink, and a celebration.

***

When I got back out to the theater entrance, I made my way through the crowd toward Kit. She was having an animated conversation with Reg, a man who in Little

Dipping owned a Volvo dealership but in Padua assumed the role of Lucentio. Reg still wore his costume and clutched a brown velvet cap with an enormous feather that he used to punctuate his words. On the way there I passed David, who was busy chatting with Macie Brown. He gave me a smile, and I gave him one back. I was tempted to stop and congratulate him on the birth of his two new children, but that could wait.

"Reg was just saying how much he misses me—er, us," Kit said.

"Yes, my dear." Reg nodded. "I'm afraid the lady who took your part just doesn't have the . . . talent you brought to the role, Kit." He leaned in close to her as he spoke. "I don't know why Jeffrey didn't keep you on and assign Christelle to another part."

"I'm no actress." Kit beamed. (Seriously, was she kidding? She didn't believe that for a minute.) "But it's so nice of you to say so."

I wondered if she was referring to his mention of her talent, or having Jeffrey kick poor Christelle to the curb. From the corner of my eye, I could see David had released Macie's grip on him and was heading our way. "Kit, we should be going," I said. "But we'll see you tomorrow, Reg."

"Ahhh." The Volvo dealership man gave a sweeping bow. *"Good night, good night! Parting is such sweet sorrow, that I shall say good night till it be morrow."*

"Holy cow!" I grabbed Kit's arm and steered her toward the exit.

"G'night, Lucentio," she called behind her.

Once outside we headed to our car. "What was the rush?" Kit asked. "And why aren't we going to the pub?"

"Because David and Heidi will be there."

"Oh, right. How was your little chat with the child bride?"

"She's not quite the child we thought and—hey, how did you know we chatted?"

"I saw her head into the bathroom after you."

"Well, thanks for rescuing me."

"Rescue you? Do you recall the size of that bathroom? I wouldn't have been able to wedge a dollar bill between the two of you. Just tell me what she said."

As we buckled our seat belts and Kit put the car into drive, I gave her, word for word, every detail of our conversation. She nodded as she listened. And when I was done, she smiled.

"Oh, I forgot." I leaned back in my seat. "She's got a huge rock on her finger."

"Yeah, but look what it's attached to." Kit swung the car toward the exit. "So David is about to become Baron von Trapp."

"Yeah, that's about it."

We looked at each other and burst out laughing.

CHAPTER TWENTY-SIX

Val," Kit whispered in my ear, so loudly I thought my mom, who I had on the phone that was pressed to my other ear, would surely hear her. As if my mother wasn't upset enough. "Our appointment's in fifteen. We're going to be late," my impatient pal said.

"Shh," I whispered back.

"What?" my mother asked, through sniffs.

"Nothing. I just sneezed." I waved my friend away. We had appointments to get our hair styled at The Cut Above in just fifteen minutes, but my mother had called a half hour earlier and was so distraught I couldn't possibly break off the conversation until she was ready.

And it seemed, finally, that she was ready.

"I better go, Valerie," my mother said. "I hear William Stuckey yelling for his socks. And I already helped him put them on." A sob caught in her throat. Sort of a coda for all she'd just presented to me.

"He's getting worse faster than I thought he would," she'd said when I'd first answered her call.

"Mom?" I'd just finished getting ready for our hair appointments and was going to relax with a cup of tea until it was time to leave. "What are you talking about?" But the immediate sinking feeling in my stomach made me realize I knew exactly, if not specifically, what she was talking about. "Is it William?"

"Yes, Valerie. He's slipping away from me. Sometimes he doesn't even know who I am. Why, he called me *Eleanor* yesterday. That was his first wife." My mother sounded too concerned about her husband to have even a trace of jealousy.

Before I could respond, she shared a few more frightening episodes they'd experienced in just the last twenty-four hours. She'd caught him leaving their home in the middle of the night, for one thing. When she asked him where in the world he thought he was going, he'd retorted, "What the hell business is it of yours? And who the hell are you?"

"And William Stuckey *never* swears, Valerie. Neither did your father. And I'm not about to start putting up—"

"Are his kids still there?" I asked, thinking I should hurry back to the States. Thinking William's swearing was the least of our worries.

"Yes, they're lining up a place for him to move to. A place with something they call a memory unit. Somewhere close so I can visit him every day. They don't think it's safe for me to be taking care of him. But first we're going to get a second opinion from another neurologist next week. So they'll stay until then."

"Are they sure it's necessary to move him? Oh, Mom, you'd miss him so much. I mean, isn't this awfully sudden?"

"Well, probably not as sudden as you think. I suppose I was in denial for a while and didn't even admit to myself how his mind was . . . was failing. And when I did begin to suspect something, I didn't say it out loud to anyone, certainly not to you. What could you do from so far away? Oh, what does it matter now."

I hated the sound of resignation in her voice. My mom is a fighter. I didn't want to see her give up so easily. But I latched on to the appointment with a new neurologist and refused to give up myself. That and the fact that Kit was now tugging at my shirtsleeve made it possible for me to let my mother hang up when she insisted she felt spent and needed to try to take a nap.

After she convinced William he already had clean socks on.

***

At nine fifteen Kit and I were seated in the waiting area of The Cut Above against my better judgment. But at least I'd convinced Kit that we were going to get our hair only styled, not cut, never mind the name of the salon. I wondered as we sat leafing through British fashion magazines how I'd let her talk me into having *anything* done at Claire's shop. And by Claire, no less.

But Kit had assured me it would look suspicious if only one of us had her hair done. "Besides, let's face it, Val; of the two of us, you're the one who could do with the styling. I've told you a million times, you should go to Wayne."

Yes, of course, I could go to Wayne, her flamboyant hairdresser, but I could also use the price he charged as a deposit on a Lake Shore Drive condo. "Aren't you worried Claire will screw up Wayne's creation?"

"*Style*, Val. No scissors involved. Wayne will never know. And it only makes sense that we both get our hair styled," she'd insisted.

But to me, as I sat with a few quiet minutes to think, it made no sense at all.

I'd been surprised Claire had even agreed to squeeze us into her schedule so last-minute. But a look around her shop—shabby without the chic and void of any other clients when we entered—informed me she probably needed the money we'd pay her.

Kit's bright idea was that we'd have a good half hour—apiece—to talk to Claire. She couldn't bolt from us as she always seemed to do just as we were getting somewhere. Because Claire was connected to almost all of Kit's top suspects (Devon, Alistair, and yes, Doreen, as well as Claire herself), Kit felt certain she held a key. Whether Claire knew that or not.

"Who's first, ladies?" It was a Claire we hadn't seen before, as we looked up from the *British Vogue* that Kit held, her right pointer finger tapping a hairstyle she thought perfect for me. The Claire who stood before us now presented the pleasant stylist-to-client side of her personality, one we had never had even a glimpse of.

She loomed over us in killer high heels, the kind her daughter Doreen favored. And she was wearing all black—leggings and an oversize T-shirt with the image of a witch about to do something witchy. The gaudy diamond earring I'd seen at church had been replaced by a large silver crucifix.

Still, it was easy to see where Doreen got her pretty face, although Claire's beauty was faded by age and hardened by her choice of makeup.

Kit rose, and I followed her as she followed Claire. We'd agreed we would both hang nearby while the other had her hair done—to facilitate the interrogation.

But it turned out that we learned way more than we'd thought possible—without asking a single question.

"You can stay out there with the magazines until it's your turn," Claire said to me with a bright if fake smile, right after Kit lowered herself into the chair so Claire could wrap a cape around her shoulders.

"Oh, I'll just sit here, if you don't mind." I perched on the chair at the next station, which a sign on the mirror identified as belonging to Stylist Kaitlynn. "Unless you expect Kaitlynn soon?"

"No. Not today. She didn't think we'd be back in business so soon. But of course we are. It's nothing but coincidence that Vera . . . met her fate here."

And then it became impossible for Kit or me to say another word to Claire because she touched a button on a miniature earpiece partially concealed in her right ear. She was rudely, but probably wisely, on the phone for the rest of our visit, immersed in what I eventually decided was a desperate-sounding call from Doreen.

From the one-sided bits and pieces I could hear, it was clear that both Claire and Doreen were upset with some *he*— Alistair Carlisle, I figured. It didn't surprise me that Claire would be angry with her ex-husband, and as for Doreen, well, she *was* a teenager—one who was dating an older man, no less.

Poor Kit. She wasn't happy with the situation at all and didn't appear pleased that I seemed so willing to forego the plan to quiz our stylist. "Um, Claire?" she spoke, when Claire turned off the blow-dryer and grabbed the flat iron.

But Claire just put a finger up to her lips and kept talking on her phone.

She didn't end her conversation when she finished with Kit and motioned for me to follow her to the row of sinks to have my hair washed. Or when I followed her back and sat in the chair Kit had vacated. Or when The Duchess arrived for what was apparently her standing appointment and greeted us warmly.

Speaking in a hushed tone as her eyes took in the sight of Claire from head to toe, Pinky's wife said, "That one would never have dressed like some gothic teenager when Vera was alive."

"Vera?" I asked. "Why would Vera care?"

The Duchess looked at Claire, who now stood a few steps away and was gesturing with her hands to her unseen caller.

"Be back in a tick," Claire said to us. "I'm telling you, you can't trust him," we all heard her say as she disappeared through a door into a tiny room that appeared to hold boxes and supplies.

I turned to The Duchess. "Go on."

"You do know this salon was owned by Vera, right?"

Kit and I looked at each other. "No," Kit said. "But then why would we?"

"You see," The Duchess continued, "Vera owned half the village, if truth be told. The old girl was loaded." She stopped speaking to give her glossy blond hair a pat. "I was thinking after you left the other day," The Duchess went on, "that I actually do have a theory about Belinda's research, more than I let on, anyway. Pinky says I should tell you. He calls you two Rizzoli and Isles, by the way; he thinks he's so bloody clever."

She stopped and glanced at Claire, who was coming out of the storeroom but still talking on her phone. "You see, even with all her dosh, Vera had something wrong with her. Or rather, something that was likely to go wrong in the future. Her mom and some other relatives died from it, and I hear her sister isn't none too good."

Instinct pushed me up and out of my seat. I performed the universal charade of needing to use the bathroom, and Claire nodded, without missing a beat in what sounded like a one-sided conversation by now. I gave a teensy nod to Kit, which of course she immediately translated to *follow me—and bring The Duchess with you.* Soon we were around the corner and out of Claire's sight. Barely, given the size of the small salon.

"Sorry about that," I said. "Please go on, um, Duchess."

"I'm still trying to think what she called it, what Vera called it. It was something Belinda was researching, something that sounded simple, although it sounded like it was made up. I'm tellin' you, nowadays it seems like almost anything can be a bad disease. Oh, that's right. I remember the acronym was the same as my cousin Frannie's initials. FFI. Frannie's name is Frances Fiona Inverness, so the acronym was FFI, but the name of the disease is . . . um . . . fatal family, um, fatal family . . . hmm . . ."

"Fatal familial insomnia," Kit said, putting her iPhone back in her pocket and looking stunned. "Ya mean people can actually die—"

"Ladies!" We turned and saw Claire, looking alarmed, as if correctly guessing we'd been discussing something not for her ears.

"Yeah, I had to use the ladies' room," I said, as I scurried back to my seat so she could finish my hair. Better, I hoped, than she had Kit's, whose shiny tresses were normally smooth, silky, and stylish. Now—*on purpose?* I wondered—they were poufy and shaped into the bubble haircut I saw in photos of my mom from when I was a baby. *Poor Kit,* I thought. *Poor me.* And back in Chicago, Wayne would be stabbing his neck with his scissors if he could see his highest-tipping client.

I knew we'd soon be washing and restyling our own hair.

But first we had some more digging to do. I had a feeling we needed to learn more about fatal familial insomnia.

CHAPTER TWENTY-SEVEN

The first thing I noticed, with great relief, was the Range Rover Sean was driving. Obviously, it was better suited to my body type than his microscopic MG.

He arrived at noon, and Kit and I watched from the window as he parked his vehicle on Magpie Lane several cottages down from ours. He jumped out of the driver's side, looking dapper in a crisp blue cotton shirt, open at the neck, and casual linen pants. He was actually smiling, and I felt a little sick.

He whipped off his aviator sunglasses as he made his way up our sidewalk. "Hiya," he said, when Kit opened the door to him.

"Hi yourself." She stepped aside to let him into the tiny hallway.

When he came fully into the living room, with outstretched arms ready for a hug from me, I really wished he wasn't so damn nice.

"So, where are you kids going?" Kit sat on the arm of the sofa.

"I thought we'd start by driving to a little village I know about an hour away and have some lunch. It's smaller than Little Dipping, if you can believe that, but equally as charming. Then maybe we'll take in Arundel Castle. I think you'd like that."

"Because all Americans like castles?" someone said, and then I realized it was me.

Kit flashed me a *what the hell is up with the attitude* look, and I turned away to avoid her questioning glare. "Were you born in Sussex?" she asked Sean.

He laughed. "No. I'm a Londoner, born in the East End."

"Oh, we just love London," Kit said. "And Arundel Castle sounds cool, doesn't it, Val?"

"Yes, it does. So, Sean, we better get going." I grabbed my purse from the corner of the couch.

He returned his sunglasses to his face and gestured toward the front door. Again, he looked happy, really happy, and I gave him my biggest smile.

"All set?" he asked, after he had buckled me into the Range Rover, rather like an anxious mother securing her baby into a car seat.

"Yep." I glanced at my watch.

Sean walked around the vehicle to the driver's side and climbed in. But before turning on the ignition, he swiveled to face me.

"You sure you have time for this?" he asked in a soft voice.

"What do you mean?"

"You were checking your watch just now. You know, Val, if you—"

"Sean, I was just—"

"Checking the time?"

"Right. Is that so bad? Please don't read anything into it."

210

He sighed. Then he looked in the rearview mirror, his lips set in a firm line. "Val, I realize I sort of pushed you into this. If you didn't want to go, you should have said so."

"No, it's fine." I turned my head and looked out the passenger window.

"Oh, well, if it's *fine*, then that's different."

I sighed and turned my gaze back to him. "Look, Sean, you're a very nice man, and I—"

"Wait. You're not going to say *it's me and not you*, I hope."

"Actually, I wasn't, but maybe I should."

"Okay, what were you going to say?"

I thought of Luke again. *Oh crap. Is this going to be bad for him? Am I going to get him fired?* "I guess I was going to say . . . you're a very nice man—"

"Okay, you actually did say that already. Continue." He had returned his sunglasses to his face, and he was staring out through the windshield. "We're not having our first fight, are we?"

"Maybe, but it will probably be our last."

"Because we won't see each other again, or because we'll make up and never have another disagreement?"

I studied him as he gazed down Magpie Lane. He had a nice profile, but his lips were still pinched together, giving him a defeated look.

"Sean," I began again. "You're a . . ." Luckily, I was able to stop what had become my refrain. "Here's the thing. Eventually—in fact, soon—I have to return to the States. I had a lovely evening with you, but my time here is so precious, and I want to spend every moment I can with Emily and Luke."

"So you don't have time for me, is that it?"

I took a few seconds to think about it. "I guess that's what I'm saying."

He turned fully toward me. "Val, I wasn't planning on monopolizing all your time. I understand your commitment to your daughter—"

Whew. "Oh, Sean, I'm so glad, because the last thing I want to do is offend you—"

"I'm not in the least offended."

"Well, good." I took a moment to marvel at how well he was taking this. "So you see, I don't know when I'll be able . . . er . . . when I'll have time again . . . I mean, on this visit . . . which of course will be the only time I'll be . . ."

He opened his door, stepped out, and walked around the vehicle to the passenger side. Then he opened my door and extended a hand toward me.

"Wait," I said, "I didn't mean for—"

"Val, really, I don't want you to do anything against your wishes. I did push this on you. I never gave you a chance to graciously decline. And let's face it, we were the product of someone else's matchmaking. You probably went along with it only because I'm Luke's boss and you were afraid I'd fire him if you didn't agree to run away with me."

"You won't, will you?" I took his hand and stepped down out of the Range Rover.

He laughed. "No. I promise. And I take it you won't agree to run away with me."

"No," I said. *Was I going to regret this?*

I immediately headed back to the cottage and felt enormous relief rush through me as I saw Sean's Range Rover pass by on the street. It was like leaving the dentist's office with no cavities. But poor Sean didn't deserve to be compared to tooth decay.

I let myself in and headed to the kitchen. I saw Kit sitting at the table, sipping tea, the pressed flower and her smartphone in front of her. She turned her attention from them to me, frowning. "Val, what is it? Are you okay? What's going on? Did Sean Meacham . . . did that guy—"

"Nothing is going on, Kitty Kat." I took a seat across from her.

"So what are you doing here? Why are you back?"

"We just agreed that perhaps it wasn't the best idea—"

"We, or just you?"

212

"Okay, just me." I rose to get a cup and returned to pour some tea from the teapot.

For a second she was silent. Then she said, "Okay, tell me what's going on with you. Because you were acting like a very bad teenager before you left."

I gave an exaggerated sigh. "Kit," I said slowly and patiently, like that same very bad teenager explaining her malicious actions to a police officer. "How can I put this? Sean is a terrific guy—the best. But here's the thing . . ." I stopped speaking.

"I'm waiting to hear the thing." She was drumming the top of the table with her fingertips.

"Okay. Don't you think it's a little odd that he would want to take *me* out? I mean, look at him. He's gorgeous, he's British, he apparently has an endless supply of vehicles. Why would he give me five minutes of his time?"

She gave an even bigger exaggerated sigh than I'd just laid on her. Then she jumped up, returning a few seconds later with the sherry bottle and two glasses. "Okay," she said, pouring. "Now . . . how can I put this? You are a helluva woman, Val. Why wouldn't any man—British, American, or Zulu tribesman—want to take you out?"

"Okay, the Zulu tribesman, possibly. But come on; Sean Meacham can have any woman—"

"But apparently, he wanted you."

"I don't buy it. And anyway, I'm not cut out to be courted—"

"*Courted?* What are you, Amish, all of a sudden?"

"No." I laughed. "You know what I mean."

"Actually, I don't."

"Well, pour me another sherry, and I'll explain it."

"Please, not again. Ya know, I blame that damn Culotta for this . . . this attitude of yours."

The strange thing was, she was probably right; well, not about blaming him for anything. But my erstwhile relationship with Detective Culotta had been on my mind ever since Sean had come, however briefly, into my life.

Again, I was overcome with a sense of reprieve, basking in complacency, relieved at not having to dress up, say the right thing, and worry whether or not butterflies were flooding my body. In general, it boiled down to the fact that I couldn't be bothered to date someone new (which probably meant I was somewhat of a moron). "He promised he wouldn't fire Luke," I said, trying to add some levity to the situation.

"Oh, Valley Girl." She poured us both another glass. "What am I going to do with you?"

I took up my drink and tapped the card that held the pressed flower. That's when I noticed for the first time that the flower was actually attached with cellophane to *two* pieces of card stock. Either that or it was a piece of thick cardboard that looked like it could easily be split in two. "So, what were you doing with this?" I picked it up.

"While you were speed dating, you mean?"

"Yes, exactly."

"Still trying to figure it out. Is it somehow related to Belinda's research? I mean, this supposedly has sedative characteristics, and she supposedly was researching a condition where people die due to lack of sleep. So is it a very big leap—?"

"You are talking about this FFI?"

"Yep; I googled it, and it seems to me Vera was lucky she was murdered. It says here . . ." She paused and tapped her phone " . . . that there's no cure, death usually happens between seven months and three years of onset, and during that time the inflicted suffers from progressively worsening insomnia that leads to hallucinations, delirium, confused states like those of dementia—all that and then death. Yep, seems to me like a slashed throat would be preferable."

"Kit!"

"I'm just sayin'. And I'm sayin' I think this flower might have been something Belinda was working on, if not for a potential cure, then at least to alleviate symptoms, maybe give the poor gal some sleep and slow down the progression."

"So, is that flower what Claire was looking for, do you think? You think Doreen knew about it and told her? Could that be what their phone call this morning was about, too, what Doreen seemed to be having a fight with her dad about? Something is up there."

"Oh, do ya think?" Her eyes widened, translating her words into *no shit*.

"You know what I mean."

"I do. And I don't trust Doreen one little bit."

"I'm still not so sure you're right. Maybe she just had an off day that once. We've seen her be really nice."

"She's an actress, Val. I'm telling you, I don't trust her."

I'd been absent-mindedly—or nervously?—picking at the tiny space between the layers of cardboard. "What in the—" I now held a tiny piece of paper that had been hidden between the layers.

"What have you got there?" Kit asked.

"I have no idea."

"Let me see it." She took it out of my hands.

"Be careful. It's going to tear—"

"Well, well, well," she said. "What *do* we have here?"

I went around to her side of the table, and we put our heads together. But we couldn't decipher what appeared to be hieroglyphics or chemical notations—something too scientific for either of us to recognize.

"Ya know, we just gotta figure out how to connect all the dots. And I think these are some important new dots we have here."

"Why do *we* have to connect the dots?" I asked.

"Because I know you won't feel safe going home and leaving Emily behind with a murderer on the loose. And Larry's expecting me home as planned."

Hah! I knew Larry was the last one Kit would worry about if she decided to extend her stay abroad. I also knew she loved a good mystery. And we'd landed in the middle of an irresistible one. To her. For my part, it made me feel far sicker to my stomach than Sean's advances had.

So much for feeling complacent. Well, it had felt good while it lasted.

***

I awoke after a short nap, brought on by the third glass of sherry we'd consumed, to hear Kit coming in the front door. I made my way down to her. "Where were you? I didn't even know you were gone."

"Pippa says hi." My pal was sitting on the couch next to a Knit One, Purl Two shopping bag. "I exchanged the sweater I bought Larry," she continued, responding to my raised eyebrows. "His reward."

I sat down next to her but kept my eyebrows raised.

She gave a huge sigh and withdrew a handsome cream-colored wool sweater from the bag. "You were right, Val. OMG, will you lower your eyebrows already? They're gonna freeze in that position."

"Well, then tell me what the heck you're talking about. Reward Larry for what? The last I heard, you were hardly ready to reward—"

"That's what I'm trying to tell you, dum-dum. I decided you were right, and I called and told him so. While you were getting your beauty sleep. After I realized that you just couldn't get a spark going for ol' Sean, that it really *isn't* easy to find someone you want to be with . . . Ya know, for all his faults, Larry's that one for me. And so I thought, why not let him retire."

She sighed again, as if picturing such a scenario and still having misgivings. But then she broke into a big grin. "But guess what? When I told him all that and gave him my blessing for retirement, he announced he'd already changed his mind, didn't know what he'd been thinking, yada yada yada."

I couldn't help but wonder if what he'd been thinking was what it would be like to have more time at home with Kit. The word *high-maintenance* came to mind.

"So—" She held up the sweater in front of her, and I again admired the rich, lush yarn woven into perfect stitches. "Here's his reward!"

I gave her a big hug and then stood up. "Good girl. Now, we gotta scoot. Time to get ready for the thee-ay-ter," I said, feeling almost giddy with happiness for my friends.

***

We arrived a half hour before the performance was to begin and made our way toward the dressing room to have a brief chat with Emily. I prayed that Luke wouldn't be around so I could avoid explaining my nondate with Sean.

But Kit made a detour when she spotted Alistair Carlisle standing at the edge of the stage, all but hidden by the curtains. I followed before I had time to realize what we were doing.

"Hey, Alistair," she said.

He looked up, startled. I told myself not to read anything sinister into that. Our rush to approach him had turned Kit's excited voice into a screech, so of course he would look startled. I needed to remember that all fathers and daughters have disagreements. The fact that we'd overheard an angry phone call between his ex and their daughter that mentioned his being untrustworthy didn't mean any of them was a killer.

"Ladies." Alistair's face became composed, and now he appeared delighted to see us.

"Is Doreen here? How is she?" Kit asked.

"She's fine. Why wouldn't she be? I'm meeting her here; I thought she might be backstage."

"Let's hope you catch her in a good mood," Kit mumbled to me. I had my doubts, too, considering the one-sided phone call we'd overheard.

But for now I was more concerned about seeing Emily before we had to take our seats. I grabbed Kit's arm and made excuses to Alistair.

***

Emily was standing at the door to the makeshift dressing room, looking lovely with her crown of flowers and her velvet bodice. Very Elizabethan except for the cell phone pressed against her ear.

"Mom," she said, as soon as she saw me. I watched her turn off her phone, and I steeled myself for some kind of reproach from her regarding her husband's boss. But fortunately, none was forthcoming. In fact, she had far more important things on her mind. The play, to be precise. "Jeffrey!" she called, looking past me. I turned to see the director heading our way. "We were beginning to worry," she said.

"Sorry, I got delayed." He sounded breathless as he nodded at Kit and me.

But before I could even wonder, let alone ask, what Emily was worried about, the two of them took off toward the stage, with Jeffrey clapping his hands and yelling his trademark, "*People, people, listen up.*"

"Break a leg," I called, but I don't think anyone heard me.

CHAPTER TWENTY-EIGHT

Sipping tea and listening to Emily's play-by-play of the night's performance was turning out to be my favorite part of our visit. Having actually been a cast member, however low my status might have been, I found it so interesting to hear who flubbed a line or who missed a cue. Or what audience reaction led to a subsequent equal if different reaction onstage. Who knew physics and plays worked so similarly?

"Did you catch it when Ernie called me Emily instead of Kate?" My daughter looked amused.

"No, not at all." I glanced at Luke and Kit for confirmation.

"Actually," Kit began, and I kicked her shin under the kitchen table. "Actually," she started over, "I didn't notice."

Emily laughed and reached over to pat Kit's arm. "That's so sweet, but I know you probably did."

"So no big deal, right?" Kit laughed. "But I did notice there might have been a problem with the props. I'm assuming there should have been something coming out of the jug when that serving person was supposed to be pouring beer, or ale, or whatever it was."

"Ha. Yes." Emily giggled. "We had a little problem with all the props. Apparently, Sylvie, the prop woman, left half of them at home. I was hoping no one noticed, but Jeffrey was fit to be tied."

"Well, I didn't notice a thing," I lied, recalling my favorite: the supposed sound of a trumpet offstage to announce the arrival of one of the characters.

"Hey," Luke chimed in, as if plucking the thoughts from my mind. "What happened to the trumpet? It sounded like someone was faking it back there."

Emily burst into laughter. "Oh yes. It was Jeffrey. Da da da dum," she mimicked.

"Sylvie forgot the trumpet?" Luke asked in amazement.

"Not forgot; she brought it, all right, but apparently when she took it home last night, her six-year-old plugged it up with bubble gum, and it wasn't discovered until the crucial moment, hence Jeffrey's remarkable recovery."

"I thought someone stepped on a cat," Luke said, implying we shouldn't equate remarkable with good.

"Riiight." Emily laughed some more. "But it wouldn't have been so bad if he'd managed to give his trumpet impression before Lord Whatsit told Sirrah to go see what trumpet 'tis that sounds."

Kit and I joined in their mirth. And then I added, as Luke refreshed our teacups, "Did Doreen show up? We saw Alistair before the show began, and he was looking for her."

"No," Emily said. "At least I never saw her. She told me she'd stop by, and I reserved a seat for her, but she didn't show."

I wanted to share with my daughter the disgruntled phone call we'd overheard—one side of, anyway—earlier that day. But Emily, unlike her mother, is not a big fan of gossip, especially when it's thirdhand. So I remained silent and picked up my cup to take a sip of tea.

Kit, however, has no problem whatsoever with gossip, thirdhand or even fourth. "What's up with Doreen and her dad?" she asked.

"Aww." Emily smiled, thankfully misinterpreting Kit's supposed knowledge of the young woman's relationship with her father. "Alistair dotes on Doreen, doesn't he? He's very eager for her to start college, and she's looking at Edinburgh, where they have fantastic drama opportunities. She's so good, that's totally where she belongs. You've heard of the Edinburgh Festival, of course?"

Kit and I both nodded, indicating we had both so heard of the festival, chatted about it daily, and were not in the least bit completely clueless.

"Does Alistair want her to go there?" I asked, since I did have a clue that he wasn't totally okay with it.

"Oh, I think he'll agree to whatever she wants. She's a little spoiled."

Just then Kit's phone rang. "What the—" She reached for her purse strap that was slung across the back of the chair. "It's nearly eleven; who'd be calling this late? It better not be Larry, because—oh." She held the phone at arm's length, and we all saw a picture of Ivy in her provocative pose, wearing Kit's shoes and fancy robe. "Ivy, honey, are you okay?" Kit said into the phone.

We watched as Kit listened. And from the frown on her face, one thing was clear: Ivy was not okay.

CHAPTER TWENTY-NINE

I'm too upset to sleep." Ivy's voice on the phone sounded so childlike, just the way an eight-year-old's *should* sound. Not at all the same as when she was babbling in person.

Kit had placed her phone on the kitchen table and turned it on speaker. She, Emily, and I huddled around it, while Luke busied himself boiling more water. "Hey," he said, from his position at the stove, "you three look like the witches in *Macbeth*. You know, *double, double toil and trouble*."

We all three stared at him, as Ivy's voice wailed from the phone. "Oh nooooo; Luke, is that you? Don't you know you are never supposed to quote from that play? It's extremely bad luck! Emily, please make him stop."

Emily put her hand over her mouth to suppress a giggle. "It's okay, Ivy. The curse applies only if the word *Macbeth*—"

"Nooooo, you are not supposed to call it that; you have to say *The Scottish Play*."

I was impressed by Ivy's knowledge of Shakespearean folklore but decided maybe all English children are familiar with The Bard. Did American eight-year-olds know that Tennessee Williams wrote *A Streetcar Named Desire*? Was it even remotely the same?

"Right; you're right." Emily said. "But the curse applies only if *Mac*—if the title of The Scottish Play—is said in the theater."

"Are you sure?"

"Yes, I'm certain. Kitchens are totally safe," Emily assured her. (And now I was impressed with my daughter's knowledge.)

"That's all right then." Ivy sounded relieved.

"But why are you calling so late, Ivy? And why are you so upset?"

"Because Mummy told me that Doreen is going to Scotland to university, and I won't see her for a long time, and I'll really miss her, 'cuz she's my only friend—apart from you, Kit. You are my *best* friend." We all three stared into the phone, silently watching it, as if Ivy's picture would suddenly morph into the real thing and we'd be faced with the infernal question of whether or not we had any cake.

I saw Kit take a big gulp of air before she responded. "Honey, first of all, Doreen is not leaving tomorrow—"

"She's going very soon. Mummy saw her tonight in the place she stays at sometimes, and she said Doreen was leaving. Very soon."

"Where is your mom now?" I asked.

"In her room; I think she's asleep, and I have to be very quiet 'cuz I'm not supposed to make phone calls except in an emergency, and she'll be really cross with me."

"Ivy," Kit spoke again, "I don't think you have anything to worry about. Why don't you try to go to sleep now, and we can talk tomorrow."

"But I'm soooooo upset," the child wailed again, making me think her mother had either taken a handful of sleeping pills or been hit over the head with a hammer.

"Yes, we can hear that you are, but I promise it will all be much better tomorrow. You can talk to Doreen and find out what she's planning, and then maybe you can go visit her in Scotland—"

"I don't like Scotland; they eat haggis, which is disgusting, and they talk funny."

"Oh, Ivy," Emily said, "I think they have a lovely accent."

"Kit has a lovely accent, and she's from Chicago."

Luke sat down at the table with a fresh pot of tea. "You have a real admirer, Kit," he whispered, refilling our cups with more damn tea.

"I know." Kit's tone of voice and the nod of her head implied Luke was stating the obvious.

"Gotta go," Ivy said, and she ended the call before we could say good-bye.

***

"Tell me again why we're doing this."

Kit sighed, driving slowly and looking for Coventry Lane. "Because—is this it? It looks different in the light." She frowned. "We're doing this because I just want to be sure that Doreen is aware of how upset her little sister is. And I want to ask her what she knows about the flower—"

"Of course you do. But first of all, how do we know she's even here?"

"Because Ivy said Claire visited her here last night. Were you even listening, Val?"

"Yes, I was listening. I could hardly *not* listen. But . . ."

"What?"

"Well, Kit, I know you have a real fondness for Ivy—"

"And she for me. Here's the cottage."

"Right. You're Florence Henderson, and Ivy's one of those Brady Bunch girls—"

"Which one?"

"I don't know; I don't even remember their names."

224

"Not Marcia, Marcia, Marcia; she was the oldest. I think Cindy was the youngest."

"For heaven's sake, it doesn't matter which one. I'm trying to tell you that while you definitely have a lovely, special relationship with Ivy, you have to remember . . ."

"What, Val? What do I have to remember?"

"Well, that Ivy is, you know, a little dramatic and maybe doesn't always tell the truth."

"She's eight."

"She's a kleptomaniac."

Kit pulled the car to a stop outside Doreen's hideaway cottage. She switched off the engine and turned to look at me. "We'll just stop in and say hello. What's wrong with that?"

As I watched her take off her sunglasses and store them in their holder, I felt a little guilty. Had I said too much? Was I just being mean about her relationship with Ivy? The adoration of a child, any child, is special, and I should have been celebrating Kit's obvious pleasure. Not trying to dampen it. "You're right, Kitty Kat. Nothing wrong with that. And why don't we stop at Marbles on the way home and buy Ivy a cake."

"Yes. Good idea. The best damn cake they've got."

CHAPTER THIRTY

When Doreen didn't answer our loud knocks on the door of Alistair's family cottage, we quit whispering and spoke in hushed voices. The circumstances just seemed to call for lower-than-normal volume.

"I don't think she's here," I said.

Kit shook her head. "Ya think?"

I knocked again, so loudly Emily probably could have heard me back in Little Dipping. Except that I felt certain Emily was still sound asleep, resting up for tonight's performance.

"Yes, I think." My curtness was aimed at our failed mission, not really at Kit. "I'm still wondering . . ." My voice remained low but lost its irritated tone as my disturbing thoughts returned.

"Wondering what?" Now Kit sounded irritated as she spoke into the silence that had hung in the air as I continued to wonder.

I leaned against the door I'd been banging on and folded my arms across my midsection. "About Claire's anger when she was at our cottage, how she said Doreen had been lying. Surely it had to do with the flower, since she'd expected to find it under your drawer. Do you think she knew its significance? And *was* that flower somehow connected to Vera's family disease? Did Claire know about that? OMG, I'm getting a headache. And probably over nothing but my imagination. Forget—"

"No, I'm sure you're onto something." She gently pushed me aside and knocked again. Louder than ever, displaying her heightened desperation for answers. "Fuck," she said, her irritation now aimed at our inability to quiz Doreen.

Then, as if deciding second best would be to get a look in the cottage, she wiggled the doorknob, and I had no doubt her next step would be to ram her clutch purse through one of the three dimpled-glass windows at the top of the door.

But it yielded to her turn of the knob.

She looked at me and gave a snort of a laugh, as if to say *why didn't I think of that sooner?*

Once inside I called out, "Doreen? Anyone home?" Following behind Kit as she did a walk-through, I glanced back to the front door so frequently I grew dizzy from turning my head. I half expected Doreen—or Alistair or even Claire—to appear and demand answers from *us*. "Kit, someone could come any second. We better—"

"Good. I hope they do. I have some questions for them."

I had no doubt.

"But Kit, we're trespassing."

"Trespassing? Val, we're investigating a murder. *Murders*, plural. Who's gonna give a damn about a little trespassing?"

Here we go again, I thought. Kit in detective mode and quite full of herself.

But she didn't disappoint.

It was the last place we looked, of course, because why keep looking after you find a dead body?

We'd entered the bedroom and noticed nothing but a messed-up bed. "So Doreen must have slept here last night," I said.

"That figures, ya know, since Claire visited her here last night. Ivy said—"

"I know. Ivy said so." I tried to hide, since I couldn't erase, the ambivalent feelings I had for Ivy. "But I wonder what happened. If she's gone, why isn't her bed made?"

Kit looked at me in shock, knowing full well it isn't at all hard for me to leave my own home with an unmade bed. Now, Kit—she's a different story.

"Okay, I guess that's not unheard of," I said, promising myself I would never again leave my *bedroom*, let alone my house, without first making my bed.

As we turned to leave the room—the bathroom being our next stop—I saw something poking out from underneath the bed. And not just anything. It was a foot. And even though it didn't have a five-inch heel on it, I knew it was Doreen's.

"Kit!" I shrieked, just before I fainted.

CHAPTER THIRTY-ONE

The Crawley House was jam-packed with diners lingering over a late lunch by the time we got there. Our waitress led us to a table that had just been vacated by two mothers, both pushing strollers with chubby babies. One baby appeared to be chewing on a sock, and the other was munching on a napkin.

"Just give us a tick, and I'll clean this off," the young waitress said, clutching two menus to her chest and indicating with a nod of her head that we should go ahead and sit.

As soon as we did, Kit reached across and took my hand. "How are you feeling?"

"Fine; I'm fine. Really." I squeezed her fingers and released my hand from hers.

"Sure? 'Cuz you had me scared back there."

"I know. I'm sorry. But I'm good now." I picked up the menu and looked at it, not really registering the words of the lunch special or what was available for dessert. All I could see was Doreen's foot. Her dead foot. And even though my first thought had been a certainty that it did indeed belong to Doreen, and only her, my second thought was Emily. What if it had been her foot? She was too close to the action, and I was terrified.

I couldn't change my focus from that dreadful experience to the menu.

"Val, Val, wake up, c'mon, wake up!" Kit's voice had been shrieking at me as I came to after fainting. Her hand was slapping my face (harder than necessary, I thought), and the bedroom was spinning.

"Wha . . . what happened?" I asked, as she helped me to a sitting position.

"Here." She pushed me gently so that my back leaned against the wall, and then she opened her tiny purse. She brought out something small, a tube about half the size of a cigarette. Breaking it in two, she held it under my nose.

"What the—" I pushed her hands away from my face.

"Smelling salts," she said proudly.

"Kit, I think you're supposed to use those when a person is still in the middle . . . of the faint? That sounds weird."

But Kit wasn't paying attention to me anymore. She'd poked her head and an arm under the bed, and I expected her to break open another tube of smelling salts for Doreen. But instead, she said, "No pulse."

Then she returned to me. "Maybe you have a concussion." She put her palm on my forehead.

I gently removed her hand, twisting out of my sitting position and using a floral wingback chair to pull myself up. "I don't have a concussion—"

"How d'you know?" She looked worried.

"Well, I don't think falling onto a sheepskin rug is how you generally get a concussion, and furthermore, you don't test for concussions the way you test for a fever." I sat down in the chair.

And that's when I saw the foot again.

Kit immediately called the police. Well, almost immediately. First she dialed 911, then realizing that wouldn't work in England, she punched the nine on her phone three times. We remained in the bedroom after the assurance that the police would be there shortly. Me on the chair, Kit kneeling on the floor in front of me, and Doreen's foot still peeking out from under the bed ruffle. Neither of us spoke for a few minutes after she shut off her phone and we began our wait for law enforcement.

"Who carries smelling salts around?" I asked, when the silence between us got to be too much.

"Aren't you glad I do?"

"Er, not really."

"Want me to go find a glass of water?"

"*No*," I said, a little too dramatically. "No, please don't leave me here."

We avoided looking at Doreen's foot, as Kit rubbed my shin. "No problem, Valley Girl. I won't go anywhere."

"Good. How long was I . . . out?"

"Less than a minute. You probably fainted because you hadn't eaten anything," she suggested.

"Riiight." I didn't mention the two slices of toast we'd both had with our coffee before we left the house. And I definitely kept mum about the bowl of cornflakes and the mango yogurt I'd consumed while she was showering.

Luckily, Detective Constable Downey arrived shortly after Kit's call. And he was followed by an army of official-looking people, a few of them wearing white coveralls like you see on *CSI* and other television crime shows. Detective Downey led us out to our car, and there he asked what had happened.

We gave him a detailed account, which didn't amount to much. Then he let us leave, but only after making us promise we would go directly to the station to give formal statements and be fingerprinted.

"For elimination purposes only," he'd said brightly, making it sound like a fun game.

But it was no game.

And I was still shaken to my core as I heard Kit place her order now with the waitress who had returned with a pencil and pad. "Just coffee for me, please. I don't think I can eat a thing." She closed the menu and looked up at the waitress.

I wanted to say *me neither*, but I found myself ordering. "Chicken noodle soup and half a cheese-and-pickle sandwich, please."

"Right-ee-oh," the girl said. "Won't be a tick." She took our menus and moved gracefully among the tables toward the kitchen.

Kit heaved a big sigh as soon as she was gone. "Wow. I can't believe this. I keep thinking of Ivy; she's going to be devastated."

"Yes," I murmured. "Poor kid."

"Hey, speaking of Ivy, look who just came in."

I turned toward the entrance of the café and saw a tall ginger-haired guy waiting to be seated.

"Ivy's papa," Kit announced. "And Claire's ex." Before I could respond, she was on her feet, waving a napkin in the air toward Devon Scoffing. "Mr. Scoffing? Over here. Won't you please sit with us?"

The man hesitated, but after a moment he pointed our way, indicating to the waitress who was trying to seat him elsewhere that he would be joining us.

"Mr. Scoffing." Kit took her seat again.

"Devon, please." He sat next to me and leaned his elbows on the table. His legs were so long, he had to be content with one sticking out sideways.

"Okay, Devon." Kit gave him a dazzling smile. "I don't think we've been formally introduced. I'm Kit James, and this is Valerie Pankowski."

Devon smiled, and his somber look vanished, making him downright appealing. "I know all about you, probably more than you'd care for me to know. My daughter, Ivy, is very taken with you."

"Oh yes, Ivy. We just love Ivy," Kit said, as the waitress appeared with my soup and sandwich and poured coffee for Kit.

Devon waited for her to leave, and then his cheerful smile gave way to a look of pride. "Yes, she's really something, all right. So, you are here on holiday from Chicago?"

"Yes. My daughter, Emily, is in the play at The Beamlight—"

"Emily, right," he said. "She's a Cubs fan, but she lives in Los Angeles. Her husband, Luke, works in Chichester."

We all laughed.

"So how do you like the Gaston cottage?" Devon asked.

"Apart from its sad history and what happened to Vera Wingate, it's pretty fabulous," Kit answered for both of us. "Did you know Vera?"

Before Devon could respond, the waitress returned and took his order for cod and chips with mushy peas.

"Vera?" Kit prompted him.

He leaned back in his seat. "Bloody hell." He looked to the ceiling as he spoke, his words coming slowly and seeming to bring him pain. "Yes, I knew her. Awful woman. She caused a lot of aggro around here; stirred up a lot of shit, I can tell you. She's one hundred percent responsible for the predicament I'm in right now, with this restraining order. Did you know I'm not even allowed to go near my own kid? And if my ex-wife isn't the world's biggest bitch . . ."

He paused, and I thought Kit might have to prompt him to continue. But he began speaking again after taking a deep breath. "I suppose you probably know—not much kept secret in this damn village—that I spent some time in prison. I was totally stitched up by that damn Wingate woman—"

"Stitched up?" Kit interrupted. I couldn't believe she was stopping him to get clarification.

"Yeah, framed, you might say. I went down for receiving stolen goods. The evidence against me was overwhelming, thanks to her. She was friends with the prosecutor, and my solicitor was useless. You get what you pay for, right? But it worked very well for Vera Bloody Wingate. It got me out of the way, which is exactly what she wanted."

"Away from what?" Kit asked.

"Belinda, for one thing," he mumbled his response, as he unwrapped his napkin and carefully laid his knife and fork on the table.

"I never knew she had such power," Kit said quietly.

"Power? She owned the whole fucking—excuse me—the whole damn village. I hope you weren't fooled by her Brown Owl crap and didn't waste sympathy on her because of all the shit about her family illness."

"About that, the family illness—"

"Yeah, some fu—damn hereditary thing. Apparently, if you get it, you can't sleep, until eventually you wind up taking the Big Sleep, know what I mean?"

"And why would she want to keep you away from Belinda Bailey?" Kit took a sip of her coffee.

The waitress appeared at that exact moment and set a plate in front of Devon: steaming fried cod and the mushy peas, which did indeed look like they had been mashed with a sledgehammer.

"So, the play's going well?" Devon cut into his cod and looked up contentedly. Clearly, Belinda Bailey was not up for discussion. "Too bad about Doreen."

Kit and I stared at him, and then at each other. Was he serious? Had the news of poor Doreen's murder reached the village nerve center already? Were we even allowed to discuss it?

"But," Devon continued, leaving us no time to respond, "Ivy tells me that your daughter is much better in the role than Doreen, and anyway, I hear Doreen's busy making plans to go away to uni, so no big deal, right?"

I wondered if Devon heard the sighs that escaped our mouths. "Riiiight," we said in total agreement.

"Doreen will make it, eventually," he added, pouring a liberal amount of vinegar over his fish. "She's a good and determined actress."

We were done with our meal before Devon and so left him to finish alone with a copy of the local newspaper, *The Little Dipping Daily*, which he'd purloined from the empty table next to ours. Despite its name, the tabloid showed up around the village only every three or four days, he'd told us with a laugh.

"So," I said, as soon as we were out on the high street, "what did you make of that?"

Kit had a fake smile on her face as she waved through the window of the café at Devon, who waved back unenthusiastically. "You mean about Doreen?" she asked.

"Right. I felt awful not coming clean about her . . . about this morning, and apparently he doesn't know the poor girl is dead."

"Hmm," Kit said, still waving, although Devon had returned to the newspaper. "I wonder. Does he really not know? Or is he faking? And if he does know, how'd he find out so bloody quickly?"

CHAPTER THIRTY-TWO

We slowly and silently walked back toward our cottage, both of us deep in thought.

"His tone was quite different today, ya know," Kit said.

"Huh?" I asked.

Thoughts of Doreen's foot and her pink toenails had just popped into my mind, so it took me a minute to follow my friend's line of thinking.

"Oh, you mean Devon's?" I asked.

"No, I mean the Archbishop of Canterbury. Of course I mean Devon's. I don't trust him. All that claptrap about Doreen. The first time we heard him mention her, when we were in the pub, he was practically spitting when he was talking to Alistair. Remember, he called her *your daughter* in a threatening tone of voice. So what does he *really* think of Doreen?"

"Wow. You're right. I'd forgotten that. Did something happen in the past week to make him like her again? Or does he know Doreen's dead, and no longer a thorn in his side? Or whatever she was that made him sound so angry that day."

"Good question."

"Well," I offered up my own answer, "I suppose since Doreen ran so hot and cold, so nice one day and not the next, it might have created equally uneven feelings about her in others. Regardless, it scares the living crap out of me to know that she is dead and Emily could also be in jeopardy. I mean, they're connected, they're friends, Doreen confides in . . . um . . . confided in Em. Whoever killed Doreen might know that Emily is—"

"Calm down, honey. I'm sure Emily is in no danger."

But the look in her eyes said otherwise. And I vowed we would not leave England until the murders were solved and Emily's safety was assured.

By the time we reached our sidewalk, I was feeling sick to my stomach with worry. "Kit, I have a really bad feeling. About Devon. About this whole thing. We need to go to Emily's cottage and make sure she's okay. She didn't answer her phone when I called her earlier." I walked on past our own cottage, heading toward my daughter's.

"Val, calm down," my pal said again. If her eyes hadn't still looked as concerned as I felt, I might have smacked her for repeating her order. "You know the phones don't work well here, Emily's *or* yours. And besides, we know Devon is back at The Crawley House, so if he's the one you're worried about—"

"Emily's the one I'm worried about. And maybe Devon's already gotten to her." I was picturing her foot poking out from underneath her bed like Doreen's, and picked up my pace to a jog that I could sustain for only a few feet. I slowed down to a brisk walk, and Kit soon caught up with me.

"Honey, I know she's okay—"

"No, you don't."

"Okay, I don't *know*—"

I couldn't walk fast and talk at the same time, so I said without malice, "Shut up."

I knew Kit understood.

Unable to bear the worry one second longer, I did what I should have already done. I pulled my phone from my purse to dial Emily's number again. I needed immediate assurance that she was all right.

When I turned my phone on, I felt both relief and fury. "Dammit, you're right!" I said to Kit. "I have a message from Emily, and I never even heard it ring. These stupid phones." With a shaky hand, I pushed the button to retrieve the voice mail.

I listened to Emily's message, twice, but no matter how tightly I pressed it to my ear, I couldn't improve the reception.

"Mom, it's me. Jeffrey wants me to meet—" I heard, before a crackling assaulted my ear, followed by a silence. Then a loud static obliterated some words before she ended the call saying, " . . . heading out now; love you."

After I relayed the garbled message to Kit, she asked, "When did she leave it?"

"When we were having lunch, I guess. We need to find her and make sure she's okay."

"Absolutely. Should we go to Jeffrey's, do ya think?"

"Yes."

***

When her knocking went unheeded, Kit turned the handle of Jeffrey's front door. "Doesn't anyone in this village use their locks?" she asked.

I followed her into the hallway. "Apparently not. Although we—"

"We shouldn't have bothered, considering the key was outside and accessible to every passerby and his dog."

"Look, no one's here," I said, "so let's go to the theater. They're probably there."

I placed my third call to Emily since I'd listened to her voice mail, and once again it went unanswered. Then I looked up and saw my friend standing at the closed door to Jeffrey's kitchen.

"Let's at least look around," she said, "since he isn't here." She stepped away from the kitchen and down the short hall. "What's with all these doors?" she asked as she gingerly opened the one to the living room. "Haven't they heard of the open plan?"

"Well, I'm sure the Elizabethans, or whoever built the homes around here, hadn't caught on to the cool factor of one room flowing into another."

"Elizabethans? I think you're searching too far back."

We stood at the entrance to the living room, and I recalled seeing it full of people at Jeffrey's cast party. It looked tidy now, with books filling the wall-to-ceiling shelves, an upright piano in one corner, and several framed prints covering the walls.

"Nice," I said, "but let's go."

"Okay, but let's just check out the kitchen."

I sighed, but before I could stop her, she hurried past me, and I heard her open the kitchen door.

"Holy shit!" she exclaimed, as I turned to follow.

This room told a different story from the almost-pristine living room. Dirty dishes were strewn over the heavy oak table. A glass lay on its side in the middle, in a puddle of spilled milk. A couple of large towels were bunched together, thrown on the floor and blocking the entrance to a door at the far end of the room.

"Looks like someone left in a hurry, wouldn't you say?" Kit kicked the towels aside and reached for the handle of the door.

"Be careful," I said, from my safe position at the other end of the room.

"Val, it's okay; I don't think—oh, it's just the laundry room." She turned toward me, looking relieved.

"Whew." I leaned against the door frame.

"What were you expecting? Jeffrey hanging from a beam in the ceiling?"

"Something like that. Look, let's go." I turned to head down the short hallway to the front door, but when Kit called my name, I turned back.

"I think the man has a serious laundry issue." She held a blue plaid shirt from an index finger, and I saw that it was sprinkled liberally with heavy drops of blood.

"Oh, *shit*," I said. *Please, dear God, let it be just a prop, just a shirt from wardrobe that's doused with fake blood*, I prayed. But what I knew was that I'd seen Jeffrey wearing that very shirt. Was it at rehearsal the night before Vera's body was found? *Oh, dear God, don't let it be Emily's blood.*

"Did Emily say Jeffrey wanted to meet her *here*?" Kit asked, sounding very serious.

"I told you. I couldn't make out—" I stopped talking and pulled my phone from my purse to listen again. As I punched the buttons, I cursed myself for not having tried again sooner. I know that reception for voice mail varies as much as reception for calls. Maybe I'd be able to decipher the words this time. As soon as Emily's message began to play, I pushed the speaker button so Kit and I could both hear.

And then we knew.

Mom, it's me. Jeffrey wants me to meet Doreen and him. He's at The Beamlight with her—

I quit listening. I quit hearing. I almost quit breathing. Because we knew Doreen couldn't be at The Beamlight. Because the last time we'd seen her she was lying dead under her bed.

As we both ran from the house, Kit barked, "Call 999 and tell Tromball to get to The Beamlight."

***

News of Jeffrey's arrest had leaked, like everything in this village, and spread like an oil spill. Many villagers had gathered on the sidewalk outside the police station and traded facts and rumors. There was a weariness that seemed to permeate everyone, and Kit and I slowly made our way back to our little cottage, taking a spot on either end of the couch.

We sat in silence for several minutes, until Kit spoke. "You want something to drink?" she asked. "Tea, coffee, sherry?"

"I'm not sure what's appropriate. Oh, Kit, I feel so terrible, for everyone, but mostly I feel . . ."

"Relieved? For Emily, at least."

"Yeah. Does that make me awful?"

"Not in the least. I feel it too."

Then we heard a light tapping at the door, but neither of us made a move to answer it. Like we had an unseen butler who would do it for us.

"May I come in?" It was Claire, standing at the entrance to the living room. I vaguely made note of the fact that we hadn't locked our door.

Claire's heavy makeup was streaked down her cheeks, her eyes glassy and swollen from crying, her too-black hair pushed back from her forehead, and yet I don't think I'd ever seen her look as soft and pretty as she did now. Immediately, an image of the always-perfect Doreen came to mind.

Kit and I both jumped up, each taking one of Claire's arms and leading her to the couch to sit between us.

"Oh, Claire," I said, "I'm just so sorry."

She nodded and reached for a tissue from her pocket.

"I must look a fright," she said. "I just left the police station and . . . I wasn't sure where to go. Ivy's at home with my mum; she came down from London, and . . . I couldn't quite face her yet."

"Would you like something to drink?" I asked. "We have some sherry."

Claire shook her head, managing a weak smile. "I guess I just wanted to say thank you—"

"Thank us?" I didn't understand. "For what? We've done nothing—"

"For being so nice to Ivy. Things were not good at home; I'm glad she made friends with you two. She's mad for Americans."

"We absolutely loved having Ivy around," Kit quickly assured her.

"Yeah, she loves it here. She told me that Doreen brought her here before you rented the place." She gave a short laugh void of any humor.

Then she sighed and continued. "I accused Doreen of fixing it so that Ivy could meet her father here. I was dead set against that, and I had a restraining order against Devon . . . but Doreen insisted they had come here for another reason, that she'd brought Ivy with her when she'd come to tape something under that dresser drawer in the bedroom. When I doubted her, she told me I could go see for myself. When I burst in here that day and made such a fool of myself, and then didn't find anything, I chalked it up to Doreen lying."

"She wasn't lying, Claire," Kit said, ready to redeem the dead girl, for at least that part of her story.

And I didn't see why we should bother to tell Claire she actually *had* been right about Ivy and Devon meeting here, with the help of Doreen.

" . . . there *was* something taped to the drawer," I heard Kit further explain, "but we'd found it and removed it."

Claire nodded her head slowly, and I wasn't sure if that was good or bad news for her.

"I know that now, of course," she said. "But Doreen was so unreliable, given to impetuous behavior and mood swings. Like when she threw her script away in the woods, probably in a snit with Jeffrey, having decided for the moment that she didn't want to be in the play and taking off—not bothering to tell anyone, of course. And I hated her crush on Jeffrey Hastings. I kept telling her not to trust him."

Ahhh, I thought. "So, that phone call you were on when you were doing our hair," I said. "That wasn't about Doreen's relationship with her father. It was—"

"I was trying to convince Doreen not to trust Jeffrey. But she was young, and thought she was in love, and his connection to the theater was too irresistible for my impressionable daughter."

Kit and I both nodded.

But Claire wasn't done.

"That wasn't the worst of it. Jeffrey was hell-bent on finding that evidence—I think it was a bloody flower and some kind of . . . formula?—once he'd discovered it was missing from his place. And he suspected that Doreen's the one who took it. So, knowing Doreen and Ivy were close, he started badgering Ivy. Actually, I guess all he had to do was ply her with that damn strawberry cake she loves so much, and she spilled the beans."

She managed a weak smile, and then she said, "I best get back home; I don't want to leave Ivy alone with my mum for too long. She's a terror. Ivy takes after her. But thank you again for being such good friends to Ivy."

"It was our pleasure," I said, surprised that I meant it.

***

"You were very clever, Kitty Kat. You had it all figured out, didn't you?" We were sipping sherry on our couch that night, hours after Claire had left and the play should have gone on.

But of course, with the director in police custody (not to mention two recent murders), the play had come to an abrupt end. The final performance, it turned out, had taken place on Thursday. The weekend's performances had been canceled. Not postponed, but canceled. Everyone insisted, the indubitable phrase *the show must go on* be damned.

"The *who*dunit was easy," Kit said. "Jeffrey told Emily he wanted her to meet him and Doreen, when we knew very well that the only place Doreen was going was to the morgue. And of course the bloody shirt. And the *why* quickly followed. Ya know, Jeffrey sold pharmaceuticals. That was the key for me. I don't know why we didn't think about it sooner, like when we knew Belinda was doing research on sleeping disorders, and we knew Vera had a familial disease and . . . there's a lotta money in all that, Val."

"So," I said, still trying to wrap my tired brain around it all. "Jeffrey killed Belinda so he could manufacture the drug she invented—do you *invent* drugs? well, whatever—and make a gazillion dollars? And when Vera—and later Doreen—suspected that, he killed them?" I shook my head. "And why did Doreen tell us she thought *Devon* killed Belinda and Vera, if she had reason to suspect Jeffrey?"

"Sometimes we believe what we wanna believe. And we deny what we can't bear to believe." Kit sighed. "Shall I top you off?" Her jubilant look was back.

But I was too tired for one more sip, and certainly too tired to grasp all that had happened. I wasn't sure if my BFF was a genius or a madwoman who had stumbled onto the truth in spite of faulty reasoning. "I gotta go to bed, Kit. I am beyond exhausted."

She looked disappointed, like she'd been looking forward to retelling—yet again—every step of her brilliant deductions (glossing over any credit due Claire, and even Ivy, for the gaps they had filled). But suddenly I preferred to be lying flat and mulling it all over in the dark—alone.

I fell asleep that night with the dreamy vision of Emily and Luke enjoying a cozy, romantic dinner. It didn't matter that Detective Tromball would take all the credit for solving the crime (without referencing Kit's help, which I chalked up to poetic justice—or karma). I was just glad my kid was safe.

But my dreams turned the sweetest of all when they took me back to my own bed in my tiny apartment in Downers Grove, Illinois, the theme song to *Law & Order: Special Victims Unit* just beginning and me looking forward to falling asleep to the sweet words *sexually based offenses are considered especially heinous* . . .

CHAPTER THIRTY-THREE

My suitcase lay in the middle of my living room floor, its contents spilling out.

Since returning home just a few hours earlier, I had removed only what was necessary to brush my teeth, wash my face, and don a clean Cubs T-shirt to sleep in.

I was already in bed, snuggled down for the night, when I heard my doorbell ring.

Crap!

Larry had picked Kit and me up at the airport and then dropped me off at home. I'd made a quick call to the office to say I was back and would be in the next day. Only Billie was around, and after commiserating with her about the passing of her beloved cat, I'd hung up, telling her I was exhausted and had to get some sleep.

Now my visitor banged loudly on the door. "Valerie! Open up."

It was Tom Haskins, my boss, my dear friend, my pain in the butt.

I checked that my T-shirt was long enough to cover my knees and obeyed his command, opening the door to his six-foot-plus frame, shaven head, and handsomely craggy face that looked irritated. He had an unlit cigar in his mouth. "Geez, Val, how long does it take to answer a door?"

"I was sleeping, if you must know, and hello to you too."

"Yeah, yeah, sleeping. Right."

"It's very late and—"

"It's seven forty-five."

"Ever heard of jet lag?"

He stepped over my suitcase and moved a messy pile of clothes from one end of the couch. Then he sat, leaning back with one arm slung over the cushions. "So, you made it home."

"Yep." I moved another messy pile from the coffee table and sat down across from him. "It's good to see you, Tom."

He grunted. A lovely sound, similar to the kind made by farm animals. I hadn't realized how much I'd missed it. "So," he said, taking the cigar out of his mouth, twirling it in his fingers. Then he used a gold lighter to begin the arduous task of setting it on fire.

I could have told him not to smoke in my home, but instead I went to the kitchen to find a saucer he could use for an ashtray.

"Tell me everything," he said, when I returned to my coffee table perch and handed him the make-do ashtray.

"Okay. Well, there was a guy—Jeffrey Hastings—who was the director of the play. Actually, in real life, he was a pharmaceutical salesman—"

"Is this the beginning, or are you starting in the middle?"

"Well, I guess you could call this the somewhere-heading-toward-the-middle—"

He waved the cigar, leaving a swirl of blue smoke. "No, start at the beginning, but don't go into too much detail."

"Okay, our landlady, Brown Owl—well, her actual name was Vera Wingate; don't even ask about the Brown Owl stuff—was murdered. But before that—two years before, in fact—another woman, Belinda Bailey, was murdered in the very cottage we were renting from this Vera. We found a little flower taped to some cardboard that also held a piece of paper with a formula of some kind written on it. It was hidden in our cottage, but not, like you might think, by Belinda, who had lived there. She was a medical researcher, working on sleeping pills—"

"I feel like I've just taken a sleeping pill myself. Would you just get to what happened while you were there? I don't need a history lesson."

"Okay. Understood. But Belinda was important to the story. She had developed a super-duper sleeping pill that, although not approved for public distribution, was being sold by Jeffrey Hastings on the black market."

"Two years ago." Tom looked bored.

"Right. Jeffrey used her formula to manufacture the pills. There's big money in sleeping medication—"

"Really?" He did a bad job of suddenly appearing interested. "So I should ditch my hedge fund and sink all my dough into NyQuil?"

"You wanna hear this story or not?"

"I do, but please speed it up."

"You have somewhere to be?"

"I've always got somewhere to be, Valerie. But I thought it would be nice to stop by and visit my favorite employee since I didn't know if she was dead or alive—"

"I called the office, but you weren't there."

"Yeah, Billie mentioned something. So, continue—but quickly."

"You want something to drink first?"

"What you got?"

I made the short trip to the refrigerator in my galley kitchen. "I have Doctor Pepper, but it's probably flat. And half a bottle of wine."

"I'll risk the wine."

I poured the ungrateful man a glass of pinot grigio, taking a sip before delivering it to him. It didn't taste too bad.

"Geez, Pankowski, when did you buy this?" he asked, not even drinking, just swirling the liquid around in the glass.

"Bad?"

"As vinegar goes, probably quite good."

I ignored him and sat back down on the coffee table. "Okay, so in a nutshell—"

"This is the *nutshell* version?"

"Yes. Brown Owl Vera had a disease in her family. It's very rare, called fatal familial insomnia. FFI for short—"

"*Really?* What made them think they should shorten it?"

"And her mom and some other relatives died from it. So naturally, she was afraid she'd be next. And it seems that the sleeping drug Belinda discovered had the potential to help sufferers of this fatal . . . this FFI. But when Belinda found out that Jeffrey was selling her drug, illegally, mainly to regular insomnia victims, he murdered her, and then—"

"Two years later, when Gray Pigeon—"

"Brown Owl."

"Right, that one; when she found out who'd killed the maker of the medical miracle, she was next for the chop."

"What a lovely way to put it. Actually, Doreen Carlisle's romantic involvement with Jeffrey led to her suspicions of the source of his secret income and his likely motive to kill Belinda. But before she could meet Vera at The Cut Above for help in putting the pieces together, Vera was murdered. Unfortunately, Doreen had shared just enough with her mom to worry her, but she hadn't shared enough in time to save herself."

I told Tom that my fear that Emily was next on Jeffrey's to-die list because of her friendship with Doreen was well founded. Jeffrey felt certain Doreen had confided in Emily way more than she actually had. But thankfully, our rush to The Beamlight Theatre with the police on our tails had kept my fear from becoming a reality. Jeffrey was captured before Emily even knew she was in danger.

There were many parts of the story that would have been too tedious to share with my impatient boss. Like the fact that the shoe found in the woods turned out to have been dropped there by Macie on one of her trips to The Beamlight with a garbage bag full of accessories. That mystery within a mystery was solved for Kit and me only when Tromball begrudgingly told us she'd heard Little Dipping's Edith Head ranting about a pair of shoes that would have been *perfect* if only she hadn't lost one of them. Tromball, of course, had delighted in keeping us in the dark.

And I didn't tell Tom about all our good-byes. On the morning of our departure from Little Dipping, we'd stopped at Claire's house. Ivy had cried profusely, clinging to Kit and making her promise she would FaceTime with her. Kit was genuinely sad to say farewell to her young friend. Just before we left, she took her strand of pearls from her pocket, the ones that Ivy had so admired, and wrapped them around the little girl's neck. I knew the pearls were expensive, but I also knew they would be treasured forever.

Our next stop in the village was at The Lady of Shallot, where Pinky and his Duchess both came from around the bar to give us warm hugs. It was the first time I'd seen Pinky look sad.

"Come back and see us," he said. "I promise we are not all murderers and villains."

We had a good if slightly grim laugh before Kit and I headed toward the door. "I'm going to miss this place," I said.

"Me too." Then Kit turned back toward Pinky and The Duchess, who were standing with their arms around each other, like parents seeing their kids off to college. "One thing," my pal addressed Pinky, stepping closer to him.

"Only one?" He chuckled.

"Yeah. You don't seem to like Alistair Carlisle; I just wondered why. It's bothered me."

"Ugh." Pinky tightened his arm around The Duchess's shoulder. "That guy."

"Go on," his wife said. "Tell 'em."

"He fancied the missus, didn't he? He's lucky I didn't smack him one."

The Duchess giggled. And we couldn't argue with that.

Our last stop was at Emily and Luke's cottage. Saying good-bye to my daughter was hard, knowing it would be a long time before we were together again. But I knew she was safe and could continue her adventure in England. And she and Luke had each other.

We'd also received good news from home. Thanks to an article my mom read about Kris Kristofferson, my stepfather's condition had finally been correctly diagnosed as Lyme disease, which can mimic the symptoms of Alzheimer's, and his prognosis was good.

Once I'd hit Tom with the high points, I rummaged around in my messy suitcase and produced a small square box wrapped in tissue paper. "Here's your gift," I said, handing it to him.

He laid his half-smoked cigar in the faux ashtray and turned his attention to the package. "Another coffee mug?" he asked.

"Damn you; why do you always spoil the surprise?"

"Let me tell you something, Pankowski. A coffee mug from you is no surprise, believe me."

He took it out and turned it around to see the image of Winston Churchill, one hand holding a cigar, the other forming a V-for-victory salute. Tom smiled.

"Do you love it?" I asked.

"Best one yet. I'll stick it next to my *Virginia is for Lovers* mug."

"Tom," I began to protest, "it's so hard to buy you anything; you've already got—"

"Everything. Yep, I know. Especially now that you're back, Kiddo."

Patty and Roz
www.roz-patty.com

About the authors ...

Now a proud and patriotic US citizen and Texan, Rosalind Burgess grew up in London and currently calls Houston home. She has also lived in Germany, Iowa, and Minnesota. Roz retired from the airline industry to devote all her working hours to writing (although it seems more like fun than work).

Patricia Obermeier Neuman spent her childhood and early adulthood moving around the Midwest (Minnesota, South Dakota, Nebraska, Iowa, Wisconsin, Illinois, and Indiana), as a trailing child and then as a trailing spouse (inspiring her first book, *Moving: The What, When, Where & How of It*). A former reporter and editor, Patty lives with her husband in Door County, Wisconsin. They have three children and twelve grandchildren.

No. 1 in
The Val & Kit Mystery Series

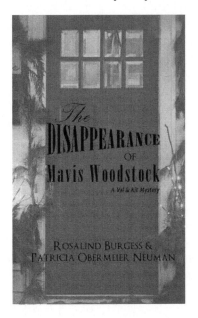

The Disappearance of Mavis Woodstock

Mavis Woodstock (a vaguely familiar name) calls Val and insists she has to sell her house as quickly as possible. Then she fails to keep her scheduled appointment. Kit remembers Mavis from their school days, an unattractive girl who was ignored when she was lucky, ridiculed when she was not. She also remembers Mavis being the only daughter in a large family that was as frugal as it was wealthy. When Val and Kit cannot locate Mavis, they begin an investigation, encountering along the way a little romance, a lot of deception, and more than one unsavory character.

What readers are saying about...
The Disappearance of Mavis Woodstock

FIVE STARS! "Best book I've read in a long time; couldn't wait to go to bed at night so I could read this book and then couldn't put it down. TOTAL PAGE-TURNER ... Cannot wait to read the next book in this series!!!"

FIVE STARS! " ... well-written mystery ... first of The Val & Kit Mystery Series. The two amateur sleuths, Val & Kit, are quirky, humorous, and dogged in their pursuit of righting what they felt was a wrongful death of someone they knew from the past. It's full of humorous, cagey, and a few dark personalities that keep you on your toes wondering what or who would turn up next. ... a fun, fast read that is engaging and will keep your interest. ... A tightly woven mystery with a great twist at the end."

FIVE STARS! "I thoroughly enjoyed this book, laughing out loud many times, often until I cried. I love the authors' style and could so relate to the things the characters were going through."

FIVE STARS! "This was a fun read! The story was well put together. Lots of suspense. Authors tied everything together well. Very satisfying."

FIVE STARS! "Enjoyed this tale of two friends immensely. Was shocked by the ending and sad to find I had finished the book so quickly. Anxious to read the next one. ... Keep them coming!"

FIVE STARS! "Mysteries are sometimes too predictable for me—I can guess the ending before I'm halfway through the book. Not this one. The characters are well developed and fun, and the plot kept me guessing until the end."

FIVE STARS! "I highly recommend this novel and I'm looking forward to the next book in this series. I was kept guessing throughout the entire novel. The analogies throughout are priceless and often made me laugh. . . . I found myself on the edge of my seat. . . . The ending to this very well-written novel is brilliant!"

FIVE STARS! "I recommend this book if you like characters such as Kinsey Millhone or Stone Barrington . . . or those types. Excellent story with fun characters. Can't wait to read more of these."

FIVE STARS! "A cliff-hanger with an I-did-not-see-that-coming ending."

FIVE STARS! " . . . well written, humorous . . . a good plot and a bit of a surprise ending. An easy read that is paced well, with enough twists and turns to keep you reading to the end."

FIVE STARS! "Very enjoyable book and hard to put down. Well-written mystery with a great surprise ending. A must-read."

FIVE STARS! "This is a well-written mystery that reads along at a bright and cheerful pace with a surprisingly dark twist at the end."

FIVE STARS! "I really enjoyed this book: the characters, the story line, everything. It is well written, humorous, engaging."

FIVE STARS! "The perfect combo of sophisticated humor, fun and intriguing twists and turns!"

No. 2 in
The Val & Kit Mystery Series

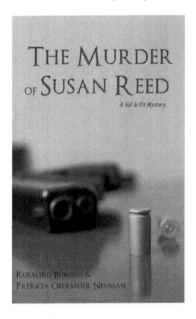

The Murder of Susan Reed

When Kit suspects Larry of having an affair with one of his employees, Susan Reed, she enlists Val's help in uncovering the truth. The morning after a little stalking expedition by the lifelong friends, Val reads in the newspaper that Susan Reed was found shot to death in her apartment the night before, right around the time Kit was so certain Larry and Susan were together. *Were* they having an affair? And did Larry murder her? The police, in the form of dishy Detective Dennis Culotta, conduct the investigation into Susan's murder, hampered at times by Val and Kit's insistent attempts to discover whether Larry is guilty of infidelity and/or murder. As the investigation heats up, so does Val's relationship with Detective Culotta.

FIVE STARS! "I couldn't wait to get this Val & Kit adventure after reading the authors' first book, and I was not disappointed. As a fan of this genre . . . I just have to write a few words praising the incredible talent of Roz and Patty. One thing I specifically want to point out is the character development. You can completely visualize the supporting actors (suspects?) so precisely that you do not waste time trying to recall details about the character. . . . Roz and Patty practically create an imprint in your mind of each character's looks/voice/mannerisms, etc."

FIVE STARS! "Even better than the first! Another page-turner! Take it to the beach or pool. You will love it!!! I did!!!"

FIVE STARS! "Great writing. Great plot."

FIVE STARS! "Once again Val & Kit star in a page-turner mystery!"

FIVE STARS! "I loved this book and these two best friends who tend to get in trouble together. Reminds me of my best friend and myself."

FIVE STARS! "Ms. Burgess and Ms. Neuman are fantastic writers and did a great job with their sophomore effort! I enjoy their writing style and they really capture the genre of cozy mystery well! I highly recommend their books!"

FIVE STARS! "Val and Kit's interactions and Val's thoughts about life in general were probably the best part of the book. I was given enough info to 'suspect' just about every character mentioned."

No. 3 in
The Val & Kit Mystery Series

Death in Door County

Val embarks on a Mother's Day visit to her mom in Door County, Wisconsin, a peninsula filled with artists, lighthouses, and natural beauty. Her daughter, Emily, has arrived from LA to accompany her, and at the last minute her best friend, Kit, invites herself along. Val and Kit have barely unpacked their suitcases when trouble and tension greet them, in the form of death and a disturbing secret they unwittingly brought with them. As they get to know the locals, things take a sinister turn. And when they suspect someone close to them might be involved in blackmail—or worse—Val and Kit do what they do best: they take matters into their own hands in their obsessive, often zany, quest to uncover the truth.

What readers are saying about . . .
Death in Door County

FIVE STARS! "I really enjoyed this book. Not only was I in Door County at the time that I was reading it and Door County has always been one of my favorite places, I am also a homeowner in Downers Grove, IL, which is where Val and Kit also live. I did read the first two books in The Val & Kit Mystery Series which I also thoroughly enjoyed. Being from Downers Grove, I got quite a kick out of the real names of most of the streets being used in the stories because I could just picture where the events were taking place. Even though all three books were mysteries, they were lighthearted enough to hold my interest. I would love to see more stories in this series."

FIVE STARS! "Whether you are a mother, daughter, grandmother, great-grandmother or best friend . . . This is a heartwarming and hilarious read that would be a perfect part of your Mother's Day celebration!!! I loved getting to know Val and Kit better. Their relationships with their loved ones had me laughing and weeping all at the same time!!! I loved ending my day with Val and Kit; it just made it hard to start my day as I could not stop reading *Death in Door County*!"

FIVE STARS! "Another page-turner in the Val & Kit Series! What a great story! I loved learning about Val's family."

FIVE STARS! "Really enjoy the Val and Kit characters. They are a yin and yang of personalities that actually fit like a hand and glove. This is the third in the series and is just as much a fun read as the first two. The right amount of intrigue coupled with laughter. I am looking forward to the next in the series."

FIVE STARS! "*Death in Door County* is the third installment in the series, and each book just gets better than the last."

FIVE STARS! "The girls have done it again . . . and by girls, do I mean Val and Kit, or Roz and Patty? The amazingly talented authors, Roz and Patty, of course. Although Val and Kit have landed themselves right smack dab in the middle of yet another mystery. This is their third adventure, but don't feel as though you have to (albeit you SHOULD if you haven't done so already) read *The Disappearance of Mavis Woodstock* and *The Murder of Susan Reed* in order. This book and all the other(s) . . . are wonderful stand-alones, but read all . . . to enjoy all of the main and supporting characters' quirks . . . I can't seem to express how much I love these books . . . Speaking of characters . . . This is what sets the Val & Kit series apart from the others in this genre. The authors always give us a big cast of suspects, and each are described so incredibly . . . It's like playing a game of Clue, but way more fun. . . . the authors make the characters so memorable that you don't waste time trying to 'think back' to whom they are referring. In fact, it's hard to believe that there are only two authors writing such vivid casts for these books. So come on, ladies, confess . . . no, wait, don't. I don't want to know how you do it, just please keep it up."

FIVE STARS! "Great read! I love this series and this particular book kept me intrigued until the very end. I found myself rooting for certain characters and against others."

FIVE STARS! "Just the right mix of a page-turner mystery and humor with a modern edge. I have read all three books and am waiting impatiently for more."

FIVE STARS! "Love, love these two writers! I'm these authors' best fan, and I can't wait for these lovely ladies to write more!"

No. 4 in
The Val & Kit Mystery Series

Lethal Property

In this fourth book of The Val & Kit Mystery Series (a stand-alone, like the others), our ladies are back home in Downers Grove. Val is busy selling real estate, eager to take a potential buyer to visit the home of a widow living alone. He turns out not to be all that he claimed, and a string of grisly events follows, culminating in a perilous situation for Val. Her lifelong BFF Kit is ready to do whatever necessary to ensure Val's safety and clear her name of any wrongdoing. The dishy Detective Dennis Culotta also returns to help, and with the added assistance of Val's boss, Tom Haskins, and a *Downton Abbey*–loving Rottweiler named Roscoe, the ladies become embroiled in a murder investigation extraordinaire. As always, we are introduced to a new cast of shady characters as we welcome back the old circle of friends.

What readers are saying about . . .
Lethal Property

FIVE STARS! "Rosalind and Patricia have done it again and written a great sequel in The Val & Kit Mystery Series . . . full of intrigue and great wit and a different mystery each time. . . . *Lethal Property* is a great read, and I did not want to put the book down. I do hope that someone in the TV world reads these, as they'd make a great TV series. . . . I cannot wait for the next. Rosalind and Patricia, keep writing these great reads. Most worthy of FIVE STARS."

FIVE STARS! " . . . Val and Kit—forever friends. Smart, witty, determined, vulnerable, unintentional detectives. While this fourth installment can be read without having read the first three books (in the series), I'm certain you'll find that you want to read the first three. As has been the case with each book written by Rosalind Burgess and Patricia Obermeier Neuman, once I started reading, I really didn't want to stop. It was very much like catching up with old friends. Perhaps you know the feeling. . . . Regardless of how long the separation, being together again just feels right."

FIVE STARS! "My girls are back in action! It's a hilarious ride when Val is implicated in a series of murders. We get a lot of the hotness that is Dennis Culotta this time around. . . . Also, we get a good dose of Tom too. But the best part of *Lethal Property*? Val and Kit. Besties with attitude and killer comedy. The banter and down-to-earth humor between these two is pure enjoyment on the page. Five bright and shiny stars for this writing duo!"

FIVE STARS! "Enjoyed reading *Lethal Property* as well as all by Roz and Patty. Written in a way that I felt connected with the characters. Looking forward to the next one."

FIVE STARS! "OK . . . so I thought I knew whodunit early in the book, then after changing my mind at least 8-10 times, I was still wrong. (I want to say so much more, but I really don't want to give anything away.) Just one of the many, many things I love about the Val & Kit books. I love the characters/suspects, I love the believable dialogue between characters and also Valley Girl's inner dialogue (when thinking about Tina . . . hehe). I'd like to also add that (these books) are just good, clean fun. A series of books that you would/could/should recommend to anyone. (My boss is a nun, so that's a little something I worry about . . . lol) Thanks again, ladies. I agree with another reviewer . . . it IS like catching up with old friends, and I can't wait for the next one."

FIVE STARS! "Reading *Lethal Property* was like catching up with old friends, and a few new characters, but another fun ride! I love these characters and I adore these writers. Would recommend to anyone who appreciates a good story and a sharp wit. Well done, ladies; you did it again!"

FIVE STARS! "As with the other books in this series, this can be read as a stand-alone. However, I've read all of them to date in order and that's probably the best way to do it. I'm to the point where I don't even read the cover blurb for these books . . . because I know that I'll enjoy them. This book certainly didn't disappoint. Plenty of Val and Kit and their crazy antics, a cast of new colorful characters and a mystery that wasn't predictable."

No. 5 in
The Val & Kit Mystery Series

Palm Desert Killing

Palm Desert Killing

When one of them receives a mysterious letter, BFFs Val and Kit begin to unravel a sordid story that spans a continent and reaches back decades. It also takes them to Palm Desert, California, a paradise of palm trees, mountains, blue skies . . . and now murder. The men in their lives—Val's favorite detective, Dennis Culotta; her boss, Tom Haskins; and Kit's husband, Larry—play their (un)usual parts in this adventure that introduces a fresh batch of suspicious characters, including Kit's New York–attorney sister, Nora, and their mother. Val faces an additional challenge when her daughter, Emily, reveals her own startling news. Val and Kit bring to this story their (a)typical humor, banter, and unorthodox detective skills.

What readers are saying about . . .
Palm Desert Killing

FIVE STARS! "Have fallen in love with Val and Kit and was so excited to see there was a new book in the series. It did not disappoint. Val and Kit are true to form and it was fun to get to know Kit's sister."

FIVE STARS! "Each book in this series is like hanging out with your gal-pals! The characters, Val and Kit, are very well developed."

FIVE STARS! "I love all of the Val & Kit mysteries! Great reading! Lots of laughs and suspense with Val and Kit."

FIVE STARS! "Everyone needs a pal like these two!! Love Val and Kit! Can't wait for their next adventure!!"

FIVE STARS! "Love the authors, love the characters. This series gets better and better!"

FIVE STARS! "Love these well-written books!"

FIVE STARS! "Val and Kit are such fun. Time spent with them is always a joy. I love the intrigue of these books, but nothing entertains me more than the wit and humor. It's so wonderful to see these great friends interact. They make you want to join them for a cup of coffee or a glass of wine! Looking forward to the next adventure."

And if you want to read about the mystery of marriage, here's a NON–Val & Kit book for you . . .

Rosalind Burgess & Patricia Obermeier Neuman

Dressing Myself

Meet Jessie Harleman in this contemporary women's novel about love, lust, friends, and family. Jessie and Kevin have been happily married for twenty-eight years. With their two grown kids now out of the house and living their own lives, Jessie and Kevin have reached the point they thought they longed for, yet slightly dreaded. But the house that used to burst at the seams now has too many empty rooms. Still, Jessie is a *glass-half-full* kind of woman, eager for this next period of her life to take hold. The problem is, nothing goes the way she planned. This novel explores growth and change and new beginnings.

What readers are saying about . . .
Dressing Myself

FIVE STARS! "Loved this book!!! Another page-turner by talented Burgess and Neuman, my new favorite authors!!! I loved reading this book. It was very heartwarming in so many ways!!! Ready to read the next book from this writing duo!!!"

FIVE STARS! "I love these authors. I love the real feelings, thoughts, words, actions, etc., that they give to their characters. I love that it feels like a memoir instead of fiction. I love that it depressed me. I want to say so much more about what I loved, but I don't want to give too much away. A classic story that draws your emotions out of you to make you root for it to go one way, then in the next chapter, make a U-turn; just like the main character. It makes you reflect on your own life and happiness. It makes you check your husband's e-mails and credit card statements. I simply love your writing, ladies. Can't wait for the next one."

FIVE STARS! "I couldn't put it down! Great book! Maybe I could relate with the main character too much, but I felt as though she was my friend. When I wasn't reading the book, the main character was constantly on my mind! The ending was unpredictable in a great way! I think the authors need to keep on writing! I'm a huge fan!"

FIVE STARS! "Wonderful book! A fast read because once you start, you just cannot put it down; the characters become like your family! Definitely a worthwhile read!"

FIVE STARS! "Delightful! I so enjoyed my time with Jessie. I laughed with her, and ached for her. I knew her so well so quickly. I'll remember her story with a smile. I hope these authors keep it coming. What a fun read!"

FIVE STARS! "Love these writers!! So refreshing to have writers who really create such characters you truly understand and relate to. Looking forward to the next one. Definitely my favorites!"

FIVE STARS! "This book is about a woman's life torn apart. . . . A lot of detail as to how she would feel . . . very well-written. I have to agree with the other readers, 5 stars."

FIVE STARS! "What a fun read *Dressing Myself* was! . . . I have to admit I didn't expect the ending. . . . It was hard to put this book down."

FIVE STARS! "Great, easy, captivating read!! The characters seem so real! I don't read a lot, but I was really into this one! Read it for sure!"

FIVE STARS! "Loved it! Read this in one day. Enjoyed every page and had a real feeling for all of the characters. I was rooting for Jessie all the way. . . . Hope there's another story like this down the road."

FIVE STARS! "*Dressing Myself* deals with an all-too-common problem of today in a realistic manner that is sometimes sad, sometimes hopeful, as befits the subject. My expectation of the ending seesawed back and forth as the book progressed. I found it an interesting, engaging read with fully developed characters."

FIVE STARS! "Great book! It has been a long time since I have read a book cover to cover in one day . . . fantastic read . . . real page-turner that was hard to put down . . . Thanks, Ladies!"

Made in the USA
Middletown, DE
05 September 2024

60407840R00161